THE POTATO THIEF

MERCY ROW SERIES PREQUEL

HARRY HALLMAN

THE POTATO THIEF

A Mercy Row Prequel

by Harry Hallman

www.mercyrow.com

Published by
Octane Interactive, LLC - Publishing

ISBN- 1985152282
ISBN 13: 978-1985152281

This book is dedicated to my wife Duoc, my son Bill,
my daughter Nancy, my granddaughter Ava
and all of my family, past, present and future.

CHAPTER 1

Letterkenny, County Donegal, Ireland - November 1881

It was a bone-chilling night. Every muscle in eighteen-year-old George Graham's body was quivering. He hated the cold, and it was always cold in Letterkenny. Summer, winter it didn't matter. Before he left school at the age of fourteen, his teacher had told him of places where it was always warm. Places where oranges, limes, and coconuts grew year-round. He had no idea what a coconut was, and to him, it sounded strange and exotic. He often dreamt of being in such a place only to wake and find he was on the cold floor of the shack his family called home.

George had eaten oranges only once in his life. One day, when George was ten years old, a man from one of the ships in the port of Dunfanaghy stopped by the family's farm on his way to Derry. He traded a dozen oranges for a large sack of potatoes. His father was so enamored with the fruit that one would think it was gold. Eight years later George could still imagine the succulent sweet and sour taste of the two oranges his father had bestowed on him.

Before his father died of consumption, the family ate mostly potatoes, carrots, and cabbage. On occasion, there was a small amount of boiled beef or pork. Now, most meals were only potatoes, and they were few and far between.

When potato crops fail, the Irish people suffer, his Grandmother, now departed, used to say. She told him of the great potato famine of 1845, and she said whole families died of starvation and disease. Before he quit school, his teacher had secretly taught her class that their Irish-English overseers, during the great famine, had exported what few eatable potato crops there were. They cared more for profits than Irish farmers lives. As a result of poor governing by the English and greed over one million poor, Irish men, women and children perished during that famine.

Since the time of the great potato famine, there had been several lesser famines such as the one that was currently occurring. The potato crop on George's family farm had failed three years in a row, making the family destitute and without food.

The church helped when it could, but the entire community was devastated, and donations to the Catholic church diminished so much they could hardly feed the priests and nuns. The local government officials and most of the upper class were unaffected. They either diverted aid shipments of food from England and other countries to themselves or were wealthy enough to buy what local food was available or even have food imported. The poor got the scraps, and they were not plentiful.

George took off his right shoe, adjusted the paper he had placed over the hole in its sole and slipped it back on. He rubbed his hands together to warm them and wished now that he hadn't given his coat to his youngest brother Sean. He had no choice. His brother was ill, and the house was cold and damp. George was the oldest of five children and as the oldest son was responsible for taking care of the family.

His sister Eileen, who was fifteen, had complicated the family's precarious situation by getting pregnant. She married, and she and her boyfriend Paddy Muldoon moved in with the family after Paddy's father kicked him out of his home saying that he couldn't feed his own family let alone another woman and a baby.

Sometimes George felt the responsibility to be overwhelming. He never complained to the others, but the burden took its toll. At one time he thought perhaps he would become a priest, but circumstances had destroyed that dream. The idea of living a pious quiet life appealed to him. He wholeheartedly believed in God's word and the Catholic doctrine and thought he would make a good priest. His faith and belief were now eating at his insides because what he was about to do was completely the opposite of God's word.

Lord, George prayed silently, *I have a problem. I believe in you. I believe in your word, but if I don't do what I must, I'll be breaking your commandment to honor my mother. If I do honor my mother, I'll be breaking your commandment not to steal. I cannot allow my mother, my brothers, and sister to suffer any longer. Because you are a loving God, I know you will understand. If not and if I must go to hell then so be it, but I beseech thee to lay your cloak of safety and love upon my family.* George made the sign of the cross and whispered, "Amen."

He slowly rose from behind the two large wooden crates he was hiding behind and looked at the O'Connor warehouse building just fifty feet away. The candlelight was flickering yellow and red in a second story window. He dropped back behind the crates, rubbed his hands again and said "Damn It" a little too loudly. He quickly put his hand to his mouth and silently addressed God again. *Lord, can you please show a small bit of compassion and make Mr. O'Connor go home?* A minute later large flakes of snow started falling from the heavens.

George looked at the snow in despair then pulled his shirt over his hair and put his head on his knees. He began to envision a warm tropical place where oranges and limes lay in abundance on a large wooden table. He was sitting at its head eating from a plate full of chicken and pork. It was delightfully warm. So warm he had taken off his shirt. The sky was blue with small white puffy clouds slowly drifting to the north. His mother was at the other end of the table, and she was smiling. He hadn't seen her smile in years, and it made him happy. He smiled back at her and took a large mouth full of roasted chicken. Suddenly, there was an explosive noise and everything dissolved to black. Then there was another loud bang.

George took his shirt off his head and peeked around the crate. Mr. O'Connor was placing a lock on the two large warehouse doors. The candlelight in the second-floor window was gone. George made the sign of the cross and silently mouthed the words, "Thank you, Lord."

O'Connor started to walk south, his boots leaving imprints in the light snowfall. He stopped suddenly, thought for a second, and instead crossed the street and went into Maggie O'Farrell's pub.

"Forgive me, Lord," George said as he rushed to a window on the back side of the warehouse. He broke the glass with a rock, unlatched and opened it. Then he jumped headfirst into the warehouse, landing on a stack of bagged potatoes. He threw four fifty-pound sacks of potatoes out the window, then walked over to an area in the warehouse where O'Connor stored the canned foods. He found a burlap sack and started to fill it with cans. First, he put in canned beef, then beans and finally some fruits.

He took note that the boxes the cans were in had British Relief Fund written on them. It made George feel a bit better knowing he was stealing from a man who was stealing a whole lot more from the poor Irish people. He justified to himself that he was just taking what was only due him.

George dropped the sack with the canned goods out the window and followed. He dragged three of the fifty-pound sacks of potatoes to the woods behind the warehouse and covered them with broken branches. He would come back in a day or two with Paddy, to get them. He returned to the warehouse and picked up the sack of potatoes and slung it over his shoulder, then did the same with the sack of canned goods. George was large for an Irishman, standing about six feet three inches tall. The hard work of farming had made him lean and fit, but the past three years of deprivation had sapped his strength, and he was struggling with the two fifty-pound sacks.

He adjusted the sacks and was about to leave when he heard Mr. O'Connor talking and a woman giggling. There were rumors that O'Connor, who was married, was having an affair with the widow Maggie O'Farrell. George hadn't believed that since O'Connor always seemed a very pious man and was prominent in the Church of Ireland. *All men are sinners,* George thought. When O'Connor and Maggie went into the building, he started off for home.

By the time he was three quarters home, he was dragging the sacks behind him. When he reached the house, George was worn out. He sat on the floor panting. After he caught his breath, he told his sister Eileen to hide the canned goods. Eileen lifted two floorboards and poured the cans into the hole underneath the floor. Then she replaced the boards. George's mother and Eileen lifted the sack of potatoes and poured them into their empty potato bin and threw the sacks into the small fire in the fireplace.

George's mother leaned over and kissed him on the head and said, "I know it hurts you to have to take this food, but we had no other choice. God will forgive you and me."

"I know, Ma," George said as he stood up. He kissed his mother and said, "I love you, Ma."

"Oh, don't be getting soft on me, George," his mother said and patted him on the cheek. "Eileen put on a pot of water and get some potatoes cooking. The boys are hungry."

George's mother was thirty-six years old, but the rigors of her life made her look much older. She was very thin, had dark circles under her eyes and her skin had a pale translucent look. It pained George when he remembered how beautiful she was when he was a youngster. *This country killed my Da, and now it's killing my Ma,* George thought as a tear rolled down his cheek.

When the potatoes had cooked, George's mother cut them into quarters and sprinkled salt on them. Eileen set seven chipped and worn plates on a small table and placed a fork next to each. There would be no fancy potato dish this night. There was no milk, cheese or butter. No vegetables or meat either, just boiled potatoes and salt. She would save the canned goods for later. Everyone ate in silence understanding the sacrifice George had made to provide this meal.

George's mother spooned several more potato quarters onto her son Sean's plate and said, "Eat up, Sean. It'll help to make you feel better."

When they were finished eating, Eileen collected the dishes

and washed them. She placed them back on the shelf. George made a makeshift bed for Sean near the hearth and covered him with a couple of threadbare blankets. George's mother and Eileen slept in the only bed, and the other children cuddled as close as they could to the fire. George watched as they fell asleep then sat down in the corner of the room. He pulled his blanket over his head, closed his eyes and envisioned himself sitting on a white sandy beach looking out onto gently rolling waves of clear blue water. On the horizon, he could see the masts of a schooner sailing slowly towards the sun. Next to him sitting on the sand was a beautiful woman with long black hair and dark brown eyes. She took his hand in hers and kissed it. The sun was warm and his heart content.

George slowly opened his eyes, and the dream faded away. He pulled the blanket from his head and stood up. He thought he heard something outside, so he slowly walked to the door and put his hand on the latch to open it. The door exploded inward hitting George in the face. He fell backward onto the floor. Blood dripped from his nose. He shook his head to clear his vision and looked up. Constable O'Brien and two of his men were standing in the doorway. All three had shillelaghs in their hands.

CHAPTER 2

Constable O'Brien walked over to George and smashed his shillelagh on his left leg. George tried to crawl away as the other constables joined in beating George on his legs and arms. He begged them to stop, but they were relentless. Finally, O'Brien held up his hand, and the men stopped.

"Where is it, George?" O'Brien asked.

George looked at O'Brien and asked, "Where's what?"

O'Brien hit George again and yelled, "You stupid bogger. You're all alike. Think you can just take from decent folk. Did you not know you were making tracks in the snow? We followed them from O'Connor's place to here." O'Brien hit George again.

George's mother quickly placed herself between O'Brien and George and yelled, "Stop it. Francis O'Brien, you're a tool for the English, and your own sweet Ma is rolling over in her grave at the way you treat your fellow Irishmen."

O'Brien said nothing, pushed Mrs. Graham aside and pulled George to his feet. He turned to George's mother, pointed his shillelagh and said, "Stay out of this, hag. If you keep it up, I'll take you in as well."

George punched O'Brien in the jaw and yelled, "Leave my Ma out of this. I stole the potatoes. No one else was involved."

O'Brien spat blood on the floor and nodded to his fellow constables. All three started beating George again. He fell to the floor and pulled his legs up to his chest to protect himself. It didn't help. Each blow sent spirals of pain through his body. George's mother tried to pull O'Brien and the others away from her son, but they were too strong and easily pushed her away. Eileen, George's sister, also tried to stop the men. One of the constables smacked her hard in the face and Eileen fell backward onto the floor.

George's mother jumped on the constable's back, pulled his hair, and yelled, "Animal. Did you not see she is with child?"

The constable flung her from his back, and she landed beside her daughter. O'Brien, seeing they may have gone too far yelled, "That's enough." He took a minute to catch his breath and pointed to the other constables and said, "Search the house."

As George lay bleeding and bruised on the floor, the two constables started searching. They pulled the family's meager possessions from shelves and drawers with little regard. Finally, one of the constables shouted, "I found them." He looked around for something to put the potatoes in, grabbed one of the blankets Sean was using and placed the potatoes in the center.

George's mother crawled across the floor to him, placed her hand on his cheek and said, "Are you all right, George?"

George put his hand on the back of her neck and pulled her closer, then whispered in her ear, "Behind O'Connor's warehouse in the trees. Three bags of potatoes under some branches."

O'Brien pulled George's mother away from him then lifted George to a standing position. George was lightheaded, and his legs collapsed from under him. O'Brien pulled him up again and motioned to the other constables to hold him. He turned to George's mother and said, "Keep your whelps away from Letterkenny. If I see them near there, I'll put them in a cell with George, and I won't be so nice about it." Then he motioned to the other constables to take George out the door. O'Brien picked up the potatoes and left the shack.

O'Brien and the two constables who were half dragging George started back to Letterkenny. George's mother ran to the door and yelled, "Francis O'Brien, may you die a thousand burning deaths and the gates of paradise never open to you."

O'Brien stopped, turned around and looked at George's mother. He held up his hand and pointed at her. "Do as I say, Mrs. Graham. You keep your bastards out of Letterkenny." He turned and started walking again.

George's mother fell to the floor and wept.

The magistrate heard George's case the next morning. Ten minutes after the proceedings started he pronounced George guilty and sentenced him to one year of hard labor at the local prison. After two weeks the authorities allowed George's mother to visit him.

"How're you, George?" George's mother asked.

"I'm okay, Ma," George lied. The truth was his prison cell was shared by ten men and was damp and filthy. There was no water to wash with, and they relieved themselves in buckets that were collected by other prisoners each morning. Collecting piss and shit buckets were considered one of the better jobs for prisoners. George wasn't as lucky. He spent twelve hours a day, six days a week busting rocks to use for repairing bridges and public buildings.

Sunday was a day off, and in an attempt to rehabilitate the prisoners they were made to attend Church of Ireland services.

Most of the prisoners were Roman Catholic and resented being forced to listen to Protestant pastors preach how their religion was the one and only true path to salvation. George had attended twice and witnessed three fist fights between Protestant and Catholic inmates.

"Ma, they feed me once a day. So that's good. Sometimes I get Indian corn and sometimes potatoes, even some meat, but not much. It's not so bad," George said. Whispering, George asked, "Ma, did you get... you know?"

"Jimmy and Paddy went last week. Thanks to you, we'll be eating for a while," George's mother whispered back.

"And how's Sean?" George asked.

"Still coughing. I took some of the canned goods to pay the doctor. He gave him some medicine to help with his cough, but it doesn't seem to help," George's mother said. "I'm so worried, George. Sean is so ill. You're in here."

George took her hand, kissed it and said, "It'll be all right. You take care of Sean and Eileen's baby when it comes. I'll find a way to help and sooner than a wink, I'll be back home. Meanwhile, Paddy and Jimmy can try to get work."

George's mother made the sign of the cross and said, "We'll pray to God for that."

Three months later Eileen's baby was stillborn. Lack of the proper food and harsh living conditions had taken their toll on Eileen and through her, the baby. They named the infant Shamus. Paddy dug a grave in a nearby field close a large oak tree George's father when he was a boy had planted. The baby Shamus was laid to rest next to his Uncle Sean, who had died of consumption a month before, and his Grandfather.

A local priest from Letterkenny, Father O'Sullivan, blessed baby Shamus and his mother Eileen wrapped him in the best threadbare blanket the family owned. Then Eileen carried Shamus to the gravesite as the family followed. She stopped in front of the grave Paddy had dug and with tears streaming down her face kissed Shamus then handed him to his father. Paddy kissed the baby, pulled the blanket over his head and laid him in his resting place.

Father O'Sullivan performed the rites, and when he finished, he said, "God's ways are mysterious, and why he takes a baby so young we may never know. But we must believe he has a reason and that Shamus must have been a special child for God to want him by his side even before his first breath of Irish air. So rejoice in the fact that Shamus is with Jesus now. He is with his Uncle Sean and his Grandfather enjoying the benefits of eternal happiness. In time, we will all join them. Please bow your head and say a silent prayer for Shamus." Father O'Sullivan made the sign of the cross and said "In the name of the Father, the Son, and the Holy Ghost," and he bowed his head.

When George learned of Shamus's fate, he was devastated. Sean's death had shaken his belief in God and Shamus's death all but destroyed it. He simply could not understand how a loving God could wreak such devastation on Ireland, his family and himself. The old refrain *It's God's will* no longer rang true for him. *If God was almighty he could stop the suffering,* he thought. *He would make the potato blight go away. God could send the English back to Britain. Why didn't he?*

George had been told all his life that men didn't cry. Men, they said, soldiered on no matter what happened. But George did cry. He cried for Sean. He cried for Shamus and most of all he cried because he had lost his faith in God.

Conall O'Leary was in a foul mood when he inserted the key and opened the cell door. He had been drinking the night before, and his head ached. This day, like most days he hated his family, his job, and the prisoners even more. *Dirty stinking Papists most of them,* he thought.

"Get the fuck up. It's time to save your souls, you worthless pieces of dung," O'Leary yelled. The men quickly formed a line knowing if they didn't they would feel the sting of O'Leary's shillelagh. He was all too ready to administer punishment if a prisoner didn't immediately do what he ordered. He had sent more than one man to the hospital and even killed an inmate once.

George didn't move. He sat bent over with his head in his hands, hiding his tears, and oblivious to his surroundings. O'Leary saw him, smiled at the prospect of giving someone a beating, walked over to George and yelled, "What the fuck are you waiting for, Graham? You want an invitation from the Queen?" He struck George with the shillelagh on his arm. George didn't react, so O'Leary hit him on the side of his knee and yelled, "I told you to get the fuck up."

Slowly, George lifted his head and took his hands away from his eyes. O'Leary said, "Are you crying? Look boys, he's crying. I'll give you something to cry about." O'Leary lifted his shillelagh and swung it at George's head.

George caught the wooden club in his left hand and twisted as he stood up. The shillelagh fell out of O'Leary's hand and hit the floor. George was six inches taller than O'Leary and months of harsh labor had hardened his body. Still only eighteen years old, George was formidable-looking.

O'Leary stepped back a pace and yelled again, spittle coming out of his mouth, "You fucking Papist bast…" He was interrupted when George quickly moved forward and placed his ample-size hands around O'Leary's neck and began to squeeze. O'Leary's eyes bulged, and he hit George with his fists to try to get him to release his grip.

George was numb both mentally and physically and heard and felt nothing. His mind was a blur of images of the constables beating him in his mother's house, his starving dead brother Sean and the innocent baby Shamus. He squeezed harder as the other prisoners cheered. After a few minutes, O'Leary stopped struggling, but George continued to hold tight. As sudden as the cheers started, they stopped. The other prisoners just stood watching as George squeezed the life from Conall O'Leary.

Finally, George let go, and the guard constable fell backward to the ground, his lifeless eyes staring at the ceiling. George sat back down, put his hands on his face and bent over.

CHAPTER 3

"Get out of here, George. The door's open. Go," Billy Flannigan yelled.

Flannigan had become friends with George over the last few months. The two had a lot in common. They were both the same age, and both raised on a farm. Flannigan ended up in prison after he almost beat a banker to death who tried to take the family farm.

George didn't move. Flannigan ran to him, shook him and yelled, "Come on, get going before another guard shows up."

George still didn't move. Flannigan started smacking George on his head and face with his open hands, while yelling, "Get the fuck up," repeatedly. Finally, George looked up, jumped to his feet and grabbed Flannigan by his neck and began to squeeze.

Flannigan croaked, "It's me, Billy."

George loosened his grip, looked around the cell still in a daze and finally said, "Flannigan," as he realized what he was doing. He quickly took his hands away.

"Go George. They'll surely hang you for this. Go," Flannigan croaked.

George looked at the body of Conall O'Leary lying on the cell floor then to the open cell door. Flannigan pushed George towards the door and yelled again, "Go."

"Come with me, Flannigan," George said.

Flannigan shook his head no.

"Flannigan, five years. You'll be in here for five years if you don't die first. Come with me," George pleaded.

Flannigan thought for a few seconds and nodded yes. Then he turned to the other inmates and said, "Follow us if you want out." Then he pushed George out of the cell, and both men started running, followed by two of the other inmates.

Another inmate who had stayed in the cell yelled, "Come on, boyos. Let's go to the church and make a bit of a ruckus." The remaining eight inmates started down the damp and dank hall towards the room used for the Protestant church services. As they marched towards the church they began to chant, "Fuck you bastard prods. Fuck England. Fuck Queen Victoria."

By the time they arrived at the church, some fights had already broken out between the Irish Protestant and Irish Catholic inmates. Guards had been summoned from all parts of the prison to help quell the violence and began to beat the inmates with their clubs.

When Graham, Flannigan and the two other escapees arrived at the rear entrance, there was only one guard. George quickly overpowered him, knocked him to the ground and the four men ran to their freedom. By the time the guard was able to sound the alarm, Graham and his companions were a mile away.

Flannigan stopped running, held his hand up and said, "George, we need to split up. It'll make it harder to track us."

"You okay with that," George asked the other two men.

“Makes sense. We’ll try to make our way to Belfast. Maybe try to find a ship to get out of Ireland,” one of the men said.

“Good luck to you boys,” George said. They all shook hands, and the two men started running to the east.

“Which way, George,” Flannigan asked.

“Dublin. There’s a port there. Maybe we can get passage to America or Canada. Lots of other Irish over there.” George replied.

“How far is Dublin?” Flannigan asked.

“I don’t know. Pretty far, I think,” George said.

“We need to find some clothes and get some food,” Flannigan said.

“How? We’ve no money,” George asked.

“Same way that got you in prison. We steal it,” Flannigan said. “Let’s go.”

The two men started running southeast.

Chapter 4

That evening Graham and Flannigan came upon the small village of Donemana. On the outskirts of the village, there was a large manor home. George knew well Anglo-Irish aristocrats owned most of the large farms. To avoid detection, he told Billy Flannigan to stay away from the house and to look for a barn.

"Circle to the northeast. There should be a barn there," Graham said.

"And how do you know that?" Flannigan asked.

"Most of the time the wind blows from the southwest, so they build the barn so it will be upwind of the house," Graham answered.

"Oh! I'm guessing they don't much like the smell of shit with their dinner. I kind of like that smell. Reminds me of home," Flannigan said and laughed.

"This way," George said.

The moon reflected off of the ice particles that were forming on the soil as George and Flannigan made their way first along the tree line and then out into the fields. They came upon a tenant farmer's mud hut and gave it a wide berth. The barn wasn't far from the hut. They circled the barn looking for any sign of people and finally found a small door at the rear of the building.

"Let's get inside. I am freezing my ball sack off," Flannigan said.

George slowly opened the door and looked inside. The moon was shining through two large openings on the second level. It was enough light so that George could see no one was in the barn. He cautiously entered. The barn had ten stalls for horses, and there was a carriage near the rear. The farm implements hung neatly on the wall, and the hay carefully stacked on a second level.

Flannigan followed George into the barn then closed the door behind him a little too hard. It made a loud noise and scared the horses, and they began to neigh. George and Flannigan ran to an empty stall and hid fearing the noise would attract attention. After five minutes or so the horses calmed down, and no one came to the barn. George pointed up but said nothing, fearing the horses would start up again. Flannigan nodded his agreement, and the two men silently and carefully climbed the stairs to the upper level. After making beds from loose hay, they fell asleep.

George had a fitful sleep having woken once to shoo away a mouse that made a playground on his chest and then again when Flannigan started talking in his sleep. He finally fell into a deep sleep only to feel a tickling on the outside of his throat. Not opening his eyes he put his hand to his neck to chase away the mouse again. Instead, he felt something cold and hard. George's eyes opened wide and saw the pointed end of a pitchfork against his throat. As he followed the wooden pole upwards, he saw a boy no more than fifteen or sixteen looking down at him.

"Don't move," the boy said.

George put his hands up to indicate that he wasn't going to resist.

"Who the fuck are you?" the boy demanded.

The sound woke Flannigan and seeing the boy threatening George with a pitchfork, he started to get up to help him.

"If you move another inch, I swear by Christ I will plunge this into his throat and then I'll gut you with it," the boy yelled.

Flannigan sat back down.

"Now, who are you and why are you here?" the boy demanded again.

George pulled his head back a little so he could talk without the spikes of the pitchfork digging into his skin and said, "I'm George Graham, and this is Billy Flannigan. We're both from Letterkenny."

"Well then George, why are you in my barn?"

"We're on our way to Dublin and needed to get out of the cold," George answered.

"Umm, considering the clothes you're both wearing you might be escaped prisoners." the boy said. "Maybe I should turn you in? Might be a reward."

George looked at Flannigan who yelled, "Go ahead, you Anglo bastard, turn us in."

The boy looked shocked and moved the pitchfork to Flannigan's chest and yelled, "I'm no fucking Anglo. You say that again, and I'll spear you like a fish."

"You said it was your barn," George said.

The boy looked at George, opened his eyes wide and said, "Well, I take care of it and the horses for the master of the house."

"Does your family farm for the master?" George asked.

"They did. My Ma and Da died of smallpox when I was elven."

"Sorry," George said.

The boy looked at George than at Flannigan and said, "I get along okay. I keep the barn clean and care for the horses and the foreman allows me to grow food and lets me sleep here."

"What kind of food does he let you grow?" Flannigan asked.

"Potatoes. What else?"

"So the foreman is so kind he lets you grow and eat potatoes and allows you to sleep in horse shit," Flannigan said sarcastically.

"I didn't say that. He's a proper bastard to be sure, and the master doesn't even know I'm around unless something goes wrong."

"Then what?" George said.

"Then I get the strap," the boy said.

"Was your Ma and Da Catholic?"

"They were, but they don't allow that here. We can only go to the Church of Ireland." the boy said.

"Let me get this straight. You can only grow and eat potatoes. You have to sleep on hay in the barn with the horses, and they beat you if you do something wrong. You get no pay, and you can't even worship as your Ma and Da did. Is that right?" George asked.

The boy looked bewildered and finally said, "Yes pretty much."

"Don't you think maybe you got that pitchfork at the wrong throat?" George said and tilted his head.

The boy looked at him for a long time, then took the pitchfork away and threw it to the floor. He sat down on the hay and said, "What else am I to do. I got nowhere to go. No family. This is," he waved his arm around, "all I have."

"No, you have us. Come with us. We're going to Dublin and then to Canada and maybe the United States," George said.

"The United States! I hear everyone has money there, and you can eat meat every day," the boy said his voice brightening.

"That's right, and there're plenty of Irish people there already," George said.

"Have you ever been to Dublin?" Flannigan asked.

"I have, twice. Went with the master's family and took care of the horses," the boy answered.

Do you know your way around the city?" George asked.

"A little," the boy said.

"Well, what do you think? You want to come with us?" George asked.

The boy looked at them both for a minute and said, "You two have been in jail. How do I know if you're telling the truth? What if I go with you and you murder me on the way?"

George laughed and said, "Do we look like murderers?"

"You don't, but," pointing at Flannigan."But he does." the boy said pointing at Flannigan and then smiled. "What'd you do anyway?"

George smiled back and said, "Well, I stole a sack of potatoes to feed my starving family. They beat me senseless and gave me one year of hard labor. Flannigan here beat the piss out of an Anglo banker who wanted to take his house. He got five years hard labor. By the way, what's your name?"

"Danny," the boy said and stuck his hand out to shake George's hand. "Danny O'Boyle." Then he shook Flannigan's hand.

"Well, what do you say, Danny O'Boyle?" George asked.

O'Boyle shut his eyes so he could think. After a couple of minutes, he opened his eyes and said, "I'll go, but not with you dressed like that."

"That's all we got, Danny," Flannigan said.

Danny thought for a minute then said, "I have a plan. We

wait here until the end of the workday tomorrow. The foreman, the drunken sod that he is, always goes into town to the pub. The master and his family aren't here. They live in Belfast and only come in the summer. Once the foreman is gone, I'll sneak into the house and grab some clothes for you and some food. Then we can leave."

"What about the servants?" Flannigan asked.

"You leave them to me," Danny said.

CHAPTER 5

Mrs. McGorry, the main house's caretaker, was just finishing washing the dinner dishes when she heard a tapping on the back door window. Cullen McCorkle, the farm's foreman and man in charge when the master and his family were not present had gone to Maguire's Pub in the village, so she assumed it was Danny O'Boyle. Danny often came after dinner to see if there were any scraps left over and Mrs. McGorry always made sure there were.

She opened the door and said, "Come on in, Danny, McCorkle's gone."

Danny started to walk through the door when Mrs. McGorry said firmly, "Hold on, Danny," and then pointed to his shoes.

Danny quickly bent down and loosened his laces, slipped his shoes off and walked into the kitchen.

"Good evening, Mrs. McGorry. You're looking younger every day," Danny said.

"You're a good liar, Danny O'Boyle. Go ahead. I saved you a piece of pie, a slice of meat and some bread. It's on the table there," Mrs. McGorry said.

Danny kissed her on the cheek," and said, "Thank you, and I'm not lying." Then he sat down and started eating the bread.

"Danny O'Boyle, did you forget something?"

Danny looked at Mrs. McGorry with concern then relaxed and nodded yes. He made the sign of the cross and said, "In the name of the Father, Son, and Holy Ghost. Thank you, Lord, for this food I am about to eat that Mrs. McGorry stole from our master."

Mrs. McGorry lightly smacked Danny on the back of the head, smiled and said, "Go ahead, eat."

Danny finished the bread, meat, and pie and sat back and said, "Mrs. McGorry, I'm leaving."

She stopped sweeping the floor and said, "What do you mean you're leaving?"

"I'm going to America to make my fortune. I can't stay here anymore," Danny said.

A tear formed in Mrs. McGorry's left eye and rolled down her reddened cheek. She dabbed the tear with her dishcloth and said, "I understand."

"I need your help," Danny said.

"We've no money of our own, Danny. You know that."

"How about rope? Do you have some rope?" Danny asked.

Mrs. McGorry looked at Danny quizzically and said, "Yes, in the cupboard."

Danny went to the cupboard, opened the door and found the rope. "Here, sit in this chair," Danny said as he placed a kitchen chair behind her.

Mrs. McGorry sat down, and Danny started wrapping the rope around her.

"That's not too tight, is it?" Danny asked.

"No, it's fine, but you better bind my hands as well," Mrs. McGorry said, now realizing what Danny was doing.

He did as she told him and asked, “Is that okay?”

“Yes, that’s fine. Now go get my husband. He’s in our room.” Danny did as Mrs. McGorry asked.

When Mr. McGorry came into the kitchen, he started to say, “What’s go…” when Mrs. McGorry interrupted him.

“Sit in the chair, Timothy. Young Danny needs our help.”

Looking concerned he reluctantly sat in a chair Danny had placed in front of Mrs. McGorry. He wrapped the rope around Mr. McGorry and then bound his hands.

“Timothy, Danny’s going to have to thump you in the jaw. Not too hard, Danny. Just enough to draw some blood.”

Mr. McGorry’s eyes opened wide as Danny punched him. A small amount of blood formed in the corner of Mr. McGorry’s mouth and streaked down his chin.

“Good. Now Danny, get something to scrape up his knuckles. Make it look like he hit you. That’s what we’ll tell Mr. McCorkle when he finds us. We’ll say you had help and overpowered Timothy. Isn’t that right, Timothy?”

Mr. McGorry shook his head yes. Danny found a rough file and ran it over Mr. McGorry’s knuckles.

“Let me see, Danny,” Mrs. McGorry said.

Danny turned the chair so she could see Mr. McGorry’s hand. “Good. That’ll do.” Danny turned the chair back.

“Now, if you’re done mutilating me, can you tell me what the hell’s going on here?” Mr. McGorry asked.

“No need for profanity, Timothy. Young Danny here is going to America. Going to make his fortune, he is. He’ll be needing to borrow a few things to help him,” Mrs. McGorry said. “Go ahead, Danny. Get what you need.”

Danny kissed her on the forehead and ran to the upstairs level. He riffled through the masters clothing and took three pairs of pants, three shirts, and three jackets. As he was leaving the room, he noticed a small case with a glass door. In the case was a revolver. He broke the glass and took the revolver and put it in his waistband. There was also some ammunition, and he took that as well.

Back in the kitchen, Danny grabbed as much food as he thought he could carry and put it on the table. He started looking around for something to put it in.

"You'll find a knapsack in the closet. While you're there, look for the cookie jar. There's some house money in there," Mrs. McGorry said.

Danny put the money in his pocket then filled the knapsack with the food. He kissed Mrs. McGorry on the head again and said, "I'll miss you. You've been like a Ma to me since my own Ma died."

Mrs. McGorry tried to hold back her tears but failed. She said, "Come back some day and tell us all about your adventures."

"I will. I promise." Danny turned to Mr. McGorry and said, "I'm sorry."

"Don't worry about it. I inherited the McGorry hard head. Godspeed, my boy."

"Before I leave, can I do anything for you? Do you want me to loosen the ropes?" Danny asked.

"No Danny. You best be going before McCorkle gets back," Mrs. McGorry said.

Danny quickly turned and ran out the door.

"Katy, you know that boy will never be back here," Mr. McGorry said.

"I know," Mrs. McGorry said as the tears rolled down her cheeks.

Danny ran back to the barn and had George and Flannigan change into the clothes he had stolen.

"I got some food for our trip. We best be going. You can eat on the road," Danny said.

George and Flannigan started for the door, and Danny yelled, "No, No. We're going in style. Do you two know how to ride?"

"We do," Flannigan answered.

"Good, then let's saddle up. I'll show you the best horses. We need to make some time tonight. McCorkle's not going to like this," Danny said.

CHAPTER 6

The three fugitives rode through the night guided only by moonlight. Fortunately, the moon was almost full, and the illumination was good. Still, it was slow going.

By sunrise, they came upon a small river. The rising sun shimmered off of the water running over the rocky terrain. After a momentary stop to see if there was anyone nearby, they passed through the trees to an open area of ground leading to the water's edge. About two hundred feet upriver George could see there were two children and guessed it was a boy and a girl about eleven years old. They were spearfishing.

The children saw them and started to run away. George yelled, "It's okay, we're friends. They're God's fish, and he wants you to have them."

The children waved, and the three men waved back.

"If they get caught the least that will happen is they'll get a good beating," Danny said.

The English imposed laws in Ireland that protected landowners from anyone poaching on their lands. Even in times of famine and strife, it was illegal to find your food from the rivers or land of the Anglo-Irish landowners. There were severe penalties that could lead to beatings, jail or even eviction from tenant farms. There was little mercy for starving Irish farmers.

"Look at that. The girl caught herself a fish. Looks like a nice size," Flannigan said.

"So she has," Danny said.

All of the sudden George jumped on this horse and headed at a gallop towards the children. Flannigan and Danny looked after him, and Flannigan yelled, "What the hell are you doing, George?"

As soon as he said it, he saw for himself why George galloped away. A couple of hundred feet upriver from the children, two men were running quickly towards them.

Flannigan yelled at Danny, "Constables. Let's go." Both men took to their horses and followed George.

Just as George got to the children, the girl saw the constables and started to run. She tripped, and the fishing spear she was holding with the fish on it pierced her leg. She screamed in pain and fell to the ground. Her brother stopped and knelt next to her.

By the time George got to the children, the constables were only about one hundred feet away. George quickly took off his coat and draped it over both the boy and girl and said, "Don't come out. If they can't see you, they won't know who your parents are."

George quickly turned and waited for the constables to come to him. When they did, he held out his hand and said, "Hold up there."

Both constables stopped, and one bent over breathing hard and the other one, obviously in better shape said, "And who the hell are you?" The constable was confused because George was dressed in fine clothing, but he did not recognize him.

"No one you would know," George answered.

"Then get out of the way and let me arrest those children," the constable said.

"No, I don't think you'll be arresting any children today," George said.

"And I suppose you're going to stop me?" the constable said in a mocking voice as he lifted his shillelagh and tapped it on his open hand.

Just then the other constable having caught his breath lifted his club and waited for his superior's orders. "Constable Ryan, go get those children."

Constable Ryan moved towards George, and when he was just a few feet away, George leaped towards him and grabbed the shillelagh. He twisted it, and Ryan lost his grip. George threw the shillelagh in the river.

"You bloody bastard, that was my Da's," Ryan said and threw a punch at George.

George blocked the punch with his left arm and hit Ryan in his eye with his right fist. Stunned, Ryan staggered back towards the river. George quickly moved towards him and pushed on his chest with two hands knocking Ryan back and into the river. While Ryan was falling backward into the water, George said, "If it's that important then you best go get it."

The other constable acted quickly and lifted his club ready to hit George on the head. Before he could swing the club, a shot rang out, and the constable stopped and backed up. Danny O'Boyle and Flannigan rode up to George and the constable. Danny said, "Drop it."

The constable looked at Danny but did not drop the club.

Danny cocked the pistol and pointed it at the constable. "I don't want to hurt you, but I will if I have to. Please drop the club before you make me a murderer," Danny said.

The constable dropped his club, and George picked it up.

"I'll remember you three. You can be sure of that," the constable growled.

Constable Ryan was hanging onto the bank of the river trying to pull himself out of the water but without success.

"Go help your friend out of the water," George said.

The constable walked over to Constable Ryan, bent over and put his hand out. As soon as the two men grasped each other's hands, George kicked the constable in his buttocks, and he fell forward into the river taking Ryan further out. The current caught both men, and they quickly moved down river.

As Danny and Flannigan laughed, George pulled his coat off of the children and said, "Let me see your wound."

The child pulled her dress up a bit and revealed two bleeding holes in her calf.

"It's not so bad, sir," the girl said.

"Can you walk?" George asked.

"Yes, sir."

Is this your brother?" George asked.

"Yes, his name is Sean, and I'm Catherine." She hesitated and then said, "Sir."

"You two best be on your way before the constables come back. Get your Ma to put some vinegar or Whiskey if she's got it on the wound. You'll be okay," George ordered.

The girl tentatively stood up, adjusted her dress and said, "Sir, can you tell me your name? I want to tell my mother who helped us.

"Just tell her three angels saved you," George said.

The girl's eyes opened wide, and she made the sign of the cross and started to limp away with her brother helping her.

"Wait," George said. "You forgot your fish and spear." He picked it up and handed it to the brother.

"Thank you, sir." the girl said and left.

George mounted his horse, looked at Flannigan and Danny and said, "Well, what are you waiting for?"

"Angels. Is that what we are?" Flannigan said and smiled.

George pointed south and said," Let's find a place to cross this river before more constables show up."

With that, the three men galloped away. In a few minutes, they saw Ryan and his boss still floating down the river and trying to find a way out. As they passed them, Flannigan yelled out, "Having a good swim, are we?"

"Go fuck yourself," Constable Ryan yelled back as the three rode off laughing.

CHAPTER 7

Dublin, Ireland - 1882

Trying to avoid anyone who might be chasing them, George, Flannigan and Danny stayed in the trees instead of traveling on the road. It was harder riding and took them longer, but it was safer. As they came close to Dublin and the forest thinned out, they had to ease back on the well-traveled road.

There were water troughs along the road, and they stopped to water and rest their horses. After the horses had their fill, Danny led them to an open area just off of the road and allowed them to graze on what grass there was. Then he climbed up a tree near the edge of the road and sat on a limb.

"Danny, what the hell are you doing?" Flannigan asked.

Well, Mr. Flannigan, I'm sitting in a tree," Danny replied a bit sarcastically.

"For fuck's sake, I can see that. But why are you sitting in a tree?"

"I don't know. I just like sitting in a tree," Danny answered.

Flannigan turned to George, who was sitting next to him, and said, "I think that boy's a bit daft."

George smiled but said nothing. He laid back on the grass and shut his eyes. After a minute or so Flannigan did the same. In what seemed like a second, but was actually thirty minutes, George was woken by Danny's frantic slaps on his face and yelling, "George, wake up. Hurry." George opened his eyes and when he did, Danny shook Flannigan and yelled, "Get up."

Flannigan, in shock from being woken from a deep sleep, grabbed Danny by his coat, pulled him to the ground. Danny yelled, "Get up. Get your stuff, we have to leave."

"Why?" George asked.

"It's McCorkle, from the farm, and he's got men with him. Let me up. They're close now."

Flannigan let Danny up, and Danny ran to the horses, with Flannigan and George following. Flannigan jumped on his horse and Danny said, "No. Leave the horses and get your stuff. We'll go into the woods over there." He pointed at a dense area of forest just a hundred feet to the south.

The three men ran to the woods and entered the thicket just as McCorkle came upon the horses. McCorkle pointed to the horses and nodded to one of his men. The man jumped down from his animal and inspected the three horses and nodded back in the affirmative.

"Everyone, go search for O'Boyle. Remember, the constables said he was with two other men and he has a pistol," McCorkle said as he dismounted. The men searched for over an hour and found nothing. Finally, McCorkle said, "Take the horses. We'll go to the docks. He thinks he's going to America so that's where we'll find him."

With Danny in the lead, the three fugitives made their way through the woods until they came to an open area. Danny peered out from the trees and said, "Okay, it's clear."

"I think this is Phoenix Park. Look, there's the Zoological Gardens to the left, "Danny said.

"What's that," Flannigan asked.

"That's a place where they collect all manner of animals. Last time I was here I saw a tiger from India," Danny said.

"What do they do with these animals?" Flannigan asked.

"They put them in cages, and people go look at them," Danny answered.

Flannigan thought for a minute and said, "It's like a prison. I don't think I like that."

"You'd like it less if you were in the cage, which you will be if we don't get into the city," George said.

"If we go straight for a couple of miles we should come to Dublin proper," Danny said.

"What're we waiting for? Let's go," George said as he walked out of the trees and into the open park. Danny and Flannigan followed.

The trio walked several more hours, with wide-eyed wonderment, passing through Dublin proper and past St. Patrick's Cathedral. The crowded streets and abundance of shops and tall buildings were unfamiliar to George and Flannigan. George became uncomfortable with the crowds and when they finally came to a less crowded section of the city near the Dublin Bay called Irish Town, he was happy. They found a pub named Brennan's that also offered rooms to rent and after paying in advance, sat down for their first meal since the evening before.

"I could eat a horse," Danny said.

"By the looks of this place you just might," Flannigan quipped.

"If you're so concerned, why'd you order so much food," George asked.

"I'm a growing boy, don't you know," Flannigan said and laughed.

An attractive young woman, holding two loaves of soda bread, walked up to their table and said, "You're a happy bunch." She placed the bread on the table and continued, "Here, this should hold you till your food's ready."

"We are happy. Very happy," Danny said.

"And why's that?" the woman asked.

"Because a red-haired, greened-eyed beauty with the complexion of a goddess just served us soda bread," Danny said and gave her a wide smile.

She smiled back and asked sweetly, "What's your name?"

"Danny."

"Well, Danny boy, you'll have to do a lot better than that. I hear every sort of silver tongue talk, and that was one of the worse yet," the young woman said and walked away.

Danny yelled after her, "What's your name?"

She stopped, turned around and said, "Kathleen, but you can call me Miss O'Toole."

Danny smiled, and George and Flannigan laughed as they tore off pieces of the soda bread.

Ten minutes later Kathleen placed three bowls of hot lamb stew on the table. "Here you go, boys," Kathleen said. "The best mutton stew in all of Dublin."

Flannigan grabbed his fork and started to eat. Kathleen reached out and held Flannigan's left hand so he couldn't eat. He looked at her and smiled.

"And what's your name?" Kathleen asked.

"William, but you can call me Billy," Flannigan said.

"Billy, may I ask you a question?" Kathleen asked.

"Sure you can," Billy answered.

"Are you Catholic?"

"I am," Flannigan said.

"Did your Ma not teach you to do the blessing before you eat?" Kathleen said.

Flannigan's face turned red, and he said, "She did."

Kathleen took his right hand and said, as she put his hand to her forehead, "In the name of the Father." She placed his hand just below her breasts and said, "The Son." Then she moved his hand to the top of her left breast and said, "And the Holy." She then moved his hand to the top of her right breast and continued, "Ghost." Finally, she moved his now-trembling hand to the center of her breast and finished, "Amen. Now, Billy, you can eat."

"Can I get you more ale?" Kathleen asked.

The three men stared at her for longer than was comfortable before Danny said, "Yes."

All three looked as Kathleen turned and walked to the bar. George let out his breath and said, "I was going to go get rid of some of this fine ale, but I don't think I should stand up right now."

"When I get like that I just give me old shillelagh a quick snap of a finger on the head," Danny said as he demonstrated in the air. "That does the trick."

Kathleen brought the three ales just as Danny snapped his finger. "What're you doing there, Danny?" Kathleen asked.

"Nothing, just showing how I get rid of a fly, that's all," Danny said.

"You haven't eaten your stew yet. Better get to it before it gets cold," Kathleen said.

Flannigan held up his fork, stabbed it in the stew and put it in his mouth and smiled.

"What are you boys doing in Dublin?" Kathleen asked.

Danny said proudly, "We're going to America. Gonna make our fortunes, we are."

"Is that so. Let me see your tickets?" Kathleen asked.

"We don't have them yet. Maybe you can help us?" Danny said.

"Maybe, what do you need?"

"Where should we go to get our tickets?" Danny asked.

"Do you have the money? It's four pounds each just for steerage," Kathleen asked.

"We do, and a bit more so we can get started in America," Danny said.

"Kingstown. It's just down the road a bit. You can walk. Most of the ships go to Liverpool from there," Kathleen explained.

Liverpool, we want to go to America, not England," George said.

"First you go to Liverpool and get a ship to take you to New York in America," Kathleen said.

"We'll be going tomorrow then," George said. "Thank you, Kathleen."

When they were finished eating, Danny pulled some coins out of his pocket and put them on the table. Kathleen scooped them up and said, "I'll be right back with your change."

When Kathleen returned, she told Danny to open his hand. When he did, she placed the change in his hand and quickly closed it.

"My Da used to say this prayer whenever one of our family traveled. I want to say it for you, so you have a safe trip. May St. Patrick guard you wherever you go, and guide you in whatever you do—and may his loving protection be a blessing to you always. Amen." A tear rolled down Kathleen's cheek as she finished the prayer. Then she turned and walked away.

Danny opened his hand. There were three coins and a piece of folded paper.

"What's that?" George asked.

Danny opened the paper, looked at it and smiled widely. "It's her room number."

CHAPTER 8

Danny O'Boyle paced the room like the tiger in a cage he had once seen at the Dublin Zoological Gardens. He slowly walked to one end of the small room, turned and walked back. After twenty minutes of this Flannigan said, "For Christ's sake, Danny, just go."

"I don't know what to do. I've never been with a girl before," Danny said.

"Well, I imagine you'll figure it out when the time comes," Flannigan said.

"Tell me. Tell me what to do," Danny pleaded.

"I don't know, Danny. I've never been with a woman either," Flannigan said.

Danny let out a sigh and said, "Just great! We're all a bunch of virgins."

"When you first see her tell her how beautiful she looks," George said.

Danny and Flannigan turned to look at George as he continued. "Ask her about herself. Where she's from. Why she's in Dublin, and especially ask about her family. Women like to talk."

"And how is it you know about being with a woman, George?" Flannigan asked.

Feeling a pang of sorrow, George said, "I had a girlfriend once. It's what she liked,"

"What happened to her," Danny asked.

"She moved with her family. I think they went to Canada."

Flannigan lowered his voice and asked, "And you had sex with her?"

"I'm not proud of it, but yes a few times," George also said in a low voice.

Danny sat down on the floor, and Flannigan turned, and both looked intently at George.

Danny said, "And?"

Graham still keeping his voice low said, "As I said, they like to talk for a while, and eventually she will lean into you, and you can kiss her. Be gentle. Girls like that too. You'll feel like your body's about to explode but hold it. Then you slowly caress her breasts and again be gentle. After that, things will just happen, and you'll find, what did you call it, your old shillelagh in her honey pot."

"There you go, Danny. It's everything you need to know, now get your ass to Kathleen's room before I do," Flannigan said.

Danny stood up, smiled and walked to the door. As he opened it he turned and said, "If I'm not back in the morning, come rescue me."

Kathleen's room was on the third floor, and as Danny walked up the steps, he found himself getting hard. By the time he reached her room, he was about to burst. He started to think about unpleasant events in his life to help him control himself. It worked a little, but when Kathleen answered the door wearing her nightdress, he started to throb.

"Danny, I thought you weren't coming. Enter please," Kathleen said.

"You look so…." Danny paused then said, "beautiful."

Kathleen was standing in the doorway, and she turned so Danny could enter, but only by sliding past her. As he turned and came into the room, she moved slightly towards him, so his erect penis caressed her lower parts. Danny began to throb even more, and he thought he would explode then and there. He immediately started to relive the time McCorkle had beat him with a leather strap for failing to clean one of the horse stalls. It helped, but just a little.

There was a small table with two chairs next to the bed. Danny asked if he could sit down thinking that would help him keep control.

"Of course, Danny. Sit please," Kathleen said as she placed a glass in front of him and another in front of herself. She poured whiskey into both glasses, being sure that Danny's glass had more of the potent liquid. She picked up her glass and said, "To America. May your trip be safe and your arrival welcomed."

Danny picked up his glass, touched Kathleen's glass and drank. He immediately began to choke.

"Are you okay?" Kathleen asked.

Danny swallowed a few times, and in a hoarse voice said, "Fine. It's strong."

Kathleen smiled and said, "So you don't drink whiskey, Danny?"

"I have a couple of times," Danny lied.

"Well, tonight you will learn to drink like an Irishman," Kathleen said as she filled Danny's glass. "Drink it down."

He did as Kathleen ordered. Danny, following George's suggestion, began to ask Kathleen about her family, why she was working at the pub, and anything else he could think of to show he was interested in her. As she answered, she kept pouring whiskey into Danny's glass, and he kept drinking.

"I'm feeling a bit faint," Danny said.

"It's okay. It's just the whiskey. It'll go away. Here, one more glass and I'll help you to the bed," Kathleen said.

Danny drank the whiskey, stood up and immediately fell back down into his seat. Kathleen took him by the arm and helped him to the bed. He flopped back on it. Kathleen undid his belt and slid his pants off. As drunk as he was Danny still had an erection. Kathleen took his hardened member in her hand and began to stroke softly.

Oh sweet Jesus," Danny said. Then he passed out.

"Danny, wake up," George yelled as he banged on Kathleen's room door.

There was no response so George banged on the door again, as loud as he could. Danny was startled and sat up abruptly. He immediately grabbed his head as a sharp pain seemed to envelop his brain. His mouth was as dry as a cotton ball and his stomach was churning.

George banged on the door again and yelled, "Get the fuck up, Danny. We need to go buy our tickets."

"For the good Lord's sake, stop yelling," Danny croaked. He stood up and almost fell back on the bed but caught himself. Danny staggered to the door as he said, "Hold your horses, I'm coming."

When he opened the door, he saw Flannigan and George standing in the doorway. Both were wearing big grins.

"Did you have a good night, Danny?" Flannigan asked.

Danny thought for a second and said, "I don't remember."

George and Flannigan looked at each other and burst out laughing.

George tilted his head and stared indicating Danny should look down. Danny appeared confused and then looked down and yelled, "Jesus Christ," and put his 'shillelagh' back inside his underwear. George bent over laughing, and Flannigan fell to the floor howling.

Danny's faced turned scarlet red, and he said, "Fuck both of you."

Flannigan tried to catch his breath between bouts of laughter and said, "Was that a bearded pissworm you had in your pants?" George burst out laughing again as did Flannigan.

"You can laugh all you want, but I was the only one with a girl last night," Danny said.

"You're right, Danny. What did you say you did last night?" George asked.

"I told you already, I don't remember," Danny said.

"Then how do you know you were even with a woman?" George retorted.

"My cock was out, wasn't it?" Danny said.

All three men started to laugh again. When they had calmed down George said, "Get your pants on, Danny. We have some tickets to buy."

"In a couple of months we'll be in America, and you can try your little inchworm out on some Yankee girls," Flannigan said and laughed at his joke.

Danny pulled up his pants and tucked in his shirt. He looked for his shoes, found them and slipped them on then picked up his jacket. "I'm ready," Danny said and patted the pocket where the money was.

He looked at George then checked his other pocket, then his jacket. He frantically began to look around the room.

"What's the matter, Danny?" George asked.

"I can't find my money."

The three men tore the room apart, but there was no money.

"Maybe Kathleen knows where it is," Flannigan said.

"George, looked at him, then at Danny and asked, "Where's Kathleen?"

"Working, I guess," Danny said and ran out the door, George and Flannigan following. He found the owner of the pub behind the bar cleaning glasses.

"Where's Kathleen?" Danny asked.

"Gone, she left early this morning," the owner said.

"Gone where?" George asked

"How should I know?" the owner answered.

"She works for you, so you should know," Danny yelled.

"She don't work for me," the owner said.

George grabbed the owner by the shirt and pulled him over the bar and yelled, "What do you mean? She waited on us last night," George said.

"She came in yesterday, said she had no place to stay. I told her I'd give her a room for the night if she worked a shift for me. We were shorthanded, you see. I swear I never saw her before," the owner said.

Danny finally realizing what had happened sank to the floor and put his hands on his face. Then he started to hit himself in the head and yelled, "Stupid, stupid, stupid."

Flannigan helped Danny up and sat him on a stool. "Look Danny, we all fell for it. Not just you."

"What're we going to do?" Danny asked.

CHAPTER 9

George let the pub owner down and sat on a barstool next to Danny.

"What's going on, boys?" the pub owner asked.

"Kathleen stole our money. We were going to buy tickets to America," Flannigan said as he took the stool on the other side of Danny.

Now understanding what had happened, the pub owner said, "Look boys, I run an upright place here. I knew nothing about this. I swear on my Mother, May she rest in peace."

"Do you have an idea of how we can find Kathleen?" George asked.

"I'm sorry, I don't. She never said anything. I'm afraid you won't find her. It's a big city," the pub owner answered. Then he shuffled through some papers under the bar, found what he was looking for, placed a piece of paper on the bar and continued. "A couple of weeks ago a man stopped in for a drink and left me his address. He said that if I knew any men looking for work to send them by."

"What kind of work," Danny asked.

"He didn't say."

"What do you think, George? We try to get some work and save enough for passage," Danny asked.

"How long will that take? I think too long, I fear," George said.

"What choice have we?" Flannigan said.

George thought for a second and asked, "What's the address?"

"It says here O'Brien's Pub on Monkstown Road. Not far from the Kingstown harbor. The man's name is Casey McGrath," the pub owner explained.

"How far is it?" George asked.

"Oh, I would guess about five miles. Just follow the coast south. People are friendly down there. Just ask, and they'll direct you," the pub owner said.

"Thanks. We best be going," George said.

The pub owner opened his cash drawer, pulled out two shillings and placed them on the bar and said, "I'm not a rich man, but I can spare this to help you get some food and maybe a drink or two when you get to Kingstown. I'm truly sorry this happened in my pub."

Danny picked up the money, put it in his pocket and said, "Thanks, that's very generous. We'll pay you back when we can."

The pub owner nodded, and George, Flannigan and Danny walked out the door.

"At least it's not raining," Flannigan said, then took a long breath of the fresh sea air. "It's a fine day for a long walk."

"Best we stay off the main road. McCorkle's no fool. He'll know we're trying to get a ship out of Ireland," Danny said.

Having to walk off the road and through mostly undeveloped wooded areas slowed them down. So did occasionally trying to find someone to ask directions. It was early evening by the time they arrived at O'Brien's Pub on Monkstown Road. It looked pretty much like Brennan's Pub they had just left.

As they entered the pub, several men sitting at the bar stopped talking and looked at them for a minute then started talking again. George saw a table towards the back of the pub and the three newcomers walked to it and sat down. Several minutes later a plump older woman set three glasses of ale on their table.

"You boys looked thirsty so I thought I might start you off with these," the woman said.

"Thanks," Flannigan said, then picked up the glass and downed the contents.

"Well, it looks like I was correct. I'll get you another," the woman said.

"Thanks," Flannigan said.

When she returned she placed the new glass in front of Flannigan and asked, "What can I get you, boys?" Not waiting for an answer, she continued, "I suggest the bacon and cabbage. We make the best in all of Monkstown as well as Kingstown."

"I'd love some of the best bacon and cabbage in all of Kingstown," Danny said.

"Me too," Flannigan added.

George nodded his head in the affirmative and the older women left saying, "Good choice."

Once the woman set the dishes on the table, she said, "My name is Mrs. O'Brien. If you need anything else, let me know."

"Would you be related to the owner of this fine establishment?" Danny asked.

"For certain I am. My husband and I own it," Mrs. O'Brien said.

"Well, I have to say you did not exaggerate about the quality of the bacon and cabbage," Danny said. He continued, "Mr. O'Brien is a lucky man to have such a young and pretty wife."

Mrs. O'Brien blushed then smiled and left without saying anything.

Flannigan looked after her, turned to Danny and said, "She's old enough to be your grandma."

"It never hurts to offer some flattery now and again. Something you should learn, Flannigan," Danny said.

A few minutes later Mrs. O'Brien returned with three more glasses of ale, put them on the table and said," On the house, boys."

Danny looked at Flannigan and raised his eyebrows as if to say *I told you so.*

"Mrs. O'Brien, before you leave would you be so kind as to tell me where we can find a Mr. McGrath, Mr. Casey McGrath?" George asked.

"You boys looking for work?" Mrs. O'Brien asked.

"Yes Ma'me, we are?" George answered.

"Mr. McGrath has a room upstairs. I'll send someone up to get him. Now finish your meal. Mr. McGrath will be down soon," Mrs. O'Brien said.

Fifteen minutes later a man, almost as tall as George, approached their table and said, "I'm Casey McGrath. Mrs. O'Brien mentioned you were asking for me. How may I help you, boys?"

George, Flannigan, and Danny rose from their seats, and Danny stuck his hand out and said, "Good to meet you, Mr. McGrath." McGrath shook Danny's hand, and Danny continued, "I'm Danny O'Boyle, this is George Graham and Billy Flannigan."

McGrath shook Flannigan's hand and then George's and said, "It's good to meet you. May I sit down?"

"Yes, sir. Please do," Danny said.

McGrath took his seat and motioned with his hand to Mrs. O'Brien. She returned a few minutes later with a bottle of whiskey and four glasses, poured each man a full measure and said in her motherly tone, "Mr. McGrath is a fine gentleman. So listen to him, and he will help you."

"I understand you boys are looking for work," McGrath said.

"Yes, sir. Mr. Brennan, who owns Brennan's Pup in Irishtown told us to talk to you about getting work," Danny said.

"Ah yes, Mr. Brennan. He's a fine gent, he is. He didn't lie to you. I represent an excellent organization that's looking for strong young men such as you. Have you heard of the French Foreign Legion?" Mr. McGrath said.

Flannigan looked at George who shook his head no, and Danny looked at Flannigan who also shook his head no. "No we have not, sir," Danny said.

"What if I told you that the French government is willing to feed you, provide your clothing and shelter you? Would that be to your liking?" McGrath said.

"Depends on what we have to do," Danny said.

"Would you like to see the world? Go to warm exotic countries?" McGrath continued, after a pause, "Look, boys, we don't care where you're from or what you've done. You don't need any papers. You just have to be eighteen or older and pass a simple medical physical. Do you think you would want to do that?"

"And what do we have to do in return," Danny asked again.

"You'll have to sign a contract with the Irish Brigade of the French Foreign Legion. You'll be soldiers then, uniforms and all. You know the ladies like a man in uniform," McGrath said.

"Would we get to fight?" Flannigan said.

"I'm sure you will."

"What about pay? Do we get paid?" Danny said.

"Yes, you get paid, and it increases as you get promotions. Since you will be traveling to Cochinchina you'll also get additional colonial pay," McGrath said, leaving out just how little the pay was.

"You said China. Do they have coconuts there?" George asked.

"Yes, they have coconuts and every other manner of fruit and vegetables," McGrath said.

"We're going to America to make our fortunes so I don't think we can join your French Foreign Legion,» Danny said.

"How old are you, Danny," McGrath asked.

"18," Danny lied.

"Your contract is for five years, and you'll only be twenty-three when you finish. You'll have seen the world, made money and learned the ways of the world. Then you can go to America. I'll tell you what. We'll give you a bonus of one pound sterling each for signing up. So what do you say?" McGrath said.

"One pound! That much?" George said.

"You'll get it as soon as you sign," McGrath said, holding up his right hand.

"Can you send it to our families for us?" George asked.

"Yes, we do it quite often. I have several forms here for you to sign. Can you boys write and read?" McGrath asked.

Each of the boys, having gone to national schools, said they could read and write. So McGrath put several forms in front of each man and said, "The first one is for sending your bonus to your family. Add their address and my clerk Mrs. O'Brien will have the money sent. The second paper is your contract. Please sign it and put your birth date. The third paper is information about your family so we can notify them in the very unlikely event you're killed while doing your duty," McGrath explained.

Danny looked up at McGrath, paused for a few seconds and then began to fill out the papers. When all three had finished, McGrath collected the papers, separated the cash transfers and placed a pound note on each.

"Mr. O'Boyle, you didn't fill out your bank transfer," McGrath said.

"I'll be keeping mine, sir. My parents are dead," Danny said and took the one pound note.

McGrath called for Mrs. O'Brien and asked her to arrange for the money to get to the families. He also asked if Mrs. O'Brien would see if Dr. Fitzgerald, who was sitting at the bar, wouldn't mind coming over to meet the boys.

"Mrs. O'Brien, could you also see that these two shillings get sent to Mr. Brennan at Brennan's Pub in Irishtown?" Danny said and handed her the two shillings Brennan had given him.

"Once the medical physical is complete you can take the oath," McGrath said.

Dr. Fitzgerald slowly walked from the bar to the table McGrath was sitting at and motioned with his hands that the three candidates should stand. When they did, he started with Danny and checked his eyes and had Danny open his mouth. He did the same to Flannigan and George.

"All three of these boys are in fine shape," Dr. Fitzgerald said.

McGrath put the three medical forms in front of the doctor and placed three shillings on them. The doctor signed each form, took the shillings and tipped his hat to McGrath and walked away.

"Now, one more thing and you'll be legionnaires. I will administer the oath," McGrath said and handed them each a sheet of paper. He continued, "Read that when you can. Now you are legionnaires. Congratulations," McGrath shook each of their hands and bid them sit down.

"Gentlemen, we leave for France two days from now. Tomorrow I'll take you to our ship, and you can stay there till we sail for France. Tonight you stay in here.

"I thought we were going to China," George said.

"Oh, we are. It's Cochinchina. You'll train for a couple of

months and then we will sail for Saigon. When we are underway to Cochinchina, you'll continue to receive military training. Here, let me pour you another whiskey. One last nip before we retire," McGrath said.

McGrath poured the whiskeys, held his glass up and said, "May friendship, like wine, improve as time advances. And may we always have old wine, old friends, and young cares."

As they started to drink the pub door opened, and Danny's whiskey spewed from his mouth and onto the table. Then he said, "Lord Jesus, it's McCorkle."

"Who's McCorkle," McGrath asked as he looked at the door where McCorkle and three other men were standing perusing the people in the pub. No one answered because they were looking as well.

McCorkle saw Danny, pointed and said something to his men. They started to walk towards the table. Two of the men were carrying rifles.

"Boys, I need an answer. Who are these men?" McGrath said.

"Nobody that means us well," Danny said.

McCorkle walked to the table and said, "Hello Danny. Did you really think you would get away?"

McGrath stood up and asked, "How may we help you, sir,"

"I wasn't talking to you," McCorkle said and pushed McGrath who fell back into his chair.

McGrath stood up again, stared at McCorkle with steely eyes and said, "I asked you how may we help you?"

"If I want to hear from you I'll ring your bell. My business is with this fucking thief and his two friends. They'll be coming with me," McCorkle said.

Five men who were sitting at adjacent tables stood up and surrounded McCorkle and his men. Two of them put knives to the backs of the men carrying guns, grabbed the rifles and handed them to Mrs. O'Brien. She took them to Mr. O'Brien, and he placed them behind the bar.

"What's your name," McGrath asked.

"McCorkle."

"Well, Mr. McCorkle, these boys won't be going anywhere with you. These boys are now legionnaires in my brigade. Let me introduce myself. My name is Sergeant Major Casey McGrath of the Irish Brigade of the French Foreign Legion, late of Algiers and headed to Cochinchina."

"Legionaries? What's that, some kind of soldier? No matter to me. They'll be coming with me one way or another," McCorkle said as he put his face close to McGrath's face in an attempt to intimidate him.

"I think not," McGrath said then head-butted him. McCorkle stepped back, blood flowing from his broken nose. McGrath followed up with a right-hand punch to McCorkle's jaw, and McCorkle fell to the floor. McGrath's five men restrained McCorkle's men.

McCorkle slowly rose from the floor and threw a punch at McGrath's face but missed as McGrath stepped aside. McGrath followed through with a right to McCorkle's head and as quick as a cobra a left to his jaw. McCorkle crumbled to the floor unconscious.

"Anyone else?" McGrath asked. None of McCorkle's men said anything. "Okay then. Pick up your boss and get along with you."

When McCorkle's men left, McGrath sat back down and said, "Men, meet Danny O'Boyle, Billy Flannigan and George Graham. They'll be joining us on our adventure. Get to know each other. You'll be together for five years as long as the Black Flag don't get you."

"What's the Black Flag, sir?" Danny asked.

"Never you mind. You'll find out soon enough," McGrath answered then asked Mr. O'Brien to bring him the rifles they took from McCorkle's men.

"I want two men on guard duty in two-hour shifts through the night. Tomorrow, I'll buy you a good breakfast, and then we go to the ship. It'll be safe there. The next day we sail for France," McGrath said.

CHAPTER 10

Outskirts of the City of Saigon, Cochinchina - September 1883

"Get it off of me. Get it off," Danny O'Boyle yelled.

George Graham flicked his finger at the six-inch centipede on Danny's back, and the insect fell to the jungle floor and crawled away.

Danny looked at George and yelled, "Jesus, Mary and Joseph, this place is worst than hell. Spiders as big as my palm, centipedes as long as my cock, rats the size of cats and snakes." Danny made the sign of the cross and continued, "Snakes that can kill a man with a single bite."

As Danny continued his rant, Flannigan picked up a small branch that was lying on the jungle floor and tickled the back of Danny's neck. Danny immediately reacted by standing up, jumping up and down and swiping at his neck. He yelled, "Damn it. What is it? George, get it off."

George, having seen what Flannigan had done, just laughed and pointed at the jokester. Danny turned and saw the branch in Flannigan's hand and jumped at him. He wrestled Flannigan to the ground and rubbed his face with mud and said, "Say you're sorry."

"No," Flannigan said and laughed.

Danny rolled off of Flannigan laughing as well.

George shook his head in amusement. He had gotten used to the pranks his friends pulled on each other. It was all good-natured, and all three men had become as close as brothers. During the trip to Cochinchina, Billy Flannigan often succumbed to seasickness and Danny always found ways to make it worse. Sometimes it was eating something that was particularly greasy which sent Flannigan to the side of the ship. Other times it was just describing the rolling of the waves. Flannigan would get even by salting Danny's wine ration or by putting dead rats, which there was an abundance of on the ship, in Danny's bunk.

The trip from Marseille to Cochinchina took forty-five days on a military steamer. They traveled across the Mediterranean Sea to the Suez Canal and then entered the Red Sea. When they arrived at the Indian Ocean, bad weather slowed their progress. After several harrowing days, the weather cleared, and they finally came to the Malacca Straights. The captain decided to replenish the ship's coal stocks, so they sought harbor in Singapore where they stayed for four days. No leave was given to the men as the officers feared that some of them would desert. Marine guards were posted to ensure no one got off the ship.

Cochinchina was a relatively short distance from Singapore, and they were very happy to see Cap Saint-Jacques and the entrance to the Saigon River. Five hours later after traversing the winding river, they docked at the port of Saigon. After a few days on shore Flannigan recovered and he, George and Danny took their posts with the Irish Brigade. Sergeant Major McGrath had taken a liking to the three boys and helped acclimate them to life in the military and the exotic land in which they found themselves.

The brigade was stationed just outside of the city of Saigon, which was the capital of the French colony and had been since 1862. In a short time, Saigon had become infused with French culture and boasted western-style cathedrals, hotels, shops and restaurants. The combination of the western and eastern cultural influences made the city a pleasant retreat. Legionnaires enjoyed the city when they weren't conducting frequent sweeps in the jungles around it, in search of rebels that threatened the southern capital city.

"I heard we might get shipped to Tonkin soon," George said.

"I heard that as well, but it's just a rumor. I wouldn't fret over it," Danny said.

"Au contraire mon ami," Flannigan said, using one of the few French phrases he had learned. "Our friend George here is not happy with our southern rebels. He wants a shot at the Black Flag."

"He does, does he? Have you not heard, George, the Black Flag takes no prisoners, and they first torture then kill anyone they capture?" Danny said.

"That would be better than dying from the rain. I can't stand this constant rain. Sergeant Major McGrath said it rains less up north," George said. "He also said it's cooler. This heat is worse than torture. Anyway, I'm not planning on getting captured."

"He has a good point, Danny," Flannigan said

"True. I have...." Danny was interrupted when Sergeant Major McGrath yelled, "Get your asses up."

The detail of twenty men jumped up and stood at attention as McGrath continued, "Flannigan, take point." Then he yelled, "Fix bayonets."

Each man quickly reached for their bayonets, which were as long as a short sword, and fixed them onto their Fusil Gras single-shot rifles.

"Everyone keep a sharp lookout. We're moving into rebel territory. Forward," McGrath commanded.

A staff sergeant would normally command details of this size. But Second Lieutenant Dubois, one of the French officers commanding the Irish Brigade, decided he wanted combat experience and was commanding the detail. Because of the lieutenant's inexperience, Sergeant Major McGrath felt it best that he come along.

The lieutenant slipped his pistol from its holster and took his place at the rear of the line with McGrath. French Officers of the Brigade were required to speak English, and Lieutenant Dubois had learned the language while attending a British University. He was a handsome man of medium height and trim body. His mustache was cut in the style of the day for a Parisian and he had a tailored uniform. It was obvious to all that the lieutenant came from a well-to-do family, and they wondered why he was in the legion instead of the regular French Army.

The brigade that the men called the Irish Brigade, in reference to a long-gone brigade of Irish Jacobites who fought with the French Army, was a collection of legionnaires who spoke English. There were British, Americans, Canadians and even a few Australians serving as well as Irish and Scotch. The one thing the legionnaires had in common, aside from language, was that most were running away from something in their homeland. Some had issues with the law and others joined just to get away from oppressive families. The Foreign Legion asked no questions, and as long as you obeyed orders and fought hard, you were as good as any other legionnaire.

The rain had stopped, but it left a muddy mess of the trail the men were following. Each step they took sunk their feet several inches into the muddy black soil. It was an arduous march. Needing a rest himself after an hour, the Lieutenant ordered Sergeant Major McGrath to give the men a ten-minute break.

"Sir, we should continue onto the village. I don't like being in the open like this," McGrath suggested.

"No, the men need a rest. Ten minutes," Lieutenant Dubois commanded.

God save me from whelps like this, McGrath thought then he yelled, "Halt, ten minutes. Keep your rifles at the ready."

Flannigan walked back to where George and Danny sat and said, "Move over, George," He continued after he sat down, "Where we going anyway?"

"The Sergeant Major said we're going to a village that was overrun by rebels. We're to clear it out," George answered.

"Again," Danny said, "How many villages have we cleaned out? As soon as we leave, the rebels come back. I don't mind telling you I'm getting tired of risking my life and limb for nothing."

"The governor says we're helping to make the natives civilized. We're giving them a better life," Flannigan said and spat on the ground.

"Like the English did for us Irish?" George asked. "The bastards took everything from us. Now we're doing the same to these people. It isn't right."

Lieutenant Dubois overheard George's comments, walked over to the three men and yelled, "Attention!"

Danny, George and Flannigan jumped to their feet and saluted.

"So, you are not happy with our Governor's position," Lieutenant Dubois said, then looked sternly at each man.

There was no answer. "No? No comments now? Let me explain something that may be difficult for uneducated men like you to understand. God has an order for all things. He has said that Christians should spread the word of Christ. It's our duty to bring his word to these heathens. Do you believe in Christ?" Lieutenant Dubois yelled.

All three men yelled, "Yes sir."

"Good, then you understand it's your duty to spread Christ's word by any means necessary. We do what we must. Understand?" Lieutenant Dubois yelled again.

"Yes sir, Lieutenant," the three men yelled in response.

"Sir, did not Jesus say, *Love one another. As I have loved you, so you must love one another*?" George asked.

Lieutenant Dubois looked at George for a second then said, "Yes he did, and we are showing these heathens love by teaching them the proper way to serve God and to live their lives. It's all part of the order of things," Dubois said.

"But…" Lieutenant Dubois interrupted George and said in a loud voice, "There are no buts. I'll think of a suitable punishment for the three of you when we get back to camp."

After the lieutenant walked away, Danny whispered, "That fella's off his nut."

Suddenly, a man rushed out of the jungle in front of George Graham. He was holding an iron-tipped spear, and it was pointed at George's heart. George parried the man's spear with his bayoneted rifle and hit him in the side with its butt. It was a glancing blow, and the rebel was able to recover quickly and thrust the spear at George again. George was bringing his bayonet around for another parry when the rebel screamed in agonizing pain as Flannigan's bayonet entered the man's armpit. Flannigan pushed hard, and the bayonet came out through the shoulder and into the man's neck severing his carotid artery. George was temporarily blinded by the man's blood as it spurted from the wound.

Along the path, the twenty legionnaires were fighting off rebels armed with spears and swords. George wiped the blood from his eyes and looked to his right. He saw Sergeant Major McGrath pull his pistol and shoot a rebel in the head. Lieutenant Dubois had fallen back into the foliage. He was sitting with his pistol pointed in the air and seemed stunned as he stared at the carnage.

Two more rebels started towards McGrath and seeing this George lunged past Danny O'Boyle in an attempt to aid his sergeant. He thrust his bayonet into the throat of one of the rebels as McGrath emptied his revolver into the second rebel's body. The rebel George killed fell at the feet of Lieutenant Dubois, and Dubois scrambled further back into the undergrowth. As the rebel fell with the bayonet still stuck in his throat, George lost his grip. He dove past McGrath in an attempt to retrieve his rifle, hit the ground and rolled crouching on the balls of his feet. Two more rebels closed on McGrath and George with swords in hand. McGrath shot one rebel and George grabbed the pistol from Lieutenant Dubois who was still frozen in fear and fired at the remaining rebel hitting him in the upper chest. The rebel fell, his arm outstretched and the sword only a foot from George.

George dropped the pistol in Dubois's lap and retrieved his rifle. Shots rang out as the other legionnaires fired at the fleeing rebels. Fifteen bloodied rebel bodies lay along the jungle pathway. McGrath walked amongst them and used his pistol on several rebels who were still alive. A couple of legionaries had minor cuts to arms. Corporal Sweeney took a spear to his eye and perished.

They left the rebels where they lay, and McGrath ordered the men to build a makeshift stretcher, and they carried Sweeney's body to the village where they placed it in a central spot. The village was typical of the ones legionaries encountered many times. The homes were built using mud walls and thatched roofs, not unlike the homes where George grew up.

The villagers had all retreated to their huts, and all the young girls of a certain age were sent off to safe areas in the jungle when they learned that French soldiers were on their way. The reputation of the French soldiers, right or wrong, was that they took whatever they desired, including the virtue of young women.

Lieutenant Dubois ordered McGrath to have his men round up the natives and bring them to view the body. They legionnaires forcibly removed the villagers from the huts and assembled them in front of Corporal Sweeney's body.

Once the villagers where settled Lieutenant Dubois, oblivious to the fact that none of the Villagers understood him, started to speak. This man. This French Legionnaire was murdered by you. You give aid to rebels who killed this man and attacked my legionnaires. It is your responsibility."

Some of the village men smiled and shook their heads in the affirmative not understanding Dubois, but thinking he might be telling them that the French were good people and here to help. This incensed Dubois.

"You will be punished,"Dubois yelled. "Sergeant Major McGrath, have the men burn down half of these abominations they call homes."

"Sir, don't do this. It just makes things worse," McGrath said.

Lieutenant Dubois said, "Do as I say, Sergeant Major or would you prefer the firing squad?"

McGrath reluctantly chose ten men, all British, to set the

fires. When the villagers realized what was happening, they began to scream and yell at the soldiers. The remaining legionnaires including George, Danny and Flannigan formed a line to keep the villagers under control. One village man slipped under George's legs and began running to his home that was now burning. Dubois seeing this ran after the man, pulled his pistol and shot him in the back of the head. A woman in front of George began screaming and crying. She was yelling something that George could't understand.

As the man lay dead, Dubois shot him again. George had just turned to see where the first gunshot came from and saw what Dubois had done.George started to go after him. Flannigan held him back and said, "There's nothing you can do now. You'll just get yourself killed."

The now dead man's wife pushed her way through where George was standing and ran to her husband who lay in a pool of blood in front of their home. She pushed Dubois away and bent over her husband crying. Dubois began to raise his pistol to shoot the woman, but before he could, McGrath ran to him and grabbed the pistol from him. Dubois looked at him and was about to say something when McGrath said in a low voice, "Don't you say a fucking word, you fucking coward."

Dubois went for his sword, and McGrath punched him in the face before he could draw it. Dubois fell unconscious to the ground.

"Form up. We're leaving," McGrath yelled. "You two go get the lieutenant and bring him here. Take that sword from him."

The two men did as told, and while they held the lieutenant, McGrath threw water on his face. Once the lieutenant was awake, McGrath took him away from the men and said, "You're going to march these men out of here, and you're never going to tell anyone what I just did. If you do, I'll have you up on charges of cowardice and murder. That will end your career. Who do you think the Commander is going to believe, a whelp with a few months service like you or me with twenty years in the legion?"

Dubois just stood looking at McGrath, his face turning a bright red. Finally, he sighed and shook his head in the affirmative. McGrath put Dubois's sword in his scabbard, emptied the pistol of bullets and handed it to him. Then he said, "If you ever pull a weapon on me again, it will be the last thing you ever do."

CHAPTER 11

When they returned to base Lieutenant Dubois had George, Danny and Flannigan tied to wagon wheels and left in the hot sun for one day as punishment for talking against the governor's rule. He never mentioned what McGrath had done, nor that he had murdered a man in cold blood. At Sergeant Major McGrath's suggestion, the brigade's commander assigned Dubois administrative duties.

During the next six months, the Irish Brigade continued their attempt to pacify the areas around Saigon. George, Danny and Flannigan became seasoned warriors having had many battles with the rebels. It was kill or be killed, as any war is, but the treatment of the farmers was distasteful to the three Irishmen who likened the French occupation of Cochinchina to that of the English occupation of Ireland. The people who suffered most were the poor farmers who saw their villages burned, their women raped and their men murdered by both sides.

The trio had befriended another legionnaire, an Irish American man named John McBride from the city of Philadelphia.

The four spent many hours talking about each other's homes and life while tramping through the jungles. John's parents had immigrated to America during the Irish potato famine and found their way to the Kensington area of Philadelphia in the state of Pennsylvania. It was an area where most Irish immigrants lived. John was born in 1859. His father was drafted into the northern army during America's civil war and was never the same after he came home. He ended up drinking himself to death by the time John was fourteen years old.

John was forced to quit school at the age of twelve to help the family as his father deteriorated. In those days the Irish, especially the Irish Catholics were discriminated against by the ruling English and Irish Protestants. It was common to see disclaimers in want ads saying "Irish Need Not Apply." Some bars and even restaurants displayed signs that read, "Negros, Irish and Dogs not allowed." So the young John could only find the lowest of jobs for the lowest of pay. By the time his father passed away, John had joined a local Irish gang and started committing petty crimes mostly in the downtown area of Philadelphia. By the time he was twenty years old, he was heading up a small crew of his own.

Unfortunately, several members of the crew had been arrested while attempting to rob a Center City bank. John got away, but understanding he would soon be arrested he decided to leave Philadelphia. He could run to the west or go to Ireland where his mother had family. He chose to go to Ireland and left his mother and his four brothers and sisters with most of the cash he had saved. In Ireland he found that things for the poorer Irish Catholics were worse than in America and using his Philadelphia ties, he started smuggling weapons from Philadelphia for a rebel group called the Irish National Invincibles.

Again, he ran afoul of the law and eventually found himself on the same ship that brought George, Danny and Flannigan to Cochinchina.

On occasion they received time off and a pass to leave the brigade area. When had the time the four men liked to visit a café owned by a Frenchman who was married to a native woman from Van Cu in Tonkin. They served a combination of French and native cuisine. George had grown fond of a dish she made. It was a soup that was popular in Van Cu made with rice noodles, spices, radish, carrots and water buffalo meat. George had asked her to try cow meat since he found the water buffalo meat rather tough and gamey. She obliged George, and she added it to her offering calling it Pho. It was only popular with her French customers as the Vietnamese were not fond of cow meat and rarely ordered it.

After a particularly difficult sortie deep into the jungles around Cu Chi, the brigade received a three-day pass. George and the others first visited the café for some Pho. The French proprietor, Mr. Blanc, was sitting behind a counter when he saw the four men enter the café. He quickly rose and greeted them.

"Good morning, my friends. It is so good to see you again. Come, sit here where the air flows best. It is cooler," Blanc said. He then guided them to a table on an outdoor covered patio. Blanc had learned English when he was an importer of opium from the British in Hong Kong. When he married, his wife made him stop his opium trading, and he took the money he made to open the café.

"Some wine?" Blanc asked.

"How about some Guinness beer?" Danny asked, smiling widely.

"Mr. Danny, you know we do not have Guinness. I do have some French beer," Blanc said.

"We'll have wine. French beer's like drinking piss," Flannigan said.

Blanc took no offense as he was used to the Irish penchant for what John McBride called ribbing.

"And four Pho soups?" Blanc asked, tilting his head.

"Mr.Blanc, do we ever order anything else?" John asked.

"No. You do not, but I have to ask, or my wife will be angry," Blanc said and smiled.

In due time, Mrs. Blanc, or Chi as she preferred to be called by her Annamite name, and her husband brought the four bowls of Pho and placed them on the table.

Chi waited for George to taste the soup then asked, "You likey?"

George looked up and kissed his finger and thumb and said, "I likey."

Chi smiled widely and said something to her husband in her native language. Mr. Blanc translated, "Chi asks for you to wait a minute. She wants to let you try something new."

Chi came back with a plate full of what looked like small fried white sausages and placed them on the table. Then she said something to her husband, and he translated, "These are called Chả Giò. It is spiced chopped pork and chicken wrapped in rice paper and fried crispy. Try it."

Each of the four men picked up a Chả Giò and took a bite. Chi waited until they finished chewing and asked, "You likey?"

All four at the same time said, "I likey," and proved it by eating all twenty Chả Giò before they started on the soup. Chi was ecstatic and almost floated back to the kitchen.

The café was situated across the street from the Notre-Dame Cathedral of Saigon. French architects designed the cathedral, and it had been dedicated in 1880. It was a beautiful French brick building, and George admired the well-kept landscape.

Whenever he was at the cafe, he would go inside the church and light candles for his father, brother Sean and his sister's baby Shamus. Then he would say a prayer for his mother and family back in Letterkenny.

George had arranged that half of his meager pay be sent to his mother as did Flannigan. This made their excursions limited to the cheapest restaurants and accommodation. That was until John McBride suggested a plan to supplement their stipend from the French government. His idea was to use his considerable skills, learned on the streets of Philadelphia, to relieve wealthy European travelers of some of their money. There were several European-style hotels in Saigon that made great targets for his light-fingered activities.

At first, George was reluctant to revisit stealing from others, but Flannigan made the point that these French bastards were no better than the English overlords they had to endure. George finally agreed. John organized the group as he had learned in Philadelphia. He and Danny would do the actual stealing because they were small and fast. George and Flannigan would be the lookouts and muscle if needed.

If they heisted jewelry, gold or silver items, they took it to Cho Lon, a suburban city of Saigon, where Chinese merchants were happy to take it off their hands for a reasonable return. After two months of illicit activity, they had accumulated a fair amount of gold coins, and it became a problem. They couldn't carry it on patrols, so they hid it under the floor of their barracks. One day Danny suggested that they arrange with the Bank of Indochina to send the money to a bank in Philadelphia that John knew. They would keep what they needed, send money to their families and the rest would be in an account that one day they could retrieve.

When he finished his Pho, Danny said, "I'll go to the bank and make a deposit and meet you at the bar in the Favre Hotel."

"Danny, can you drop this off at the postal service," George asked and handed Danny a letter.

"Sure I can. It's on the way. Another letter to your Ma?" Danny said, and his eyes glistened as he thought of his own Ma who was dead now these past five years.

"Me too," Flannigan asked and handed Danny a letter.

Danny took the letter, tipped his hat and walked off. George, Flannigan and John paid Mr. Blanc, and walked to the cathedral. Once inside each man lit candles for their departed family members and said a prayer. There were only fifteen or so other people in the church when the two men finished and started to walk towards the door leading to the outside. Two French children ran in front of them, and one dropped a small doll. George picked it up, smiled and handed it to a young woman who was chasing after them. The woman thanked him and continued running after the children.

The woman caught up with the children who were struggling to open the large door. She chastised them and kissed each one on the head.

George smiled again and said to his friends, "I want that."

"Want what, George?" Flannigan asked.

"That," George pointed at the women and two children."A wife, maybe a few children."

Flannigan looked at George and shook his head no and said, "Not me, I..." Flannigan was interrupted as the door exploded into thousands of ragged splinters of wood and glass. The concussion knocked George backward into John, and both men tumbled to the floor. Flannigan was knocked off of his feet and into one of the church pews.

It took several minutes for the smoke to dissipate, and as George regained his senses, he saw the gaping hole the explosion had made, and one door was hanging off to the side. He shook his head to clear it and checked on John and Flannigan. Both men were still recovering but were not hurt seriously. He noticed that Flannigan's face and coat were speckled with blood and his heart skipped a beat. George ran to the door to check on the woman and her two children.

George had seen some horrible things in his time in Cochinchina, but he was not prepared for the carnage. The bodies of the mother and her two children lay piled up against the pews and pieces of flesh and blood coated the back of the pews. George sank to his knees and stared in shock. He made the sign of the cross. Flannigan and John walked to George and stood beside him and stared at the scene. After a minute or so, they helped George to his feet and Flannigan said, "We need to go, George. There's nothing we can do." George didn't respond.

A man came running from the front of the church, screaming his wife's name. When he reached the back of the church and saw his wife and two children, he just stood with his mouth open as if he were screaming, but there was no sound. After a minute, he fell to the floor and put his arms around the carnage that once was his family and sobbed.

CHAPTER 12

George had the room attendant at the Favre Hotel clean the blood from his uniform. Even so, there were still some stains on the coat he was wearing. After taking a bath and dressing, he walked down the two flights of stairs into the hotel lobby. John McBride was at the front desk talking to the assistant manager of the hotel. When John saw George, he hastily walked across the lobby to meet him.

He put his arm around George's shoulder and asked, "Feeling better, George?"

"No," George replied. "I can't get the picture of those children out of my head."

"What's done is done, George. There's nothing we can do about it now," John said. "A hundred years from now the Annamites will still be trying to throw the French out of Cochinchina. It's the way of the world. The powerful conquer the weak and the weak fight back if they can."

"That doesn't make it right. It's not right what the English are doing in Ireland, and it's not right what we are doing here.

It's not right what the rebels are doing. And who suffers, who dies? The innocent farmers, poor folks and children. It isn't right," George said, his anger building.

"God's will, I guess," John said, reflectively.

"No," George said emphatically."No, it's not. It's our leader's will. It's our will. We burn a village because they tell us to, but we do it. In Ireland, I went to jail for a year for trying to keep my family from starving. Flannigan's family lost their home that had been in the family for generations. We're doing the same thing to the Annamites. It isn't right."

"Well, I am sorry for what happened to you and Flannigan, but right now I have some good news to share with you and the boys. Come on, let's get a drink or five," John said, trying to change the subject that was enraging George.

Flannigan and Danny were sitting at a table on the veranda of the hotel. A bottle of Cognac was on the table. It was three-quarters full.

"What's this? You started without us," John said jokingly, still trying to keep the conversation on the light side. "And with swill, at that. Didn't they have real whiskey?"

"And you can go fucky self, John," Flannigan said, mimicking a native Annamite accented English.

John sat down and poured George and himself a drink.

"Danny, did Flannigan tell you about the church?" George asked.

"He did. Terrible thing, that. You three could have been killed."

"That would be fine with me if I could take those children's place," George said. Then he held his glass up and said, "May God take them to his kingdom and give them peace." Each man held his glass up, looked to heaven and drank the Cognac.

"I have news from our contact. He says three English men arrived yesterday. They're on a tour of the Orient. One's supposed to be the son of an English Lord. Sounds like good pickings to me," John said and opened his palm to reveal a key.

"How do we do it, John?" Flannigan asked.

"Tomorrow they have a trip planned to go to Cho Lon on the train. They should be gone all day. I'll just waltz into the room and see what they might have to donate to the Irish cause," John answered. "Danny will go with me, while you and George stand watch in the lobby."

The next morning George and Flannigan got up early, had breakfast, and then sat in the lounge area in the lobby that overlooked the stairs. The train from Saigon Station to Cho Lon left every two hours starting at eight am. By ten-thirty they were beginning to think the English tourists would not be leaving today. At eleven-fifteen the three Englishmen walked slowly down the stairs, and it was obvious that they were suffering from hangovers. When they left the hotel, Flannigan walked to the door of the patio where John and Danny were drinking tea.

He held up his hand and John paid their bill and he and Danny left. When they reached the Englishmen's suite on the second floor, John knocked on the door twice. When he was sure no one was in the room, he slipped the key in the lock, opened the door and he and Danny walked in.

The suite was furnished with typical French accouterments. It was comfortable, but probably not what a Lord's son was used to in England. The two men rummaged through the dresser draws looking for anything of value. They found several gold trinkets, but nothing worth the effort. John began to worry he wouldn't even make enough from this job to pay the assistant manager of the hotel. Then he saw a solid-looking chest in the corner of the room. It was locked, which in John's mind was a positive sign. People generally only locked away things that were of value.

John took a small pry bar from his inside coat pocket and broke the lock. When he opened the chest, he poked around the various clothing items and found two things that made him smile. One was a sack of gold coins, mainly sovereigns with the picture of a young Queen Victoria on the front. The other was a pocket watch made by the British Watch Company, and it looked to be eighteen-carat gold.

He put them in his pocket and continued to search. After finding nothing more of value he walked to the window, opened it halfway and reached up on the outside and smashed the top pane nearest to the latch.

"Why'd you do that?" Danny asked.

"Do what?" John said.

"Open the window. Why didn't you just break it from the inside?" Danny asked.

John closed his eyes and shook his head and said, "You know Danny, for a smart guy you can be pretty dumb. If I break it from the outside, it looks like someone broke in. The glass is on the floor. If the glass was outside, they would know we got in with a key."

"Ohhhh," Danny said.

"I'll make a second story man out of you yet, Danny boy," John said, then punched Danny on the arm.

"I think not, John. My stomach's churning like my Grandma making butter," Danny said.

Check the door," John said.

Danny walked to the door and slowly opened it, peeked out and said, "Clear."

Both men left the room and John locked the door. They met George and Flannigan in the lobby, and the four men left the hotel. They caught the two o'clock train to Cho Lon and visited their contact that purchased gold. John sold the watch and the gold trinkets but kept the sovereigns. The jeweler agreed that he would melt the watch and trinkets for the gold.

John gave the sack of gold coins and the cash the jeweler paid them to Danny and said, "Put this in the hiding place until we have time to send it off to our bank in Philadelphia. Danny nodded and put the money in his pocket. The four men then walked to the train station and returned to the hotel, checked out and returned to their base.

In Cho Lon, the jeweler threw the trinkets in the melting pot. He took the watch and looked at it more closely. He shook his head back and forth and then placed the watch in the case where he had other watches for sale.

CHAPTER 13

The day after the four legionaries returned to camp, the Irish Brigade was informed that they would board ships at Saigon Harbor to take them down the river to Vung Tau and then up the coast to Tonkin. They were to be stationed outside the city of Hanoi in a fortress created by the French government to protect their interest in Tonkin. It was common knowledge that eventually the French would battle the Black Flag Army, the Chinese Army, as well as Annamite rebels.

The brigade was now restricted to the base as they prepared for travel. This caused a problem for George, Danny, Flannigan and John or as Danny had started calling them - *na Ceithre Marcach* (the Four Horsemen). They had not been able to take the money they liberated from the English Lord's son to the bank, and it was still under the floorboard in the barracks. They would have no choice but to take it with them to Tonkin. Danny split the coins and cash into four piles, and each man would carry his share. If anyone of them fell in battle, the others would at least have their split.

Sergeant Major McGrath entered the barracks and yelled, "Attention."

The sixty men in the barracks took their place in front of their bunks and stood stiffly waiting for McGrath to continue. "You have twenty minutes to pack up and get into formation. We leave for Tonkin after the commander's inspection. Take everything with you. We have no idea when we will return."

The men replied in unison, "Yes, Sergeant Major."

"These two gentlemen," McGrath pointed at two men who had followed him into the barracks, "would have a word with you. Sirs, if you please," McGrath beckoned the two men with a wave of his arm.

One of the men stepped forward and said, "Good morning. My name is George Montagu-Dunk. My father is Lord James Montagu-Dunk. Seventh Earl of Langston." Dunk paused to allow his importance to register with the men.

An Irish Legionnaire four down from Danny spit on the floor. McGrath excused himself from Dunk and approached the man. He stood silently glaring at him. Finally, the man said, "Sorry sir. I got a bug in me mouth. Tasted right awful too."

McGrath shook his head in disbelief at the man's excuse and returned to Dunk and motioned him to continue. "As I was saying, we are here in Cochinchina on holiday. Two days ago my hotel room was broken into, and I was robbed." Dunk's face turned red as he continued."The thieves took a substantial amount of money and jewelry, including this watch. He held up the watch John had taken from his room.

John moved his eyes towards George without moving his head. A small bead of sweat formed on his brow.

Dunk continued, "That same day I was in Cho Lon and to my surprise, I found my watch on display at a Chinese jeweler's shop. After my friend and I persuaded the owner," Dunk held up his fist to show the scraps on his knuckles, "he told us that an English-speaking Legionnaire had sold it to him." Dunk paused again and looked up and down the two lines of men for effect. Then he continued, "I'm offing a five-pound reward for anyone who has information about who this legionnaire might be."

McGrath said, "Does anyone have any information? If so, speak up." No one responded. After a short silent pause, McGrath said, "That's it. At ease. Get packed and get your lazy asses into formation."

"Sergeant Major, may we search the barracks?" Dunk asked.

"Is it your intent to search all the barracks, sir?" McGrath asked.

"Yes it is, Sergeant Major," Dunk answered.

"As soon as we march you may have at it, sir. For now, we must get ready for war," McGrath said and began to walk out of the barracks.

"But…" Dunk started to say but stopped when McGrath left the barracks.

The legionnaires who were packing started spitting on the floor, and Flannigan yelled, "Damned bugs," and spit in front of Dunk. Dunk and his friend quickly left the barracks.

"That fucking Chinaman. I told him to melt that watch," John whispered to George.

Ten minutes later the four horsemen were standing in formation with the rest of the Irish Brigade. Each legionnaire carried a forty pound kit on their back and was dressed in the typical uniform for tropical colonies. Their boots had leggings, and their trousers were tucked in tight to protect them from insects and snakes bites. Their tunics had long sleeves and were adorned with ammunition packs and a long sword-like bayonet. Their head was covered with a lightweight pith helmet to protect from the tropical sun.

Even before they began the march to the harbor George's undergarments were soaked through. He wished he could dress as the natives did. Most native men and women wore loose-fitting lightweight pantaloons and tops that were more suitable for the tropical heat.

The brigade commander inspected the legionaries and gave a short speech. *It was the typical speech,* George thought. *Blah, blah fight blah, for the legion, blah, the brigade blah, blah, and God.* He hardly paid attention. He had heard it all before. What he and probably every other legionnaire was thinking during the speech was *I hope I don't die. If I do die, I hope I die well and fast. I hope the food is good. I wonder what the women are like in Tonkin?*

After they boarded the troop transport steamers, they traveled down the lush Saigon River to Cap Saint-Jacques, then into the deep blue of South China Sea. The ships stayed close to the coast as they traveled north and when it wasn't raining, they experienced the beauty of the Indochina coastline's white beaches. They passed Nha Trang, Da Nang and finally arrived in the Gulf of Tonkin and the entrance to the river leading to Haiphong.

The French governor of Cochinchina decided that as a show of force, the brigades would march from the beach to Haiphong and then on to their fort outside of the city of Hanoi. The commander chose to bivouac on the gulf side of the river for a few days so the men could recover from their days on the rough seas before the march inland. Flannigan was very appreciative of this as he had again spent a good bit of time bending over the rails depositing his breakfast, lunch and dinner into the China Sea.

Once they had erected their tents near the beach, the legionaries were allowed to rest. Within minutes the camp was flooded with women holding baskets of all types of fruits, vegetables, cooked meats and fish. For a few copper coins, the locals called Phan, George was able to buy as much fruit as he could carry. He had eaten some of them before, but others he had never experienced. He had squeezed lemons and added honey and water to make a sweet juice. He had also eaten a fruit the French called mangue (mangoes). It was unlike any taste he had ever experienced, and he bought it whenever he could find it.

After spending so much time cooped up on the ships, a number of the legionnaires decided to sleep out in the open on the beach. John, George, Flannigan and Danny laid their blankets side by side and enjoyed the waning daylight hours. They took off their bayonets and jackets and lay them on the blankets beside their rifles and then sat down, finally able to rest after a demanding few days of travel.

George took in the beautiful scene in front of him. The sky was dark blue, with several puffy white clouds floating slowly to the south. The sun was setting behind him in the west, and its reflection created a reddish yellow color on the glassy blue water. There were many fishing boats and Chinese-style Junks displaying red, yellow and white sails. It was like the paintings his teacher back in Letterkenny had shown them.

In front of him, on the blanket, George's cache of fruits lay basking in the final rays of sunlight. There were bright yellow bananas, purple mangosteens, orange persimmons, green jackfruits, green mangoes and even a yellow rough-skinned pineapple. There was also a coconut with the husk still on and a strange fruit with spines on it that looked more like a weapon than food. One of his fellow legionnaires, had said the name was durian, and warned him about the fruit's particularly nasty odor. He said it smelled bad but tasted very good. George shared his fruit with his friends, and they all sat taking in the beauty of the scene and enjoying the exotic flavors of the fruit, leaving the durian for another day.

As the sunlight faded, the legionnaires lit torches. The warm glow highlighted the fifty or so men who would make the beach their bed for the evening.

"I had a dream once, where I was on a warm beach eating exotic fruits," George said.

"You had a prema… a premi," Flannigan said, struggling for the word.

"Premonition," Danny said.

"Premonition, yes," Flannigan exclaimed.

"What's that mean?" John asked.

"It's kind of when you think or dream something that comes true," Danny explained.

"I don't think it was a premonition," George said

Why not?" Flannigan asked? "Here you are, fruit and all."

"I'll tell you why. Because I was with a beautiful woman, not you ugly bastards," George said and smiled.

"And on that kindly comment from George, I suggest we get some sleep. It's up and at it again at daybreak," Danny said.

Danny fell back on his blankets, and in a few minutes he was snoring. Flannigan and John did the same. George, still feeling hungry, decided to finish off a couple more pieces of fruit.

There was a soft glowing light in the sky as the sun fell below the western horizon. George could just make out the faint silhouettes of boats heading for the shoreline. He supposed they were fishermen coming home for the evening. As the boats came closer, it was obvious they were headed for the beach, where most of the legionnaires were asleep. He stood up to get a better look and decided boats were certainly beaching right where he was. For a second he was confused, but as the boats came closer, he saw a flag on one of them. It was a large black flag with Chinese writing on it.

George yelled as loud as he could, "Attack! Attack! To arms! To arms!" Then he started to grab for his rifle, but it was too late. A Black Flag warrior was in front of him, his sword poised to strike. George grabbed the man's arm and twisted as the momentum of the man's charge knocked them both to the ground. The sword flew from the warrior's hand and then he punched George in the face. Then he put his hands to George's neck and squeezed. George couldn't breathe, and he began to feel lightheaded. He reached out trying to find his bayonet but instead felt the spiny points of the durian fruit. He grabbed it with one hand and smashed it into the warrior's head. The man loosened his grip and fell sideways. George rolled on top of him and smashed the durian into the man's face until all he saw was a bloody pulp.

He looked around for his bayonet, found it and drove it into the warrior's chest. Then he looked around to see if his friends were okay. Danny had picked up his rifle and fired at the Black Flag warriors who were now running back towards their boats. Flannigan was standing over a different warrior who was crying out in pain and the shock of having a two-foot bayonet sticking out of his gut. Danny pulled the weapon free and thrust it into the man's eye and on to his brain.

"Where's John," George shouted.

"Last I saw him he was running towards the boats with a torch in his hand," Flannigan answered.

George picked up his rifle, fixed the bayonet and chambered a round. He then started to run towards the beach. He was just a few feet away from the other legionnaires when he saw one of the boats burst into flames. He could see several of the Black

Flag warriors engulfed in flames and he heard their screams. A few seconds later John ran up to him. By then the other Black Flag boats were out in the water, and several warriors fell as the legionnaires continued to shoot after them. Then it was quiet as the legionnaires surveyed the damages.

Three legionnaires were killed and several wounded. Ten Black Flag warriors were dead, including three that were burned alive in the fire John set on their boat. Two warriors were wounded and were turned over to the command for interrogation.

George picked up what was left of his fruit, leaving only the blood-soaked durian that had saved his life, and walked slowly back to his tent.

CHAPTER 14

George's hand was bleeding where the durian spikes had punctured his skin. There were at least ten holes in the palm of his right hand, but they were not very deep. George wrapped his hand with a clean piece of cloth and sat down on his blanket.

"George, you should get that hand looked at by the medic," Danny said.

"No, it's not so bad," George said.

"At least put something on it, so it doesn't get infected," Danny said.

"That's right, George. If they have to cut your hand off, you won't be able to play with your wee willie," Flannigan said then laughed. George unwrapped the bloodied rag and threw it at Flannigan.

"I'm not joking, George," Danny said. "You need to get something so it doesn't get infected. If you don't want to go to the medic, I have something that will help," Danny said.

"What's that?" George asked.

Danny picked up one of George's lemons and held it up. "A lemon? How can that help?" George asked.

"Well you see, I was in a certain kind of house in Saigon one day and got a bit too frisky and fell off the bed. I skinned up my knee pretty bad. The old Grandma told me to put the juice of a lemon on it, so it didn't get infected," Danny said.

"Did it hurt?" George asked.

"Nah, not a bit," Danny answered.

"Okay, I'll do it," George said.

Danny took a small knife and cut the lemon in half and squeezed the juice into a cup. He handed the cup to George and said, "Go on now. Just pour it on the cuts and rub it in."

George picked up the cup, held his hand out and poured the lemon juice on his cuts. "Holy Mother of Christ," George yelled as he hopped around the room holding his hand. After a minute the searing pain started to subdue, and George stood still holding his damaged hand.

"Son of a bitch. That hurt. Why'd you tell me it wouldn't?" George asked.

"I thought it didn't. I'm sorry, George," Danny said.

"Did it hurt when you used it?" George asked.

"Ahhh, well no, you see I never used it," Danny said.

George picked up one of the lemon halves with his good hand and started rubbing it in Danny's face. Both men fell to the floor laughing.

Two days later they were standing in formation waiting to march to their new base of operations near Hanoi.

Sergeant Major McGrath addressed the men. "Yesterday we buried three of your fellow legionnaires. Several more are in the hospital. It is not acceptable to lose men, but it happens in war. We can expect more attacks like the one the other day. The

Black Flag will harass us every chance they get. So be alert on this march. If you see something strange, yell out. It is better to be safe than sorry. Legionnaire McBride, front and center."

John sharply marched to stand in front of McGrath. "About face," McGrath said to John. John turned around as did several of the other legionnaires.

"Not you, you stupid bastards," McGrath yelled. The men turned forward again and McGrath put his hand on John's shoulder to prevent him from turning back.

McGrath closed his eyes and shook his head back and forth. Then said, "Yesterday I saw Legionnaire McBride run towards the enemy with a lighted torch. He intended to burn one or more of their boats. He succeeded, and three of the enemy died." McGrath looked up and down the line of men standing at attention and continued, "It was one of the stupidest stunts I have ever witnessed."

John's wide smile turned to a worried frown. McGrath continued, "And one of the bravest. Yesterday I put Legionnaire McBride's name up for a medal of merit. Congratulations, Legionnaire McBride." McGrath took John's hand and shook it.

Five minutes later the three brigades including the Irish started marching. As they traversed the roads leading to Hai Phong crowds gathered to see the parade. Little boys cheered, but they didn't know why, and little girls cried, and they didn't know why either. It was that way all over the world. Men marched off to war, and little boys wanted to be like them, and little girls grieved for the ones that wouldn't come back.

The song started spontaneously as it always had. *J'avais un camarade* was an old song. Legionnaires had sung it as they marched to war in Mexico, in Prussia and now in the Tonkin

War. Everyone sang it in French, no matter what your mother tongue was.

I HAD A COMRADE
BETTER IT IS NOT
IN PEACE AS IN WAR
WE WERE LIKE BROTHERS
WALKING AT THE SAME PACE.
WALKING AT THE SAME PACE.

BUT A BULLET WHISTLES
WHO WILL BE STRUCK?
HERE HE FALLS TO THE GROUND
HE IS THERE IN THE DUST
MY HEART IS TORN.
MY HEART IS TORN.

THE HAND HE WANTS ME TO TAKE
BUT I CHARGE MY RIFLE
FAREWELL THEN, GOODBYE MY BROTHER
IN THE SKY AND ON THE EARTH
LET US ALWAYS REMAIN UNITED.
LET US ALWAYS REMAIN UNITED.

The camp near Hanoi was approximately sixty-five English miles or in the French metric system 104 kilometers. It would take four days at a normal marching pace. That meant the legionnaires might expect attacks for the next ninety-six hours before they were safe in the camp. The legionnaires had trained to march a minimum of eight hours a day in full gear, so that was not a problem. What was a problem, in Danny's mind, as he mulled over the facts as they marched, was the three nights of sixteen hours each that they would be sleeping and resting in the open, especially at night. That, he thought, *would be the most dangerous time.*

"Do you think the commander will post enough lookouts when we bivouac tonight?" Danny asked George.

"Why? Are you looking for a job?" George answered.

"God no. Not if I can help it. Just wondering. Did you know that we'll be spending forty-eight hours in bivouac and most them at night? It's pretty dangerous, don't you think?" Danny said.

"I haven't thought about it. If the enemy attacks, I fight. I think about how I can save my ass from getting a spear stuck up it. That's what I think about," George said.

After three days of marching and two nights of bivouac, Danny started to feel less nervous. He reckoned that if the enemy didn't attack so far, they were unlikely to do so now. The legionnaires had made better time than was expected. When they stopped for their third and last evening, they were only ten miles from the camp.

It was Danny, George and John's turn for guard duty and they took their post at two am. The other legionnaires would wake at five in the morning, eat breakfast and break down the tents. By six they would be on their way. The three men took their positions. George and John were positioned one hundred feet apart, and Danny walked back and forth between them.

As Danny came close to him, John said, "Danny, did you know there are tigers in the jungle there?"

"What do you mean? Like the ones I saw in the Dublin Zoo?"

"Yes, the ones with the big teeth. I hear the tigers in Tonkin are man-eaters."

Danny turned and marched toward George. John smiled. George wanted to get back at Danny for the lemon trick, so he talked to John about trying to scare him when they had guard duty. Danny was squeamish about the creatures of the jungle, and he thought it would be an easy job. As he approached, George said, "Did you know about the tigers?"

"I do. I didn't know tigers liked to eat people," Danny said, now looking a bit worried.

"Oh yeah, they do. If you think that's scary, I saw a snake the other day that had to be fifteen feet long. It was swallowing a full-size pig. Scared the hell out of me, it did. I bet they could swallow a small man as well," George said.

"Great! Monster snakes too," Danny said.

Danny turned and walked back to John. "Have you ever heard of the Nguoi Rung?"

"No, what's that," Danny said a bit wide-eyed now.

"The Tonkins say it's a man-beast. Walks like a man, but looks like an ape. All hairy and such, with big sharp teeth. They say the Nguoi Rung is ten feet tall and if he catches you, he takes you back to his home in the jungle and feeds you to his babies one piece at a time," John said.

"I never heard of such a thing," Danny said.

"Next time you see him ask Father O'Sullivan. He'll tell you. He's seen one. Almost scared the Christ out of him," John said.

Danny turned and started to walk back to George. As he got closer, George could see that the desired effect of the ribbing had worked. Danny looked visibly nervous.

"Switch places for a minute, will you, Danny. I want to ask John something," George said, then placed his rifle on his shoulder and walked to John.

When George got to John, he was smiling. George said, "I think he's had enough. Look at him. He's holding his rifle at the ready just in case a tiger shows up."

John smiled and said, "Or a Nguoi Rung."

"You told him about the Nguoi Rung. No wonder he's almost shitting himself," George said and laughed. "When I get back to him I'll tell him you made up the story of the Nguoi Rung. That should make him feel a little better."

George started back towards Danny. About halfway he saw Danny turn towards the jungle, crouch and point his rifle. For a split second, he thought Danny was reacting to some small animal noise he heard. Then Danny discharged his weapon into the jungle. A Black Flag warrior rushed out of the undergrowth and charged at Danny, sword in hand. Danny thrust his bayonet into the man's chest.

George dropped to a crouching position just as another warrior crashed out of the scrub. The warrior's sword went over George's head, and George thrust upward with his bayonet. It entered the man's stomach. George stood up bringing the blade up with him slicing the man up to his heart. The warrior stood stunned. George pulled the weapon out of the warrior who fell to the ground.

John could hear rifle reports from all around the camp. And, as sudden as the attack started, it stopped. Once again the Black Flag had hit and run. No legionnaires died, but several were wounded. Five Black Flag warriors were killed.

"Mary Mother of God, I thought that was a tiger or one of those man-beasts," Danny said.

George looked at Danny and said, "No, it was much worse. It was a determined enemy."

CHAPTER 15

By late that afternoon, the legionnaires were safely in their new camp near Hanoi. The legion engineers had supervised local natives in building wooden barracks, latrines and even a bathhouse. The men appreciated being able to sleep inside on cotton-filled mattresses instead of on blankets placed on the damp ground.More importantly to the men was that they now had kitchens and they ate their first hot meal since leaving Hai Phong.

The commander had wine distributed to celebrate their first night in the new camp. He also arranged to have long loaves of bread brought from Hanoi, where there was a bakery owned by natives who had been trained by French bakers. It was a feast, and while he enjoyed it, Danny couldn't help thinking that they were like lambs fattened for the slaughter. Danny, George, John and Flannigan were sitting around a small fire they built to help take the chill off of the evening air. Unlike Saigon that pretty much was hot night and day, Tonkin temperatures were somewhat more moderate. In May the evening temperatures could drop below 70 degrees.

Danny took a sip of red wine to help wash down the bread and cheese he had just eaten. Then he said, "Do you think we'll be patrolling tomorrow?"

"Don't we always?" Flannigan said.

"Why is that? What have we done to deserve the honor to go on patrol so much," John asked.

"First of all, we are legionnaires, not French soldiers. Secondly, we speak English, and most of us are Irish. You know the legion goes to frontline first, and in the legion, the Irish Bridge goes first," George answered.

"To be honest, I don't mind the patrols. It's better than sticking around the post and cleaning latrines or drilling all day. Or worse yet, having to listen to Lieutenant Le Connard pissing about every step we take," Flannigan said and spat into the fire.

Lieutenant Le Connard was the not-so-affectionate name the men had given Lieutenant Dubois after his cowardly actions and murder of a native when on patrol around Saigon. Lieutenant Le Connard loosely translated is Lieutenant Shit Head.

"I don't know why they let that bastard command again. He's useless," George said.

"Well, he's our bastard now, and someday we will deal with it," Flannigan said.

The four men sat quietly looking at the fire and listening to the night sounds for several minutes before Danny asked, "Do you miss home?"

"Sometimes I look up at the moon, and I think that it is the same moon that shines on Philadelphia and my family. It makes me feel a bit better, a bit closer. I do miss my family and my friends," John said.

"I used to dream about being in a warm tropical place eating exotic foods. Now that I'm here, all I dream about is being back in Letterkenny with my family," George said.

"How about you, Flannigan? Do you miss home?" Danny asked.

"I do, but I'm happy that I'm here. I can help feed my family. My Ma was able to get a small home, and my brothers get to go to school with the money we liberate from those tourists," Flannigan said.

The talk of home made everyone a bit melancholy and the four men sat quietly looking at the fire and thinking about home until Flannigan asked George how his hand was healing.

George replied, "It's getting better, but it hurts a little. A couple of punctures have puss coming out, "George took off the bandage to show them.

Flannigan spit out a piece of cheese he was eating and said, "Fuck George, you didn't need to show us. Now I lost my appetite."

"You asked," George said.

"I didn't say show me your putrid puss-filled hand. I just asked if it was healing," Flannigan said.

"You should go see the medic, George. I mean it," Danny said.

Okay, okay Ma. I'll go in the morning. I wouldn't want to make Flannigan lose his appetite again," George said, then pretended to wipe his injured hand on Flannigan. Flannigan yelled and rolled away from George. All four men laughed.

The next morning George asked permission to see the medic. He waited for over an hour while legionnaires suffering from a range of complaints from dysentery to hangovers were treated. As he waited, he noticed a very attractive Annamite woman caring for some of the legionnaires.

George guessed she was about the same age or a little older than him. She was about five feet tall, had long black hair that hung down to her waist, and she was wearing a long blue dress made of silk. George noticed how delicate her gait and touch were. Nothing was hurried, and each patient received the same competent and sympathetic care. It mesmerized George, and she caught him looking at her several times. He hoped she would be the one to care for him.

George never thought himself lucky until the native woman beckoned him to her treatment station. She spoke to him in French, and he put his hands up and said, “I don’t speak French.”

The woman said, “English?”

“Yes English, but I am Irish,” George said.

“Oh. I speak English, but not Irish,” the woman said.

“Yes, we Irish speak English as well,” George said.

“Oh good. How may I help you? My Name is Nguyen Thi Dat. You may call me Miss Dat if you like,” Dat said.

He had gotten used to the fact that Annamite names were backward; the last name was their first name, and the last name was their given name.

“I would like that, Miss Dat. My name is George.” he said as he unwrapped the bandage from his hand and held it out for Dat to see.

Dat softly took his hand and looked closer, and asked, “How did you injure your hand? It is an unusual wound.”

“It was from a durian fruit. Do you know that word?” George asked.

Yes, yes, I do, but how?” Dat asked.

Not wanting to tell her he smashed a man’s face in with the durian, he just said, “I fell on it.”

She released his hand, stood up and walked to a table. She picked up a bowl and filled it with water and brought it back to George.

She took his hand and said, “I must wash your wounds. Do you approve?”

"Yes," George said, bracing for the pain. And it was painful, but George did not show it, wishing not to appear squeamish in front of this beautiful woman.

When she finished cleaning the wound, Dat said, "Excuse me," then rose from her stool and walked to a small cabinet on the other side of the room. She returned with a small bottle and said, "This is a salve that will help reduce the infection. Each morning wash your hand first, then apply the salve and bandage it with a clean cloth."

Dat then opened the bottle and applied the salve to George's wound. She gently patted it on the puncture holes and then bandaged his hand.

"May I ask what is in the salve?" George asked.

"It is several different Chinese herbs mixed with honey," Dat answered.

May I ask another question?" George asked.

Dat nodded her consent, and George asked, "How is it you know English?"

Dat smiled and said, "I speak French and English. French, I learned in school and English I learned from a missionary when I was very young. He traveled here from Hong Kong with his wife and small son."

George had so many questions he wanted to ask, but he thought it might come off as rude, so he just said, "You are very accomplished, Miss Dat. Thank you for treating me."

"Please, come back in three days so I may check your wound," Dat said as she rose from the stool.

"I will. Thank you again," George said.

Dat bowed her head slightly and walked off to get her next patient.

As George walked back to his barracks, his mind was swirling with questions he wanted to ask Miss Dat. *How did she become a medic? Where did she live? Was she married? How is it she is here amongst the legionnaires? Does she have a boyfriend? Does she like Europeans?*

Three days later George was back at the medical facility, and Dat was inspecting his hand. She took off the bandage and said, "This looks very good ,Mr. George."

George smiled and said, "Thanks to your salve and you."

Dat nodded and put more salve on the wounds and applied a clean bandage around George's hand.

"Miss Dat, how is it that you became a medic?" George asked.

"My father is a doctor practicing Asian medicine, and I have assisted him since I was a child. He owns an herbal medicine shop in Saigon and one day a French doctor came to buy some herbs. He mentioned he was looking for an assistant. I thought it would be a good way for me to learn about Western medicine, so I applied for the position, and here I am," Dat said.

"Thank you for fixing me up," George said.

"You are welcome. I think you will be fine now. Just keep using the salve until you are completely healed. No need to come back. And you might want to stay away from durian fruit," Dat said and smiled. She bowed her head and said, "Good day, Mr. George."

Dat's words made George feel as if a hot knife entered his heart. *No need to come back,* he thought. But he just nodded, smiled back and left the medics area. He wasn't sure why he felt that way, as this had never happened to him before.

CHAPTER 16

For the next three weeks, George went on patrols and otherwise did his job, but he couldn't help thinking about Dat. Then fate, God or luck, George wasn't sure which, brought him back to Dat. He was chosen to be one of the twenty men that was escorting Dat and the French Doctor to the village of Hoa Dep. Hoa Dep was four miles south of their base. The wife of the village leader was Ill, and the commander authorized his medical team to help. It was part of his campaign to win hearts in Tonkin. The governor's strategy was based on rewarding the allies and severely punishing the foes.

The doctor and Dat were riding in a small carriage, and the legionnaires marched in a formation that surrounded the vehicle. George was assigned a position that was next to Dat, who was sitting on the right side of the carriage seat.

Upon seeing George, Dat asked, "How is your hand, Mr. George?"

"Good morning, Miss Dat. Good as new," George answered and flexed the previously injured hand to prove it.

"Good," Dat said.

Lieutenant Dubois, who had been assigned to lead the patrol, walked up behind George and smacked him on the back of the head and said, "No talking in the ranks Graham."

Dubois turned and looked at Dat and said, 'I'm sorry, miss." Before Dat could answer, he fell back, and George could hear him berating another legionnaire.

When they arrived at the village, George helped Dat down from the carriage. Dat thanked him, and she, the doctor and Lieutenant Dubois entered the village leader's home. The legionnaires took positions around the home and stood at ease. Thirty minutes later Dat came back to the carriage and selected three of the medications she had brought with them and returned to the house.

Several of the village women handed out salted lemon drinks to the legionnaires and offered them small cakes made from rice flour. The village boys played at marching back and forth pretending to be soldiers, while the older girls helped their mothers to prepare the afternoon meal. Girls as young as eight years old carried their baby brothers and sisters around on their hips. It all reminded George of when he was a youngster, and he thought, for the first time, *that people from this faraway exotic land were not so different than his people. All they wanted to do was farm, take care of their families and live in peace. Like Ireland, and due to nothing they had done wrong, now they were subject to war and a foreign overlord.*

Two hours passed before the doctor and Dat finished administering to the village leader's wife and returned to the carriage. George helped Dat onto the carriage and took his place on the right side. Before they started the long march back to camp, Lieutenant Dubois tapped George on his shoulder and said, "You're on point, Graham."

Not wanting to leave Dat unprotected, George, hesitated and Dubois pushed him hard and yelled, “Are you deaf man? Take the point now, before I have you on a wagon wheel again.”

George turned to face Dubois and stared at him for a few seconds. His face was red and his eyes piercing. Then he said, “Yes sir.” George reluctantly walked to the head of the column. Once there he turned to see that the lieutenant had taken his place next to Miss Dat and was talking to her.

Ten minutes after George took the point, he saw two elderly native men and two teenage boys standing on the right side of the road. As he approached them they started to yell, “French, go home.” They were speaking heavily accented French.

George readied his rifle but just marched past them. As the carriage with Dubois walking beside came to the protesters, Dubois reached out and pushed one of the elderly men. The man fell backward and hit the ground. One of the teenage boys threw himself at DuBois while screaming something in Tonkin. Dubois pulled his revolver and pointed it at the boy just as Graham ran up to him and said, “I’ll handle it, sir.” hen he stood between Dubois and the boy he was now holding back.

Another boy about thirteen years old screamed and jumped on George. The boy had a small knife in his hand, and as George was trying to control the other boy, the thirteen-year-old swung the knife and caught George just below his ear. Before George could react, the knife had created a five-inch cut in George’s neck. George quickly dropped the first boy and grabbed the arm of the thirteen-year-old before he could do more damage. He swung the boy around and held him.

Dubois pointed the revolver at the thirteen-year old’s head and pulled the trigger. The blood from the boy’s destroyed head splattered over George’s face. Dubois then shot the other boy in the chest. The two elderly men screamed and rushed to the two the boys. Each held one in their arms and rocked them back and forth while crying and screaming in their language.

George grabbed Dubois by the shoulder and said, "They were boys. Only boys." DuBois pushed George away, pointed the revolver and yelled, "Grab me again and you will join them."

Dat jumped from the carriage, and as she did, she pushed Dubois's gun away. She then bent down to the boy with the head wound. By then the French doctor had joined Dat, and she looked at him and shook her head. The doctor kneeled by the old man holding the boy who was shot in the chest. He examined him then stood up and said, "He's gone." Dat translated for the old man, who already knew the boy had passed.

Dat looked at George, saw his wound and said, "Come sit in the carriage. I'll tend to that."

George walked past Dubois and purposely knocked him with his shoulder. The blood from George's wound splashed on Dubois' uniform, and Dubois's face reddened in anger, but he did nothing.

Dat sat George on the seat opposite of hers and opened her small case of medicines. She took a clean rag and wet it and patted the blood from George's wound. After a short inspection, Dat said, "It's not so bad. Not too deep," and then rubbed a concoction of honey and herbs on the cut.

"Why did he kill them? They were just children." George asked.

"Some men like to kill," Dat said. "He will meet his karma one day."

"What do you mean karma?" George asked.

"Buddhists believe that if you do bad or good, someday you will be rewarded with like actions," Dat said.

"Christians say you reap what you sow," George said and paused for a second and continued, "I hope karma will allow me to help when the lieutenant's time comes."

CHAPTER 17

When they returned to camp DuBios had George tied to a wagon wheel for two days. He was given no food and only minimum water. Sergeant Major McGrath had been in Hanoi for a week and didn't return until a day into George's ordeal. He was eating lunch in the mess when Flannigan told him about George's punishment. McGrath picked up his plate and walked to where George was spread eagle on the wheel and said, "What the fuck did you do now, Graham?"

George told him the story and asked McGrath to report the murder of the two children to the commander. McGrath promised he would and before he left he put a piece of cooked chicken in George's mouth and said, "I'll be back later with more."

Dat also visited George and attended to his wound. She made George eat a native bun filled with sweet bean paste, and she gave him an herbal tea designed to help heal his wound.

"I'm sorry, Miss Dat. I'm sorry you had to see those boys murdered. We're not children killers. I hope you know that?" George said.

"I do. I know you are not a child killer. There are men like the lieutenant in every race. They kill with imm… What is the word in English? Ah yes, impunity."

"I don't know what that means," George said.

"It is like they kill but never get punished," Dat said.

"That won't happen if I have anything to do with it," George said.

Dat smiled and put the herbal teacup to George's lips and said, "Drink the rest."

When George finished, Dat started to stand up, and George said, "Do you think you could ever love a white man?"

Dat sat back down. She Blushed and didn't say anything for a few seconds then replied, "Love is love. What does it matter if it is white or brown?" She kissed George on the cheek, stood up and walked away.

Ten minutes later, when Sergeant Major McGrath returned, George was still smiling.

"You know, Graham I think you're the first man I have ever seen who was happy to be strapped to a wagon wheel," McGrath said.

"What did the commander say?" George asked.

McGrath sat next to George, took a flask from his pocket, opened it and put it to George's lips. George drank and coughed.

"It's Irish whiskey, George. Take another," McGrath said and put the flask to George's lips again. "You're going to need it."

"The commander sided with the lieutenant. He says the boys attacked a legionnaire and they got what they deserved. He also said that you're lucky he doesn't bring you up on charges for accosting an officer. I'm sorry, George," McGrath said.

George's face turned bright red, and bile rose in his throat. He spat on the ground and said, "That's not right. That bastard murdered two children. You have to do something."

"It isn't right, but I can do nothing. He's the commander of the force. He's God here," McGrath said.

"Devil is more like it," George said.

"Here, eat this," McGrath continued as he put another piece of chicken to George's mouth.

"No. I've lost my appetite. I could use another sip of that Irish," George said.

McGrath took out the flask and gave George two more swallows of whiskey and said, "Try to get some sleep. You'll be off the wheel in the morning. I'll get you a couple of days off to recuperate."

George had no idea how he was supposed to sleep with his arms and legs strapped to a wagon wheel. He tried and dozed off a few times, but by two in the morning he was wide awake. He felt vulnerable to any insect, creature or person who might want to harm him, so he remained vigilant. Not that he could do anything about it if they did.

Around three in the morning Danny, Flannigan and John opened the tent flap, looked around for guards. It was a moonless night and very dark. There was only a small fire burning about ten feet in front of George. Seeing no guards, they silently walked to George. As they approached him, they gave him a sign to be quiet, and then untied his arms. Danny helped him sit up.

"Oh, that hurts. My back feels like someone drove nails in it," George said.

"Here, drink this. It'll make you feel better," Danny said and handed George a bottle of wine.

"You shouldn't have come here. If night watch catches you, you'll be on wheels beside me," George said.

"Fuck the legion and fuck Dubois. We're the Four Horsemen," Flannigan said and smiled.

"We brought you something to eat," John said and handed him a sandwich.

The three men watched George devour the sandwich and wash it down with wine. George handed the wine to Danny who took a long swig, then passed it to John who did the same and passed it to Flannigan. Flannigan put the bottle to his lips, and then turned it upside down and said, "What the hell, there's none left." The others started to laugh at the disappointed look on Flannigan's face.

"Did you hear that?" George said.

"No, what," Danny said.

"Listen," George ordered.

George could hear the faint sounds of men yelling. It was coming from the other side of the camp.

"Untie my legs. Hurry up," George said.

Danny was having difficulty undoing the knots, so Flannigan unsheathed a razor- sharp knife he always carried and cut the ropes. George jumped up and would have fallen if Danny didn't catch him. His legs were wobbly from almost two days bound to the wheel.

"Give me your knife, Flannigan," George ordered.

Once George had the knife he started running toward where the shouts were coming from. Flannigan picked up the wine bottle by the neck and said, "Go back to the tent and get your weapons and follow us. He then started running after George and easily caught up with him. He grabbed George by the arm and helped him run.

When they arrived at the medical tents, they saw several legionnaires lying in the dirt. Sergeant Major McGrath and Lieutenant Dubois were holding off three natives armed with spears and knives. Dubois had his sword in one hand and his pistol in the other, but he was not engaging. McGrath was moving forward. Four other legionnaires were fighting off six natives near the entrance to the medical tent.

Flannigan ran to help the four legionnaires as George came up behind one of the warriors fighting McGrath, grabbed his head, and cut the man's throat. Dubois, seeing this panicked and his arms were flailing as he turned to run. As he did his pistol discharged and the bullet hit McGrath in the leg. Pain shot up McGrath's body, and he lost his balance. Seeing a momentary opportunity, the warrior McGrath was fighting thrust his spear into his chest. McGrath stood for a few seconds with a look of shock on his face, and then collapsed. George, who was close to the warrior, sank his knife into the back of the man's neck. He pushed him aside and as the man lay gurgling blood, George grabbed the spear and impaled the third warrior. The spear went through the man's stomach and out of his back.

Meanwhile, Flannigan seeing the legionnaires were in trouble smashed the empty wine bottle into the head of one of the warriors. The man went down like a sack of rice. He grabbed the man's knife and went after a second man, cutting him across his stomach. The man dropped the spear he was carrying and fell into a kneeling position. Flannigan retrieved the man's spear and went after a third warrior. Flannigan plunged the spear into the man's throat.

Seeing the carnage Flannigan was inflicting the three remaining warriors fled into the trees. Flannigan yelled to the three legionnaires, "Go get them." The three soldiers ran after the warriors, rifles at the ready. The warrior who Flannigan had disemboweled was still trying to put his intestines back into his body. Flannigan looked the man in the eye and then cut his throat. He then walked over to the man he had knocked out with the wine bottle and cut his throat.

All of this occurred in minutes, and as fast as the action started, it ended. Lieutenant Dubois walked up to George, who was now kneeling by McGrath's body. The spear had pierced McGrath's heart, and he had died instantly. George stood up, turned and glared at Dubois. George stood half naked with the enemy's blood dripping from his chest and face, glaring at Dubois. He looked like a demon from the depths of hell.

Dubois stepped back in alarm. George quickly stepped forward and grabbed Dubois by the throat and yelled, "You sniveling fucking coward. You got a man killed who was a hundred times the soldier you are."

Dubois' face was turning red, and he lifted his revolver and placed the barrel on the side of George's head and gasped, "Let me go."

Flannigan saw what was happening and rushed over to Dubois and George. He snapped to attention, saluted and said, "Sir, the Commander would like to see you. He's behind the medical tent. He said to have you hurry."

Then Flannigan said, "George," and gently pried George's hands away.

Dubois straightened up and croaked, "I'll deal with you later, Graham," then started towards the rear of the medical tent.

"I'll go with you, sir," Flannigan said and fell in behind Dubois and picked up the spear he had discarded. As soon as they were behind the tent and away from the legionnaires that were now assembling on the front side of the medical tent, Flannigan thrust the spear into Dubois's back. The spear blade came through Dubois and out of his chest. He dropped to his knees and fell forward. The spear held him in a kneeling position as his life's blood flowed down the spear and formed a sticky red pool.

Flannigan said, “That’s for Sergeant Major McGrath.” Then he spat on Dubois, picked up the lieutenant’s revolver and shot three times into the jungle. Still holding the revolver, he came to the front of the medical tent. The commander was standing over McGrath’s body. There were now fifty or so legionnaires standing behind him.

Flannigan approached the Commander, snapped a salute, which was returned and said, “Lieutenant DuBois is dead, sir. We went to secure the rear of the medical tent, and a native came out of the trees and speared the lieutenant. It was right awful, sir. I shot at the bastard, but he got away.”

The Commander looked at Flannigan and nodded his head. Flannigan asked, “Sir, may I check on my tent mate?

“Yes, go ahead.”

Flannigan walked to the medical tent where he knew George would go to look for Dat. The clinic area was in disarray. Medicines pulled out of the cabinet lay on the floor, and tables were overturned. He walked back to the living quarters and as he entered, he slipped on something wet on the floor. Flannigan landed on his rear end and cursed. He tried to get up but his hand, which was in the substance, slipped and he fell back again. He looked at his hand and saw it was red and he could smell a copper odor. He realized it was blood.

He followed the stream of blood and saw it was coming from the company doctor. A stab of fear went through Flannigan’s body as he considered that George might also be dead. He stood up and surveyed the room. In the left side corner of the tent, he saw George kneeling on the floor holding the lifeless body of Dat. George was sobbing.

CHAPTER 18

Two days after the attack on the camp and the death of Dat, a quick investigation determined that the assault was perpetrated by Black Flag warriors and men from the village of Hoa Dep. Sixty legionnaires of the Irish Brigade were assembled and briefed by the commander on their duty. And that duty was to get retribution for the death of the doctor, his assistant and six of their fellow legionnaires.

"Before you leave on your glorious mission to preserve the honor of the legion I want to commend two of your fellow legionnaires for bravery above and beyond the call of duty. Legionnaires Graham and Flannigan, front and center," the commander snapped.

George, who was thinking about Dat, didn't move so Flannigan pushed him and then both men marched to the commander and saluted. The commander returned the salute and told them to about-face. They did as ordered and faced the other legionnaires.

"Two nights ago, Legionnaires Graham and Flannigan, without concern for their safety, came to the aid of their fellow legionnaires with no weapons other than an empty wine bottle and a small knife. They dispatched at least six Black Flag warriors and in doing so saved an unknown number of lives. I have recommended both of these courageous men for the medal of merit and both are promoted to the rank of corporal. Now show your appreciation for their valor," the Commander said and then yelled," Hip, hip, hurrah!"The legionnaires yelled, "Hip, hip, hurrah! Hip, hip, hurrah! Hip, hip, hurrah!"

The commander shook George's, and Flannigan's hand then turned to the legionnaires and yelled, "Now go for the glory of the Legion."

The men responded with a spontaneous roar that could be heard throughout the camp. When George and Flannigan returned to the detachment, the captain in charge called the legionnaires to attention and gave the order to march. The line of three men abreast and thirty-three deep simultaneously stepped forward. Behind them were three caissons drawn by horses and full of ammunition and three older versions of the Gatling machine gun bought from the United States.

The drummer played the standard marching beat, and when they exited the camp the captain yelled, "Easy march," and the men relaxed, and the drummer beat slower. One of the men starting singing, "We leave for Mexico." It was the beginning of an old legion song from the Mexican War.

The rest of the legionnaires took up the song but changed Mexico to Tonkin.

WE LEAVE FOR TONKIN,

WE LEAVE THE SAIL TO THE WIND,

FAREWELL, THEREFORE, FAIR EUGENIE,
WE WILL BE BACK IN A YEAR.

EUGENIE WITH TEARS IN HER EYES,
WE COME TO BID YOU FAREWELL,
WE LEAVE EARLY IN THE MORNING,
BY A MOST SERENE SKY.

IT'S NOT CONVENIENT AT ALL,
WHAT TO THINK ABOUT LOVE,
ESPECIALLY WHEN IT IS WINDY,
OVER THE FORECASTLE.

When they finished one of the Irish legionnaires started to sing GarryOwen, an old Irish drinking tune that was once adopted by the U.S. Seventh Cavalry. It had become famous for being the last song that played before George Custer led his men to disaster at the fateful Battle of Little Bighorn.

GarryOwen was a song well known by the English-speaking Irish Brigade that made up the detachment. The men puffed up their chests and sang with gusto. When legionnaires finished, they relaxed once more and became silent. Their thoughts turned to the families they left behind and the possibility that they would never see them again.

George Graham's mind had been in a fog since Dat's murder. On the one hand he couldn't believe she was gone, but on the other hand, he knew it was true. He expected to see her again but knew he never would. He had no appetite, and his sleep was restless. His sense of loss was so intense he thought he would never recover and as he marched he felt nothing of the physical world, just numbness. Unfortunately, this was not new to George.

He had the same feeling when his father died, and when his brother Sean and his sister's baby Shamus, departed this life.

Left foot, right foot, left foot, right foot, George plodded along oblivious to the time, tempered weather, blue sky, green jungle and the cheerful bird calls. As they marched, Flannigan tried to talk to George, but George wouldn't answer. Finally, Flannigan gave up.

When the detachment arrived at the Hoa Dep Village, they found the village women and children standing side by side across the village center. Children were crying as mothers tried to console them. Behind the line, there were approximately fifty Black Flag and Tonkin soldiers. Some had rifles, and others carried spears and swords. Twenty village men, old and young, stood on the left flank of the line. They carried an assortment of farming tools, and some had old rusty swords.

The legionnaire captain had his men line up thirty across in two lines. The Gatling machine guns were brought up behind the second line. The captain then had his interpreter issue his demands.

"Put your arms down and deliver the men responsible for the attack on our camp and no one need be hurt." Before the interpreter could say anything else a shot rang out. He grabbed his chest and fell to the ground. Two more shots sounded, and two legionnaires fell.

The captain was momentarily confused. If he shot back, he would certainly hit some of the women and children and if he didn't, his men would be slaughtered. Before he could act there was a loud roar from the enemy line and the village men rushed at them urged on by Black Flag warriors amongst them.

"Fall back behind the machine guns," the captain ordered and the disciplined legionnaires quickly stepped backward, with their rifles pointed at the natives. Once the Gatling guns were in the clear the captain yelled, "Fire."

The village men who were charging started to fall as the three Gatling guns spewed death. The last of the fallen men died just ten feet from the legionnaire's line. At the same time, the Black Flag warriors opened fire. One of the Gatling gun operators screamed and fell across its hot barrel. Several legionaries in the line fell as well.

The legionnaire captain wildly looked around trying to focus on a solution that would avoid him from firing back at the women and children that were shielding the Black Flag warriors. A sergeant who was standing next to the captain suddenly grabbed his neck and fell to his knees choking on his blood. The captain looked at the sergeant and yelled "Fire."

The Gatling guns roared in obedience as did the rifles of the legionnaires. A few minutes later the captain yelled, "Ceasefire." Every man, woman, child and Black Flag warrior save two who had run into the trees, where dead or dying. It was a horrendous sight, and George, Danny, and several other legionaries vomited not because of the gore, but because they had killed innocent women and children. A number of the legionnaires made the sign of the cross, no doubt asking for God's forgiveness.

The captain chose several men and told them to burn the entire village. As these men did their work, the captain had the wounded and dead legionnaires placed on the caissons. When he was sure all the huts were burning, he called the men to attention and slowly started marching back to the camp. The bodies of the villagers and Black Flag warriors were left where they fell in the blood-soaked soil of their home. It was a warning that the French soldiers administer instant and devastating retribution.

As they marched back to camp, George's despair changed

to anger and guilt that he did nothing to stop the slaughter of innocent farmers and their childern. Stories his grandmother told him of riots and rebellion during the Great Famine, and the British military's ruthless response flooded his mind. More and more he thought that what was happening in Indochina was what happened to Ireland. And he didn't want any part of it.

When they finally arrived back in the camp, the captain announced that the men would all receive a three-day pass but they would be restricted to the camp. Someone had set up a tent pub of sorts for enlisted men. The pub served warm beer, wine and Cognac. Flannigan bought four bottles of wine. He found an out-of-the-way place and George, Danny, John, and he laid down a few blankets, sat down and opened the bottles.

"Graham held his bottle up and said, "To Sergeant Major McGrath. May you have an eternity of green recruits to yell at." Each man spilled a small amount of wine on the ground, clicked bottles and drank deeply.

Flannigan thought about toasting Dat, but he knew that any mention of her name would turn George into poor company for the evening. Instead, he said, "To Lieutenant DuBois. May he burn in hell."

"As we surely must," Danny said.

"And what do you mean by that, Danny boy?" Flannigan said.

"You know damn well what I mean. We killed innocent women and children. And for what?" Danny said.

"What the fuck could we do? Just stand there while the Black Flag killed every legionnaire?" Flannigan said.

"We wouldn't have been there if it hadn't been for that puss bag DuBois. The commander is at fault also. If he weren't hell-bent on teaching the natives a lesson instead of punishing a murdering sod, those villagers would still be alive. It's one thing to kill soldiers, but women and children," Graham paused and shook his head. "No, that is not right."

"So you think we're going to hell?" Flannigan asked Graham.

"No! No, because there is no hell. There is no heaven, and there is no God," Graham said.

Danny and John immediately made the sign of the cross but said nothing. Flannigan said, "Well, on that we agree."

"I'm telling you boys right now if I get the chance, I am going leave this cesspool," Graham said.

"What do you mean, leave? Leave what? Tonkin, the legion?" John asked.

Graham looked at John and said, "All of it."

"And just how do you think you'll manage that?" Flannigan asked. Graham shrugged his shoulders indicating he didn't know.

The four men sat on their blankets, sipping from their bottles of wine for over five minutes before Danny broke the ice. "To tell the truth, George, I've been thinking the same thing. I'm tired of people trying to kill me because I associate with the French. I'd die for Ireland, but I don't want to die for France. And besides, I have a lot to atone for, and I can't do that here. I'm with you, George."

"It's time I got back to Philly," John said.

George, Danny and John looked at Flannigan and waited. Flannigan took a swig of wine, shook his head and said, "Of course, I'm with you. Didn't I follow George out of jail, across Ireland and halfway around the world? George is one Fenian that can't get along without me."

Flannigan put his arm around Graham's shoulder and held up the bottle and said, "To Philadelphia. The place where my future wife resides."

"Okay, that's that. George, how do we do it?" John asked.
"I have no idea," George said.

CHAPTER 19

It wasn't uncommon for legionnaires to desert. Most had no allegiance to France. What they cared most about was the pride for the legion and their fellow legionnaires. When they became at odds with what the legion stood for, friendships were the only bonds that tied them to service. In George's case, his friends were willing to desert as well, so the ties that bound George to the legion dissolved.

It had been three weeks since the four men had decided to attempt to get to Philadelphia and so far they could come up with no feasible way to accomplish their goal. Flannigan had suggested that they go north to China and then Hong Kong where they could find a ship to America. The problem was France and China were on the brink of war, and their chances of arriving in Hong Kong alive were nil.

They considered going west in an attempt to get to Burma which was a British colony, but the distance through dense jungles was insurmountable. South to Saigon was out of the question because of French rule. The only possibility was to try to sneak on a ship in Haiphong Harbor. If they were found before the ship left, they would be turned over to the legion. After a mock trial, they would face execution for desertion. If they were found by the ship's crew while at sea they could be thrown overboard or if they were lucky, set off at the ship's next port of call. They had no other options, so they decided to become stowaways.

Danny said it was God's work when their sergeant was asked to provide twenty legionnaires to supervise and guard the unloading of two ships carrying supplies for the legion. The ships would dock in Haiphong within the next few days, and the men were to leave immediately. George volunteered himself, Danny, John and Flannigan.

When they arrived at the Port of Haiphong, the ships had not docked yet, so they had a day or so with no duty. They spent their free time surveying the various ships and talking to crews. Most of the ships were owned by French companies; a few were British. One was from the United States. The British ships were going back to Hong Kong, and the American ship was bound for Saigon, then Madagascar, Gabon and then France. All of these were under French rule. By default, the British ships were their best bet. If they could get to Hong Kong, they should be able to find a passage to the United States.

British ships were in and out of Haiphong on a regular basis which meant they could take some time to ready themselves. First on the list was to convert any foreign money they had from their business ventures in Saigon to gold. They already had a substantial amount of gold as well as the money they had stashed in the Philadelphia bank. That amount would give them enough for passage and to establish them in the States. Their families were doing well with the money they had already sent them so they wouldn't miss the small amount they received from their legion pay. The Four Horsemen were ready to make their move.

As so often is the case, life has a way of changing even the best laid out plans. On their third day in Haiphong, two American ships arrived at the harbor. These were the ships for which the legionnaires had been waiting. The cargo was a mix of various armaments from the United States. There were ammunition, small arms and some cannon and Gatling guns that were surplus from the American Civil War. The ships were owned by a Boston-based shipping company.

After talking to various crew members and the second officer George found out that the ships were bound for South Africa, then Nigeria and Spanish Morocco. After that, they were to head to the port in Biscayne Bay in Florida to offload their cargo, pick up various fruits and bring them home to Boston. George couldn't believe it, and Danny once again said it was God's intervention.

George excitedly asked if he could talk to the captain in charge and was granted a meeting. The captain had left the ship and wouldn't return for three hours, so George had the men start unloading the cargo.

When the captain returned and was told a corporal with the legion wanted to see him, he readily agreed. After all, his contracts with the French were very lucrative, and perhaps this corporal had freight the legion needed to ship.

"Sir, I understand you'll be heading back to Boston when you're finished here?" George asked.

"Eventually, yes. First, my ship will go to South Africa then Nigeria. Our second ship will go to India and then return to Hong Kong. I could certainly stop in Madagascar or the Congo if you need to ship goods there."

"No, we don't have cargo," George said. He looked the captain in the eyes and said, "Do you ever take passengers?"

"I have," the captain said then paused for a few seconds and said, "depending on who they are."

"My three friends and I would like to book passage on your ship," Graham said.

"Are your friends legionaries also?" the Captain asked.

"Yes sir, they are."

"Is this an official trip?" the Captain asked.

"No, it is not, and it is not to be discussed outside this room," George said.

"Then my answer is no," the Captain said and stood up to signal the meeting was over.

"Why is that, sir?" George asked.

"I don't believe the legion officers would think kindly of me if I assisted their legionnaires to desert. If the French military found out I would never get another shipment from them," the captain said.

"What if I made it worth the risk," George said and set a bag on the table. "There's a lot more where that came from."

The captain sat down and opened the bag. He spilled the contents on the table, and his eyes opened wide as the gold coins and nuggets glimmered in the candlelight. Then the captain said, "It is a very big risk."

George spent the next hour negotiating the fee. He agreed to give the captain half of the gold the four men currently had on hand, which was equal to the profit he would make for two cruises. The four of them would sleep in the crew quarters and eat with the ship's officers. The food was better in the officer's mess, the captain explained.

They would not be able to disembark at any port, and when customs officials came aboard, they would be hidden.

When they finally made it to Florida and were on their way to

Boston, the four men would be provided a lifeboat and let off at the entrance on the New Jersey side of the Delaware Bay. From there they could row a couple of miles past Cape May Point and land in a desolate area. After they sink the boat, they would make their way to Cape May City and board a train to Philadelphia.

Once in Philadelphia, John would arrange with his contacts at the Washington Avenue Immigration Station to have papers made for each man making them legal immigrants. The money in the bank would be split four ways, ensuring each man would be able to establish themselves in their new adopted country.

They had discussed what they would do with their money many times during the last year. Danny wanted to go to school. He had never gotten past his 7th year, and he hoped someday to even go to college. George planned on sending most of the money to his family in Ireland and didn't know what he wanted to do with his life. Flannigan said he would stick with George to see what happened. John wanted to create an organization to help support the effort to free Ireland from British rule.

There were only seven days to get their affairs in order before the ship sailed and their new lives would begin. They would need to deliver the armaments to the camp, dig up the gold and cash they had hidden, and then leave the camp somehow without anyone noticing. If they left the same evening that they returned, it would give them a full day to convert the money and buy civilian clothes. The risk was high for they surely would be missed at morning assembly.

The evening of the day they returned to camp, Danny dug up the money and gold that he had buried behind the barracks building. The gold split between the four men making the weight of the precious metal manageable. They dressed in the full kit and uniforms so that if they were stopped, they could claim they were on patrol. At three in the morning, Flannigan climbed up the pole that held the main telegraph wire used between the camp and Haiphong. He cut the line and ran to the back of the barracks where the others were waiting for him.

George handed Flannigan his rifle and kit and the four men headed for the camp entrance. They were sure the officer of the watch would be napping in the office as was his custom. They only had to deal with the two Marine guards at the gate. It was dark, and the only light was from the stars that shone brightly in the clear sky. When they approached the gate, they were challenged by one of the guards.

"Halt. State your business," the Guard said in French.

"Patrol from Irish brigade. Bloody lieutenant woke us. Need to find our fucking man who's missing. Bouncing on some floozy in whore town, I guess," Danny replied in broken French.

Every legionnaire and regular knew about whore town. It was a tent village created by a couple of enterprising French prostitutes from Saigon. They recruited local women as well as French, English and Spanish prostitutes from the houses in Saigon.

The guard laughed and motioned for his counterpart to open the gate. As the four men walked out of the gate, the guard yelled at them, "Say hello to Yvette for me. She tastes so good." Then he stuck his tongue out. When Danny didn't reply the guard said, "Fucking Irish."

Danny said, "Fucking French." The four men walked into the darkness.

They now had only four days to travel a hundred kilometers back to Haiphong and then exchange their money and get civilian clothes. Every fifteen kilometers Flannigan would climb a telegraph pole and cut the line. They stopped to rest, eat and sleep for as shortest intervals as they could. Once as they were only ten kilometers from Haiphong, they had to go into the jungle and wait for a detachment of French military carrying telegraph wire to pass. They were probably sent to find the breaks in the line and repair them.

Once they passed, Flannigan climbed the next pole he saw and snipped the wire. He laughed and said, "Now they'll have something to fix on the way home."

The first thing the four men did when they entered the city was to find a clothier. It was no easy task as most did not cater to Western fashion. Finally, they found a tailor who spoke broken English and that sold used clothing he had exchanged with seamen who had bought new clothing from him. They each bought a shirt and trousers, which were in pretty rough shape. Wearing these clothes would make them look like they were from one of the ships. The tailor told them that he could also make them new suits. They explained that they were leaving the next day at noon and didn't have time to wait. The tailor assured that he could get the suits finished and delivered before they departed. He said his three daughters and wife would help him sew the clothing.

The men agreed, and the tailor showed them an 1880 version of a Montgomery Ward catalog. John asked where he obtained the catalog and the tailor said a crew member from an American ship gave him the book. They paid for the clothing, and after the tailor measured them, they changed in the back of the shop. The tailor promised to have the suits to the ship before noon the next day.

They departed the shop, leaving their uniforms and kits and only took their weapons. The tailor suggested that they could exchange their French paper money with a Chinese merchant a few blocks away. They exchanged what paper money they had for gold coins, getting a fraction of what it was worth, and headed for the ship.

The SS Lincoln was a sail steamer, meaning it had steam engines but also use sails to augment the coal they burnt. This allowed the ship to travel longer distances as they did not have to stop for coal. If the winds were light, they could use the steam engines to keep up speed. It was an attractive ship, painted white with black trim. The smokestacks were high to keep the grimy smoke from destroying the pristine look of the ship and the lungs of the crew.

The captain of the ship collected his hefty fee and showed them to the crew's quarters. The bunks were small, and most were in an open area towards the bow of the ship. The captain worked out that the four men would have bunks in an area that was somewhat secluded. The weapons they brought with them were locked in an aft storage space.

George, Danny, John and Flannigan were taken to the officer's mess, where they had a typical American breakfast. That included crisp bacon, eggs and pancakes with maple syrup. Coffee was available day and night. The first officer suggested that George and his friends stay below decks until they sailed.

At about ten in the morning, one of the crew members delivered a large package that was dropped off by a native. Each man tried on their new custom suit and was surprised that they fit so well. They carefully put them away for when they arrived in the United States.

George lay down in his bunk and closed his eyes. In what seemed like a couple of seconds but was, in reality, an hour and a half, the second officer came running to their bunks and yelled, "Come with me, boys. Quickly now."

George jumped up and hit his head on the upper bunk.

Rubbing his head, he slipped on his shoes and followed the officer and his friends. The second officer rushed them through the guts of the ship and into a room just behind the engine compartment. The room was full of engine parts, chains, and two large wooden crates. The officer pulled two pins from the side of one of the crates, and the wooden front opened. He entered and pulled two pins from the inside back of the crate. The wood swung outward revealing a metal door. The second officer opened the door and said, "In you go, gentlemen."

When he started to close the metal door Danny blurted out, "What's happening?"

"Your friends are searching all the docked ships. Just stay here and be quiet. I'll let you out when we're underway," The second officer said and closed the door leaving the men in the dark. He placed a large lock on the doors, then replaced the rear wood of the crate and pushed in the pins. Then he threw a couple of bungles of rags in the crate and replaced the front and returned to the upper decks.

George, Flannigan, Danny and John felt around to see if there was anything to sit on. There were some boxes and some bales that seemed soft, so they sat on them. George laid down on several bales and fell fast asleep. It was total darkness and very eerie. They could hear movement on the floor and knew from experience that they were sharing the room with rats.

"What's that smell? It kind of smells sweet," Danny asked.

"I smell it too," John said.

"Maybe the rats got into the sugar, and they have sweet shit now, "Flannigan said and laughed.

Flannigan sniffed the air a few times and said, "I know that smell, but I can't place it."

It was quiet for a minute or so, and then Flannigan yelled,

"Oh my lord. It's opium."

"Shhh. Keep quiet. What do you mean opium?" John whispered.

"You know opium. You smoke it," Flannigan said.

"How do you know about opium?" Danny asked.

"One of the girls at Madam Genevieve's house in Saigon smoked it when I was with her," Flannigan answered.

"Ahhh, our good captain is a smuggler," John said.

John pried the lid off of one of the boxes and felt around. There were a number of smaller packages wrapped in some oiled cloth. He opened one and felt a sticky substance. He smelled it and rubbed his fingers together and said, "That's opium alright. They sell it in Philadelphia in Chinatown. I don't know how many crates he has of this stuff, but it's worth a fortune."

The others sat in silence as George slept. After fifteen minutes or so they heard the metallic twang of the bulkhead door opening. Men were talking, but it was muffled and was intelligible. Flannigan, who was sitting next to where George was laying, moved and in doing so hit George with his hand. George woke startled and started to yell, "Whaaa," Flannigan quickly put his hand over George's mouth to stifle the noise.

In the main room, the ship's first officer was escorting a French Legion Officer and five of his legionaries. They told the first officer they were searching for four deserters that they believed to be in Haiphong. All departing ships were to be searched first.

"What's in these crates?" The legion officer asked.

"Just some rags, now. They used to have engine parts in them, "the first officer answered.

"Open this one, please," the legion officer ordered.

The first officer motioned to one of his crew to open the crate. The crew member pulled off the front of the crate and put it to the side. Inside were two bales of rags. The French Legion officer entered the crate and looked around. He kicked one of the bungles of rags, turned and walked out and said, "Now the second crate, please."

The second crate was full of various metal parts, and the French Legion officer satisfied that no deserters were in the room, left. The crew member replaced the front of both crates then closed the bulkhead door when he left.

Danny let out a breath and said, "Thank God."

Thirty minutes later John felt the movement of the ship and said, "And here we go."

After an hour or so the ship's movements became more intense and Flannigan began to complain about feeling ill. A few minutes later the bulkhead door opened again, and finally, the doors to the secret room opened, and the light poured in.

The second officer said, "The captain sends his regrets for having you locked up, but he's sure you understand. You can come out now."

Flannigan was the first out and was holding his stomach. His sea sickness was kicking in. George was next to exit the storage hold, and when he reached the open spaces, he stretched his shoulders and arms. Because of his height, he had been crouching when standing in the confined room. Danny came next and then John.

"The captain would like to see you on the bridge. If you'll follow me, I'll guide you there. By the way, my name is Francis Muller, Second Officer," he said and held out his hand.

George shook Muller's hand and said, "George Graham, late of Ireland. Good to meet you, Mr. Muller."

Muller turned to John and took his hand. John said, "John McBride from Philadelphia."

"You don't say. I grew up across the river in New Jersey. Good to meet you, John." Muller then took Danny's hand and Danny said, "Danny O'Boyle, Ireland."

Flannigan held out his hand and said, "William Flannigan, but everyone calls me Flannigan. Now if you don't mind, I need to get to the deck and deposit my breakfast in the sea."

"You do look peaked, Flannigan. Come with me. All of you," Muller said.

As they made their way topside, Muller said, "Flannigan, we have something that may help. While you're visiting with the captain, I'll make you the potion."

"Oh, sweet Jesus. If you can take away this feeling, I will be indebted to you my entire life," Flannigan said.

As soon as they got to the deck, Flannigan ran to the side and vomited. Danny yelled out, "Flannigan, do you have room for some nice greasy pork." Flannigan heaved again.

The captain greeted the four passengers when they entered the bridge. He explained that they would travel past Singapore, across the Indian Ocean to their first stop in South Africa.

"South Africa is a beautiful country. Sorry gentlemen, you'll have to enjoy it from afar. Too bad. Perhaps one day you'll have the opportunity to return," the captain said.

Danny was mesmerized by the view from the bridge. The sky was a deep blue and puffy white clouds drifted by as the ship sailed south along the Indochinese Peninsula. The ocean was blue and studded with white caps. For Danny, the motion of the ship was calming, and he was thoroughly enjoying his visit to the bridge.

"Sir, it's so beautiful. I truly envy that you get to enjoy such splendor every day," Danny said.

The captain laughed and said, "Mr. O'Boyle, you're right. It is beautiful, but the sea is a fickle companion. One minute you have splendor like this and the next you're fighting gale winds and thirty-foot waves. I dare say, Mr. Flannigan might not agree that today is so beautiful."

Flannigan was leaning against the rear bulkhead holding his stomach. His face was ashen white and his demeanor foul. He gave a half smile and waved his hand.

"Anyway, as I was saying, the sea is fickle, but I worry more about pirates," the captain said.

"Pirates? I thought they were long gone," George said.

"Not in these parts, Mr. Graham. There are plenty of Asian pirate gangs. In fact, the Black Flag warriors you no doubt faced were pirates before they became an army. The biggest threat is from coastal pirates who plunder from Madagascar to Nigeria. When we enter those waters your military skills could become useful," the captain said.

Muller entered the bridge carrying a tray with a large pot and cups. "Sorry to interrupt, sir. I made some ginger tea for Mr. Flannigan and of course, for anyone else who would like it," Muller said.

"Splendid idea, Mr. Muller," the captain said.

Muller set the tray down and poured a cup and handed it to Flannigan. Flannigan sniffed the concoction, and said, "Smells good."

"Drink it up. I'm sure it will help you. It's a tea made from raw ginger, lemon, and honey. Seafarers have been taking it for many years. Anyone else want a cup?" Muller said.

No one did, so Muller put the pot down on the tray and said, "This is all yours, Mr. Flannigan."

"Thank you, Mr. Muller. If this works I owe you in a big way," Flannigan said.

"Gentlemen, unless we tell you otherwise you may be on the deck, in the officer's mess or your quarters. Please refrain from going to the engine room, cargo holds or the bridge unless invited. Mr. Muller will inform you when meals are served. And we have a small library in the officer's mess. You may find occupying yourselves with a good book makes the time go by faster. I'll see you at the evening meal, but for now, I must get back to running this ship," the captain said.

"This way, gentlemen, "Muller said.

"Captain, may I speak to you privately?" John asked.

The captain looked surprised and said, "Certainly, but please make it brief as I have lots to do." He opened a door and continued, "Come into my office."

Once they were alone, John said, "Captain, when we were hidden away in that dark room, we saw you were hiding opium."

"I wouldn't say hiding as much as keeping it safe, but yes, you are correct." the captain said.

"As far as I know, the sale of opium is legal in the United States. Is that still the case?" John asked.

"It is, but as you may know, there is always talk of making it illegal," the captain answered

"Would it be possible for me to buy a quantity of your opium? I have some connections in Philadelphia's Chinatown, and I think I can sell it to them." John said.

"That may be possible. The U.S. has a pretty steep tariff on importing opium and if I sell you some and you get off at Cape May, you'll avoid paying it. It makes my opium worth more, don't you think?" the captain said.

"Which is why you really keep it hidden," John said, smiled and continued. "I think we can come to a reasonable price for both of us."

The captain smiled and said, "Deal."

When John and the captain finished their negotiations, they returned to the bridge and Muller took the men to the officer's mess, where he had the cook prepare the lunch. By then the ginger tea had a positive effect on Flannigan's seasickness, and he was hungry.

As the men ate their lunch, Danny perused the small library the captain had mentioned. He was thrilled about the availability of so many books. He had only read one book in his entire life. The master of his farm would never allow his servants to read his books. Now he could read as much as he liked.

"Look at these books," Danny said. He was excited. "They even have Moby Dick. I heard of that but never saw the book." The others nodded and continued to eat.

Danny chose *20,000 Leagues Under the Sea* by Jules Vern as his first book to read. By the time they reached the coastline of Madagascar, Danny had read *Journey to the Center of the Earth, David Copperfield, Frankenstein, Adventures of Huckleberry Finn, The Three Musketeers, Kidnapped, The Legend of Sleepy Hollow, The Prince and the Pauper and even Darwin's The Origins of the Species and The Descent of Man.* George chose *Moby Dick* to read and was only halfway finished. John and Flannigan busied themselves playing cards or dice with the crew.

The trip thus far had been enjoyable. The seas were as calm as anyone would have expected and they only experienced three days of rain. When the four men were not reading, gambling or drinking, they would go topside and enjoy watching the various animals of the Indian Ocean. They enjoyed the dolphins the most. They would swim in the bow wave and then just to show their superiority would quickly swim ahead of the ship. They jumped and played in the sea as if to show off to the creatures that stood to watch them from the rail of the ship.

Once, they saw an amazingly large fish surface and blow air through a hole in its head. The captain explained that it was a blue whale, and it was not even a fish, but rather a mammal like a cow or a dog. As they got closer to land, there were gulls, albatross, and even a pelican or two glided effortlessly through the azure-colored sky.

It was all so serene and beautiful, especially when they were totally under sail power. The belching black smoke and dreadful sound of the steam engines were gone, and all that could be heard was the swish of the wake of the ship.

Flannigan's seasickness abated with the help of daily doses of ginger tea, and he was now thoroughly enjoying sea travel. George still had pangs of regret, sorrow and guilt over Dat's death, but he was learning to cope with it. John had taken the time to solidify his deal with the captain. They agreed that as often as the captain's ship passed the coast of New Jersey on his return trips from Asia, he would supply John with opium.

As the four friends enjoyed the temperate weather on deck and antics of the dolphins, Second Officer Muller ran up to them and said, "The captain would like to see the four of you on the bridge."

They had not been asked to the bridge since the beginning of the voyage. George asked, "What's it about?"

"The pirates, I suppose."

CHAPTER 20

"Gentlemen, thank you for coming. It may come that we will need to take advantage of your particular skills." the captain said.

"Skills! All we know how to do is shoot rifles," Danny quipped.

"Precisely, Mr. O'Boyle. They are skills we may well need before this journey's finished. You see we're now in the domain of pirates. From Madagascar to the Congo these waters are infested with brigands. These are not the kind of pirates Mr. Stevenson writes about. They don't come at you with sails fluttering in the wind and cannon blazing. These are local pirates infused with the scum of Europe and America. Instead, they sneak up to your ship in the dark of night in their small but swift boats. They board your ship when most are asleep, then overwhelm and kill the crew. When they take all that they desire they scuttle the ship, so it appears it just vanished in a storm," the captain explained.

"What would you like us to do, Captain?" George asked.

"I have had your weapons brought to the bridge," the captain said and pointed to the rifles stacked against the bulkhead. "If you agree I would have the four of you supplement our night watch."

"And do what?" Flannigan asked.

"Keep an eye out for any boats that approach. It won't be easy. These bastards use black sails and boats that make it very hard to see them until they're upon the ship. If you see them, sound the alarm and kill as many of the bastards as you can," the captain said.

"That we know how to do," John said and laughed.

"I purchased a Gatling gun. Can you operate it?" the captain asked.

"I used one a couple of times," Flannigan said.

"Good, we'll place it aft. That's back of the boat. They are most likely to attack from the back and sides of the ship."

"Starboard and port, right?" Danny said proudly.

"Correct." the captain said.

"He's a reader," Flannigan said as if explaining why Danny knew these things.

"Thank you, gentlemen. At sunset, please report to Mr. Muller. He'll be on watch with you. Now go get some rest," the captain said.

After pulling night watch for ten days, George started to wish they would get attacked. The most exciting thing that had happened was Danny shooting at a dolphin he mistook for a pirate boat. Fortunately for the dolphin, he missed.

The four of them rotated positions every few hours, and George was so bored that he looked forward to the walk to the next station. The four crewmen that were on night watch did so from high positions, so there were rare opportunities to talk to them. Muller knew that George and his friends weren't used to this kind of solitude and made a point of visiting each of the men as often as he could. One evening Muller told George they had rounded the Cape of Good Hope and entered the Atlantic Ocean. He pulled out a flask and handed it to George and said, "It won't be long now. Soon you'll be in your new home."

George smiled, grabbed the flask and took a large swig. He knew Muller was just trying to make him feel better. It might have worked if Danny hadn't calculated just that morning that it would be from 40 to 50 days before they got to Cape May.

"Thank you, Muller. You're a good man," George said.

Every three or four days they would test fire the Gatling gun to be sure the salty and damp sea air wasn't harming the inner workings. This gave each of the men the opportunity to learn how to work the weapon. They already knew the gun could wreak devastation, as they had seen them in action in Tonkin. Still, the utter power of the weapon amazed them.

The Gatling the captain had obtained was an older model with a straight feed. The bullets fell into place as each barrel of the gun rotated. Because there were ten barrels, none got overheated, and you could fire as fast as you could turn the crank and change the feed.

The only problem with the Gatling was that it was too heavy to move quickly. It would only be effective for pirate boats coming up from the rear. During a dark overcast evening, it might be impossible to see the blackened sails and painted pirate boats until it was too late to use the Gatling.

Danny, having run through all of the novels in the small library, started reading science and history books, of which there were only three. One of the books was the history of the war between Mexico and the United States. He remembered the story of the siege of Veracruz and how the United States used rockets. A passage in the book mentioned that the rocket attack lit up the fort. He mentioned this to Muller, who said they had no rockets but did have several Very pistols they used to shoot flares in case of an emergency.

They tested the flares and found they worked well to light

up the ocean if even just for a short time. Two of the Very pistols with a supply of Very flares were stored near the Gatling gun.

"How long has it been since we passed Madagascar?" George asked Danny one morning at breakfast.

"About 12 days," Danny replied

"So that means we are maybe 3 or 4 days from the Congo, right?" George asked.

"About," Danny said.

"Captain says after the Congo, pirate attacks are unlikely and we can get back to sleeping nights instead of days. I don't know about you, but I am sick of staying awake all night with nothing to do but stare at the stars." George lamented.

"I'm starting to wonder if there were ever any pirates. The captain was probably just trying to keep us out of his hair during the day," John said.

"Well, whatever his reason it's dark again, and we're on watch. C'mon...let's get moving," Flannigan said.

The four men took their positions. George was on starboard, John on the bow, Flannigan on port and Danny at aft with the Gatling gun. By midnight moving clockwise they changed positions. George checked the Gatling gun. It was loaded and ready. He looked out over the ocean. There was nothing to see. It was a cloudy night and occasionally he heard a dolphin playing in the water, but that was all. He sat down on the deck, closed his eyes and thought about Philadelphia.

George, when he was in Ireland, had heard stories that Irish Catholics weren't welcomed in parts of the United States. He wondered if he would be able to get a job. He had money in the bank, but he planned to send that to his mother, so a job was important. If there were jobs for the Irish, what could he do? All he knew was potato farming and soldiering.

Muller walked up to George, kicked his foot and asked, "Are we sleeping on the job there, George?"

George opened his eyes with a start and said, "No, just day-dreaming. Ahh, night dreaming, I guess."

"What did she look like?" Muller asked.

"No, not a girl. I'll be honest, Muller, I'm worried about getting work in the States. What can I do, but shoot a rifle and kill people," George said.

"Well, if you want to pick up the rifle again, there is plenty of work out west. You can join the army and fight the redskins, become a lawman or maybe even a highwayman," Muller said and chuckled.

"No, I'm done with the army. I have no grievance with any natives. Christ, I'm a native myself, a native of Ireland, who has been invaded by the English. It's why I'm here on this ship. I don't want to hurt any innocent people just so some other government can control them," George said.

"Well, you're a big strong man. I'm sure you'll find something. I'll be on my way now. See you on my next rounds. Keep your eyes open, George," Muller said and walked away.

George stood up and looked out on the ocean. He stiffened thinking he heard something but then relaxed. *It was probably just dolphins again,* he thought. He leaned over the rail and stared at the ocean again and saw nothing. Then he heard the noise again. It was different than the dolphin sounds. It was a series of sounds like something slapping the water. It was very faint, but he had good hearing, and he definitely heard something.

He looked for Muller, but he was gone and probably talking to Flannigan. He thought about sounding the alarm, but then remembered the Very pistols. He opened the box the pistols were in and grabbed one and loaded a flare. He pointed it high over the aft rail and fired. The white flare went high in the sky, exploded and started to fall. George looked out over the ocean, and his eyes widened. A second later a bullet hit the rail in front of him.

He quickly stepped back as three more shots rang out, fortunately missing him. He grabbed the Gatling gun, pointed to the five boats full of men he had seen, and started to fire. *No need for an alarm now,* he thought.

The light of the flare was fading out, and he wasn't sure if he was hitting anything or not, but he kept firing. He reloaded and fired again. It was so noisy that he could hear nothing but the repeated blasts of bullets coming out of the barrels.

Muller and Flannigan heard the shooting and leaned out over the rail looking for the pirates. As they did, five feet from them a grappling hook came over the rail and snagged it. Then another one did the same fifteen feet towards the aft. Muller ran to the first grappling hook and tried to release it, but it was too taunt. A second later a man's head appeared on the rail. He was wearing all black, and he had a rifle strapped to his back and a large knife in his hand. Muller grabbed his pistol, but he was too late. The man flung himself at Muller, knocking him backward. The pistol fell to the deck. The man thrust the knife towards Muller's chest. Just before the knife sliced through Muller, the side of the man's head exploded. Flannigan had seen what was happening and had been able to shoot the man.

Another man was coming over the rail where the second grappling hook was attached. The man screamed and fell back into the sea. A guard from the ship's crew who was stationed above the deck had shot the man in his chest.

Danny O'Boyle heard Gatling gun reports and his first instinct was to help George. But then he remembered what the captain had said about the pirates may try to board the ship on the port and starboard sides. He grabbed his rifle, which had his bayonet affixed and pointed it at the rails. At the same time, a grappling hooked clanged against the deck and caught hold on the rail. He waited until he saw the head of a man climbing the rope then he thrust the bayonet through the man's eye. The man silently fell backward, and Danny leaned over the rail to be sure he was gone and as he did, another grappling hook was tossed from the boat. It grabbed the rail and Danny's left hand. The pain was excruciating, and Danny almost dropped his rifle but was able to hold onto it with his right hand. Then another grappling hook came over the rail just ten feet away from Danny. He could feel the pressure increasing on his left hand and knew someone was climbing up the rope.

Danny was panicking. He couldn't use his rifle with one of his hands trapped. He put the rifle against the rail and pulled a knife from his belt and tried to cut the rope. Every time he leaned over to cut the rope, someone in one of the boats shot at him. The man climbing the rope was getting closer. Danny dropped the knife and grabbed his rifle, flipped it over with one hand, then pointed the bayonet downward over the rail and pushed it hard. It hit something, someone screamed, and the next thing Danny knew was his rifle being pulled out of his hand. He heard a large splash and then a smaller splash and hoped the first one was the man who had been climbing the rope.

As soon as John heard the Gatling gun, he yelled at the crewman who was on duty above him that he was going to help Danny. As he ran aft towards Danny, the ship started to heave first to the port then to starboard, then back again. The helmsman had started zig-zagging to make it more difficult for the pirates to board the ship. John almost fell, caught himself and as he came up to Danny, a man was climbing over the rail. He was heading for Danny. John stopped ,took aim and fired. The man's forward motions made him fall at Danny's feet. John ran up to him and plunged his bayonet into the man's heart.

The Gatling gun was still churning, and single shots could be heard all over the ship. A few minutes later the guns became silent. John lifted the grappling iron that was trapping Danny's hand.

"Looks like you got lucky, Danny boy. The spike didn't go through your hand," John said.

"It's broken. I can't move it," Danny said.

John pulled a pistol that Flannigan had given him, handed it to Danny and said,

"I'll check on George. You okay here?"

"Yeah, okay. Go," Danny said.

John ran back to George and found him standing by the Gatling shaking his arms.

"George, you okay?" Danny asked. "What are you doing?"

"Trying to get the blood back into my arms. Turning that crank isn't easy. My arms feel like a million pins and needles are sticking in them," George answered.

"You're okay then?" John asked.

"Yes, fine."

"I'll check on Flannigan," John said and took off to the starboard side. As he approached, he saw Flannigan standing over a man lying in a pool of blood on the deck. The captain was talking to three of his crew who had two black-clad pirates bound and sitting on the deck.

"John, help me with this guy, will you," Flannigan said as he grabbed the man by his arms. John grabbed the dead man's feet, and together they tossed him overboard. John made the sign of the cross.

"He doesn't deserve that, John. Son of a bitch would have killed you, me, all of us, and never thought anything of it," Flannigan said.

The captain was yelling at the two pirates, but John and Flannigan couldn't hear what he was saying, just an occasional curse word. Finally, he stopped yelling, reached down and picked up one of the pirates and held him over his head. He tossed the pirate over the rail into the South Atlantic Ocean as if he was a ragdoll. The crew members that were with the captain did the same with the second pirate. After a minute or so the screaming stopped.

"I wouldn't want to get on the captain's bad side, that's for sure," John said.

CHAPTER 21

For two days after they passed the Congo, the captain kept the night watch as it had been. After that, he relaxed the watch and thanked George, John, Danny and Flannigan and told them they could stand down. To be safe, he asked them to keep their weapons until they docked in Spanish Morocco.

When they arrived at the port in Nigeria, Muller took the four men to the same hiding space they were stuck in when they left Haiphong. This time they were sure to take some food and a couple of candles with them. Danny brought a copy of Noah Webster's Dictionary from one of the crew members and read it by candlelight. He practiced his vocabulary with the other three so much they wanted to take the book away from him. The final straw came when he asked them if they knew the definition of animadvert.

"Do you know what animadvert means? Danny asked.

"Oh Christ, not another word from Mr. Dictionary," Flannigan replied.

"A N I M A D V E R T," Danny said.

Here, let me see it," John said as he grabbed the book from Danny. John then laid the book on a bale of cotton and sat on it.

"Hey, give me my book back," Danny yelled.

"Not until you promise to stop trying to teach us words we'll never use," John said.

"I swear, John, I'll shove a book up your ass if you don't give it back," Danny yelled.

"At least that way you'll never be able to get it again," John said.

Danny's face turned red, and he jumped up and towards John. George stopped him in midair and sat him down and said, "Danny, listen to me. It's one thing to know big words and another to know when to use them. If you want average people to understand your meaning you have to use words they know. Save the big words for the professors and uppity-ups. Do you understand what I'm saying?"

Danny nodded that he did. George then said, "John, give Danny back his book, please."

"Not until he swears to God he won't keep asking us what his fancy words mean," John said.

George walked over to John, picked him up and sat him on the floor. He picked up the book and took it to Danny.

"You okay now, Danny?" George asked.

"Yes."

"How about you, John?"

"Yeah, I'm good," John answered.

"To consider," Danny said.

"What? Flannigan asked.

"Animadvert. It means to consider.

John pulled a handful of cotton from one of the bales and threw it at Danny. The soft materials only made it halfway and landed on Flannigan's head, making him look like an old Irish judge. All four men started to laugh.

John had felt something hard when he pulled the cotton from the bale. He looked down and saw a piece of metal sticking out, grabbed it and said, "What have we here? It looks like the captain smuggles more than just opium. These bales have rifles in them," John said.

The stay in Nigeria was brief, and they soon found themselves traveling up the coast of Africa again. Their final destination before heading to Florida was Spanish Morocco, and once again the four ex-legionnaires went into hiding. Muller brought them food three times a day and stayed to converse with them. Muller liked all of the men, but he had a special connection with Flannigan after he saved Muller's life when the pirates attacked.

Muller would describe the parts of Philadelphia he had visited and told them stories he had heard working on the Camden docks when he was a child. Muller particularly liked to brag that there was no farmland in the world that compared with New Jersey. "Jersey tomatoes," he would often say, "Were better than sex."

"That may be, Mr. Muller, but I am looking forward to partaking of the latter again." Danny said.

"Well, Danny boy, Mrs. Palmer and her five daughters seem to do very well for you," Flannigan quipped. Danny turned red as the others laughed.

"Flannigan, Mrs. Palmer seems to like you much better than me. Probably because she prefers men with small wees," Danny said. Now it was Flannigan's turn to have red cheeks.

Flannigan continued to drink the ginger tea Muller had suggested for seasickness. Many in the crew started calling Muller Ginger because he was always making the concoction. The tea worked, and Flannigan had not been seasick since the beginning of the voyage. By the time they were halfway across the Southern Atlantic Ocean, the large rolling waves also had the others drinking the ginger tea.

They had seen many wonders on this trip, including shark attacking another shark, very large whales, and a fish that was floating on the surface of the water that was at least ten feet long and twelve feet wide. Muller said it was called a sunfish. What they enjoyed most was watching the flying fish jumping from the water and sailing through the sky and then dropping back down into the water. Once, one of the flying fish landed on the deck of the ship. Flannigan had picked it up and dropped it back in the water saying, "Off you go to your Ma."

The flying fish had disappeared the further they traveled from land, but now they were starting to reappear. George asked Muller about it, and he had said that they tend to be more plentiful closer to land. This confused George as he thought they were still pretty far from Florida. Muller explained that they had a course change and that they were going to Cuba first. They had picked up some freight the Spanish wanted to be delivered to Cuba, so since they were near the captain took the job.

This was the first time any of the four ex-legionnaires had heard they were going to Cuba. It didn't bother them because it was just another stop before they could take up their new lives in Philadelphia. In fact, only Danny knew there was even a place called Cuba and that it was a colony of Spain.

One day Muller told them that they would be in Havana at about noon the next day. In the morning they would have to go back to the hiding place. He bid them get a good night's rest and that after a day in Havana they would sail to Florida.

While the ex-legionnaires slept, the captain brought the ship as close as he could to the islands off of the Cuban mainland. When they were several miles from the Island of Cayo, he had the ship slowed down. Two thirty-foot boats pulled alongside and hooked up to the larger ship. Several minutes later hand-picked members of the crew started to lower bales of cotton to the waiting boats. The final item to be lowered was the captain's Gatling gun. A chest was tied to a rope the captain had lowered to one of the boats, and the captain and first mate pulled it aboard.

The boats pulled away, and the captain had the ship resume normal speed. By daybreak, Muller roused George and told him to gather the men. It was time to go into hiding.

Again they brought some candles, food and this time some playing cards one of the crew loaned to them. Danny, as usual, brought a couple of books. He was now rereading them. Muller shut the door before they could light the candles, so it was pitch black as they tried to retrieve the matches. Flannigan, remembering where the bales of cotton were, fell back on one. To his surprise, he hit the floor.

"Fuck, that hurt. Some bastard moved the cotton," Flannigan yelled.

George had by then found the matches and lit one of the candles. The one candle dimly lit up the room, and they could see that all the bales of cotton with the rifles in them were gone. All of the opium chests were still in place.

"I am assuming that the captain offloaded them during the night when we were asleep. But why? To who?" George asked.

"My guess is Cuban rebels. I read in one of the old newspapers the cook gave me that there have been attempts to free Cuba from the Spanish rule," Danny said.

"Then I say, good for the captain," John said.

CHAPTER 22

When the ship left Havana, George and the others were allowed out and told that by morning they would have to go back to the hiding place. Travel from Havana to Biscayne Bay was only a day-long trip. In the morning the four men got up early. For George, Danny and Flannigan it would be the first time they saw America and they were excited.

It was beautiful. The glistening blue water contrasted against the white beaches and the green tree line flowed into the blue sky that hosted puffy white clouds. For George, it looked like a painting. It brought back memories of his frequent daydreams when he was in Ireland. *This is the place in my dreams,* he thought. He closed his eyes and imagined himself with his Ma, and the rest of the family, sitting on the white sand. *Someday I'll be back,* he thought. *And my family will be with me.*

"Okay gentlemen, time to get back in the hole. We'll be in Biscayne Bay for two days. For Christ's sake be quiet. Yesterday, I could hear you in the hall. These American customs agents don't screw around," Muller said.

The only good thing about being in the hidden compartment again was that this would be the last time they had to do it. They understood the need, but the conditions were pretty bad. Sure they had food and drink, books for Danny, cards for the rest, but after a half a day the compartment smelled like a cesspool. The combination of body waste and sweat didn't make a good perfume. More than once they considered smoking some of the captain's opium so that they could sleep through the ordeal. Danny insisted that it would not be in their best interest to steal the captain's drugs.

The next day Muller finally unlocked the door and said, "You're free. This is the last time you'll see the inside of this place."

The four men stepped out of the crate, and each took a deep breath. It smelled like coal dust, but it was better than smelling piss and crap all day.

"The captain would like to see you on the bridge. First, he would like you to take a bath. He's arranged to have a large tub placed on the deck and had it filled with fresh water. Captain says it won't do to have you stinking to high heaven when you first meet your new country mates," Muller said.

Muller led the men to the deck, and sure enough, there was a large tub big enough for two people. Muller suggested that the men give him their clothing and he would have the cook boil and wash them. The four men stripped to their birthday suits, and none of them was especially shy about it. They all had lean, muscular bodies from their time in the military.

George and Flannigan won the draw of the cards and were the first to the bath. There were two bars of Ivory soap floating on the water, and both men scrubbed their hair and lathered their bodies. Danny and John stood nearby naked. Some of the crew started whistling at them in jest, and Danny and John responded by sashaying around the tub. This elicited even more catcalls and lewd comments.

When George and Flannigan finished bathing, they were given large pieces of cloth to dry themselves. Since they didn't have their clothing back, they just wrapped the towels around their bottoms and waited. Danny and John skimmed off the floating grime then got into the water. When they finished, they also wrapped the towels around themselves.

Muller took them to the bridge and showed them to the captain's quarters. The captain was sitting at a table that had five plate settings. He poured each man a glass of whiskey and bid them sit down.

"How were your baths?" the captain asked.

"Thank you, Captain. We appreciate that you thought about that. We all feel like new men now," Danny said.

"To be honest, I did it as much for myself as for you. You were getting pretty ripe." the captain said."

"Thank you for this lunch," George said.

"I'm glad you could dress for it," the captain said and laughed then continued, "We'll have your clothes at the end of the day."

"Captain, I have a question," John said.

"I thought you might," the captain answered.

"We noticed that the bales of cotton were missing when we went into hiding. We know there were rifles in those bales. What were they for?" John asked.

"John, I don't normally talk about my business, but I'll answer you because we're partnering with other things and you deserve to know what your partner does. I'll also tell you because I would like the four of you to stay on with me, as security guards," the captain said.

This surprised all four men, and John answered him. When

it came to things of an illegal nature, the group always deferred to John as he had more experience in such matters.

"Sir, we're flattered and will give that consideration. Of course, we first have to get settled in Philadelphia. I am sure you understand," John said.

"I do," the captain said.

"May I ask where you get your arms?" John said.

"I picked this shipment up at our first stop," the captain said.

"I assume the weapons were for the Cuban rebels?" John asked.

"That's correct," the captain answered.

"Would you have an interest in weapons I can get from the U.S.?" John asked.

The captain's eyebrows raised and he said, "I could be if the price is right."

"Can we get together after lunch and I'll tell you how you and we're all going to make a lot of money?" John said.

After lunch Danny excused himself explaining that when he got settled in Philadelphia, he planned to go back to school and then on to college and wouldn't have time to be involved in John's schemes. Everyone understood and even envied Danny's desire to better himself.

John explained to the captain his background in gun running and why he had the contacts they needed to be able to supply the necessary weapons. They agreed that the money made from the sale of the weapons would be split four ways after expenses. He had two stipulations. John wanted to ship weapons to Ireland, and the opium part of the business would remain a deal between John and the captain.

George was at first relieved that he would have a job, but nervous because his job was against the law. He mollified himself by now planning to have his whole family immigrate to the U.S.

He would buy them a nice home, and his mother could live the rest of her life not worrying about money. Flannigan said he would do the same if his mother would make a move to the U.S. He wasn't sure she would because his mother was a suborned woman and might not want to leave her friends.

After almost three months of sea travel, they finally reached the Delaware Bay and Cape May. The captain slowed the ship as the crew lowered one of the lifeboats. The four ex-legionnaires had said their goodbyes to the various crew members they had become friends with and packed the few processions they owned.

The captain handed John a carpet bag full of opium and said, "I'm going to miss the four of you. Good luck in Philadelphia and when you have the goods we need, contact me at the address I gave you. I'll be taking a few months off before the next trip to Asia."

"Before we leave I have an important question to ask you, captain," John said.

"You do? I thought we had all questions answered," the captain said.

"Just one left. What is your name? We have always just called you captain," John said.

The captain laughed and said, "Sean Murphy," the captain replied.

"I knew it. You're a mick," John said and shook the captain's hand again.

"My family was from Galway. We've been in the U.S. since 1801," Sean said.

Captain Sean Murphy slapped John on the back and said, "Down you go." John grabbed the rope and slid down to the boat. George and Danny followed.

Flannigan shook Muller's hand and said, "If you get home, come by and see us. Captain Murphy will know where we are." Then Flannigan took the rope and dropped to the boat.

George and Flannigan took the first turn at rowing. It was a while before they reached land because the tide was going out and slowed them down. They had to switch places three times, but finally, they found a small secluded beach and pulled in. They took an ax to the boat's bottom and slid it out into the bay. It was decided that they would sleep on the beach until daylight and then walk into Cape May. The September weather had a slight nip to it, but they were too happy to notice it.

In the morning they made their way to a small trail and headed southeast as Captain Murphy suggested. The first mile was difficult because they had not walked on dry land for three months. But, by the time they reached Cape May proper they were fine. The town impressed them as did some of the fine homes they passed. They found a hotel called Congress Hall that was bigger than any hotel they had ever seen. Since it was Friday, they decided to stay the weekend and leave on Monday. The hotel arranged a tour for them and obtained first class train tickets to Philadelphia. At first, the hotel suggested a boat tour, but they emphatically declined.

That Monday, dressed in their suits they had made in Haiphong, the four friends boarded the train at the New Jersey Railroad Station in Cape May. Three hours later they stepped off of the train into Philadelphia. They were finally in their new home.

CHAPTER 23

Philadelphia. PA, USA - October 1884

The ex-legionnaires' first month in Philadelphia was both exciting and nerve-racking. George, Flannigan and Danny found a city infused with what many people called the pursuit of the American Dream. People were building amazing new structures, such as the new city hall, and otherwise trying to cut out their piece of that dream. Even the poorest immigrants living in the city's less fortunate areas believed that hard work would ensure a better life. There was a special kind of optimistic attitude that even in the face of years of discrimination against Irish Catholics couldn't dim. That attitude was contagious.

Their only fear was being stopped by authorities and getting deported back to Ireland before they could get their papers. John connected with his friend at the Washington Avenue Immigration Station the first week they were in Philadelphia and paid the appropriate bribe. It, however, took a full thirty days before the papers were available. John took the opportunity of getting new papers to change his name so he could circumvent any legacy from his past criminal life. He was now John O'Shaughnessy, late of County Limerick, Ireland. Danny had the new papers make him two years older.

John arranged with his mother to have the four men temporarily live in her small home in the Kensington section of Philadelphia until they found their own places. The home on Mercer Street was only eight hundred square feet, and including John's family, nine people were living there. On the plus side was that the home was located in the Irish section of the city called Kensington. The men felt at home amongst their Irish Countrymen and fellow immigrants. Danny was particularly impressed with how industrious everyone seemed to be. Kensington was bustling with people hustling to and from the numerous factories, many of which were making textiles. It was the workingman's part of the city, and that appealed to Danny.

Three months after they arrived, George purchased a home in Kensington on Sergeant Street that was 1,122 square feet and that he knew would seem like a palace to his family. He sent them money for passage and was now just waiting until they obtained permission to immigrate. Danny enrolled in school and was on his way to obtaining his high school diploma. He had already decided that he would go to the University of Pennsylvania after he graduated. When George and Flannigan moved, Danny kept a room in John's mother's house because he had fallen for John's younger sister Hanna. Flannigan didn't know what he wanted to do. He tried to have his mother and the rest of his family immigrated to the U.S. and told them he would buy a nice home for them. His mother didn't want to move, and his siblings decided to stay with their Ma. So Flannigan took a room with George. He sent his family money regularly.

John reconnected with Captain Murphy and made the first delivery of weapons destined for the Cuban rebels. Murphy, once he realized that John was able to deliver the weapons, took only freight jobs throughout the Caribbean. In that way, he could concentrate on the lucrative gunrunning a business to Cuba. He arranged for the captain of the second boat that traveled to Cochinchina with him to bring back opium John could sell to his connections in Chinatown. Danny had opted to concentrate on his education and decided not to join in the smuggling venture. John, George and Flannigan did well the first months and decided that as long as this continued, they would help Danny with his goal to graduate college. He was after all one of the Four Horsemen.

The first shipment of weapons was reasonably easy to obtain. The second and third shipments became more difficult to find. The sellers were asking for more money and supplying fewer weapons. John also wanted to start shipments to Ireland and had arranged with two ship owners to smuggle them. John knew that if he were to be successful, he would have to find other sources of weapons. He started to build connections with those in charge of military facilities such as the Frankford Arsenal, the Schuylkill Arsenal, Fort Mifflin and other forts and arsenals in New Jersey, Delaware and Maryland. Some of these connections were Irish American Catholics, and it was easy to get them on board by telling them the weapons were for the Irish rebels. The non-Irish were told the guns were for the Cuban rebels, and since the U.S. and Spanish relations were tense, they were more than happy to help out, for a price, of course.

John was also able to enlist executives from three arms manufacturers to work with him. After six months there was no shortage of weapons to be smuggled into Cuba and Ireland. He was so successful that he stopped buying from the original suppliers. This, of course, caused a rift between John's gang and the suppliers' organizations. John mollified them by promising to supply them with a certain quantity of arms at below market price that they could sell in other areas of the country. That worked, and everything began to work like a finely tuned clock.

As demand grew, John had to organize and get more men to join his effort. George took over relationships with the arms manufacturers, and Flannigan dealt with the arsenals and military. John talked Danny into handling the financial end of the business, at least on a part-time basis while he was in school. The Four Horsemen were back together, and they were building their particular piece of the American Dream.

The transfer of weapons had to be accomplished in such a manner that the authorities had no idea that internal contacts at the arsenals and arms companies were involved. To do this John's men had to rob shipments transferred to or from the facilities and in some cases robbing the actual facility. The waggoners were almost always in on it and this, for the most part, went smooth. It did, however, require a large commitment of men to help them. Fortunately, there was no shortage of men who were willing to do anything for a chance to have a high paying job. Even in 1884 Irish Catholics were still suffering from discrimination that started with the first large wave of Irish Catholic immigrants in 1850.

Most jobs the Irish filled were low paying hard labor. John's organization paid well so even if it was illegal many flocked to his group. He had the pick of the toughest and smartest of the lot. One of his neighbor's kid badgered John day and night to let him help. The kid was pretty big for a fourteen-year-old, tough as nails and smart. John saw something in him and hired him to help Danny with the books. The kid didn't like it since he really wanted to be in the field where the action was, but he agreed.

Danny found the kid to be a fast learner and very bright. After six months he was able to handle all journal entries and help with inventory. The kid had no desire to go back to school, even though Danny constantly tried to talk him into continuing his education. That irked Danny as he saw a lot of potential in this kid and he didn't want to see him toting a gun and robbing arms wagons. Of course, that was exactly what the kid wanted to do.

By the time the kid was sixteen, he had become the fifth wheel when John, Danny, George, and Flannigan went out on the town or saw the sights. They all liked him. The kid was a smooth talker, good looking and attracted women of all ages. He fit like a glove and became the fifth horseman. In 1886, two years after the ex-legionnaires arrived in Philadelphia, they were living the American Dream. George's family settled in, and he had even been able to buy his sister and her husband a house on the same block as his mother's house.

Danny was finishing his first year at the University of Pennsylvania and was engaged to John's sister Hannah. John had built a fairly large organization and felt like he was doing some good by supplying the oppressed people of Ireland and Cuba weapons so they could liberate themselves. Flannigan was still living in George's mother's home, and he sent all but a small amount of his earnings to his family in Ireland. The kid was promoted to second in charge in George's part of the organization. He was almost as tough as George, and George agreed, he was smarter. At the age of sixteen the kid, Charlie Byrne looked the same age as the older George, Flannigan and Danny.

George was shy with women, but Charlie made up for it by

being glib, gracious and flattering. When they went out together, there was never a shortage of women who wanted to meet them. Danny, being engaged didn't go out on the town as often as the others, and Flannigan preferred not to get entangled in relationships and found his female companionship in the various houses of ill repute in Philadelphia. John had met a fine woman from the neighborhood named Coleen and was talking about marriage. This often left just George and Charlie together on their entertainment excursions. They formed a special bond because Charlie made up for George's reserved demeanor with his sometimes outlandish behavior and propensity to get into bar fights.

George was one of the few people that could sometimes get Charlie under control. If he couldn't then George was the perfect fighting partner. At six foot three inches tall and two hundred and fifty pounds of muscle, few men would even try him. If they did, they quickly found themselves on the ground nursing a sore chin. Charlie was no weakling either, and while he was not George's size, he made up for it by being both ruthless and relentless. It wasn't long before the duo was given either deference or a wide berth.

There was an incident in 1888 that solidified the Johnny O. Gang's, as others now called the group, reputation in Kensington. On George's 26th birthday the five men, George, John, Danny, Flannigan and Charlie went to a music hall located on Front Street and frequented by Irish Catholics. They were enjoying the old Irish classics, reminiscing about home and drinking fine Irish whiskey. The band had just finished playing an Irish Jig when ten loudmouth men came into the establishment and sat at a large table. The band started to play a slow tempo classic Irish religious song titled *Be Now My Vision.* In reverence to the song's subject, the audience quieted down and enjoyed the melodic tone of the tenor's voice.

A minute into the song one of the ten men yelled out, "Play something lively. For Christ's sake, I feel like I'm at a funeral."

The band ignored the man and continued playing. The man yelled out again, and again, the band ignored him. John got up from his table, walked over to the man and said, "If you would please be quiet the rest of the patrons would appreciate it."

"And who the fuck are you? The head Mick?" the man said.

"I'm just a fella trying to enjoy the music," John said calmly and then yelled, "So if you don't mind, shut your fucking blow-hole."

The man jumped up and threw a punch at John. John leaned back and felt the air from the man's fist passing by his face. He then, using an open hand, slapped the man in the face. When he did this the other nine men at the table stood up and went after John. George, Danny, Flannigan and Charlie saw this, leaped up and joined the donnybrook. It was five against ten, but in short order seven of the intruders were lying on the floor unconscious. The other three put up their hands indicating they had enough. Charlie, not giving a damn and his blood boiling, went after them, but George stopped him then said. "You three, grab your friends and get out."

Each of the men helped up one of their friends leaving four still lying on the floor. George took two of the still unconscious men by the collar and started to drag them to the door. As he did, he said, "Charlie, Flannigan get the other two." They did as George asked. When all of the unruly intruders were out of the hall, John motioned to the band, and they started to play an Irish Jig.

CHAPTER 24

Kensington, Philadelphia, PA - 1890

By 1888 the Johnny O. Gang was out of the opium business. It just wasn't profitable. As a legal drug the competition was fierce and the supply easy to get. Both factors made it less expensive. The gunrunning business, however, thrived during the years since they started. The Cuban resistance had silently been stockpiling weapons for years, and in 1889 the demand increased. John surmised that within the next five years there would be a rebellion that if won by the rebels would pretty much end the need for his services. If the Spanish crushed the rebellion, it would be the same result - no more gun smuggling.

The Irish gunrunning part of the business had begun to slow down to a small degree. There was the talk of allowing Ireland to rule themselves, but still be under British control. By 1889 it still had not happened, but the effect was that there was less activity by the rebels and there was less need for weapons. John O'Shaughnessy had spent many hours searching for something he could do to have a diverse source of income for the gang if the gun business dried up. In 1889 he found it.

An acquaintance of John's owned a small construction company that mainly repaired older homes in North Philadelphia. John paid him a favorable sum of money and took over the operation. He put the now twenty-year-old Charlie Byrne in charge of the company mainly because he knew Charlie had the smarts and would to do whatever he had to do to make the business work.

After Danny O'Boyle graduated from The University of Pennsylvania, with a business degree, he landed a job with the office of the mayor of Philadelphia. His intelligence, wit and persuasive personality quickly gained him the mayor's trust, and he became a most valued staffer. He used this power to help John's company land a large contract to build new row homes in lower Kensington in North Philadelphia.

A rival of Danny's filed a lawsuit suggesting that Charlie had won the business unfairly by bribing the city officials. A month before the case was to go to court, George Graham and Flannigan arranged a meeting with the man and suggested that if he refuted his claims, he would live to see 1891. Three weeks before the trial the case was dropped by the district attorney. Charlie began construction a month later.

The Johnny O. Gang's largest competitor for gunrunning to Cuba was Tom Blair. Blair operated out of Atlanta, Georgia and smuggled guns to Cuba from various spots along the Georgia coastline. They maintained a peaceful relationship through the years, but lately, mostly due to the Johnny O. Gang's escalation of smuggling to Cuba, Blair had become hostile.

One of John's contacts at a local gun manufacturing company was found floating in the Delaware River with his throat cut. A week later a shipment of weapons was high jacked on route to

Murphy's ship. Two men were killed. Blair never tried to hide the fact that he was responsible. He even wrote John a letter and said, "Share your resources, and it stops," and signed his name.

John was beside himself with rage and wanted to retaliate, but Danny cautioned that a war between the two gangs would severely hurt their cash flow. "Peace was profitable," Danny said.

John took his advice and asked Charlie Byrne to travel to Atlanta to discuss options with Tom Blair. A meeting was set up, and Charlie and Flannigan took a train to Atlanta. Blair lived in a newly built brick row home on Baltimore Street just on the outskirts of the city of Atlanta. Brick row homes were unique in Atlanta but were ubiquitous in Philadelphia. If Blair was trying to impress the two Yankees by meeting at his home, it didn't work. Even so, Blair was very proud of his home and insisted Charlie and Flannigan take a tour.

"The fourteen homes on Baltimore Street were built by a developer from Baltimore. Hence the name of the street," Blair said as he toured them through the first-floor dining room and then opened the wide sliding doors to reveal the sitting room.

"Clever," Flannigan remarked.

Blair ignored him and continued, "The mantle on all the fireplaces are made from marble brought from Italy. And as you can see the hardwood floors are fitted with precision."

"Shiny too," Flannigan said dryly.

"The basement level is the cooking area and where the housekeeper lives. I'd take you down there, but it might be a bit hot for your Yankee blood. Would you like to see the second and third floors?"

"We're good. You have a very nice home here," Charlie said.

"I wonder if your man thinks so," Blair said as he looked at Flannigan.

Charlie elbowed Flannigan who said, "Yes, yes very nice home."

"Mr. Flannigan is not my man, he's my partner," Charlie said.

"Oh, is that so? Forgive me, sir. Did I detect an Irish accent, Mr. Flannigan?" Blair said and before Flannigan could answer he continued, "Are you one of those Irish Cath-o- licks?"

"That I am. Are you one of those heathen fucking Baptists?" Flannigan said and took a step towards Blair. Two of Blair's men who were standing in the doorway started towards Flannigan. Blair held his hand up to stop them.

"Well, Mr. Flannigan I am a Baptist and I certainly like fucking, so I do believe you are correct," Blair said and laughed. "Please gentlemen, sit down."

Flannigan and Charlie each sat on overstuffed chairs that were situated near the fireplace. Blair poured whiskey into the three glasses that were sitting on a small table and handed Charlie and Flannigan each a glass. He took one himself and sat on a large sofa of the same design as the chairs.

"To success, gentlemen," Blair said and tapped each man's glass. The three men drank the contents and Blair said, "Kentucky Bourbon. Nothing like it."

Charlie put his hand on Flannigan's chair arm to signal him not to say what he thought he might say about Irish whiskey being the best in the world. There was no use in antagonizing Blair. Charlie could be a hothead, but he knew when to act and when not to. They were there to avoid war not start one.

"Mr. O'Shaughnessy's telegram said he had an offer for me. Perhaps it is time you tell me about it," Blair said.

"Five percent of the take from our Cuban sales. You take it; we avoid a war that would be very costly for both of us," Charlie said.

Blair smiled and said, "Oh, that just will not do. Make it thirty percent, and we have a deal. And that includes your Irish sales as well," Blair said.

Flannigan's face got beet red. Charlie said, "How much of that bourbon have you drunk, Blair. That will never happen? I can go to six percent but only of the Cuban sales."

"Never say never, Mr. Byrne. I'll do twenty-five percent of Cuban sales. That is my best and final," Blair said.

Charlie realized that Blair was not serious about negotiating and said, "I'll take your offer back and present it to Mr. O'Shaughnessy," Charlie said and stood up.

Flannigan stood up as well but pretended to trip, hit the table, and the bottle of bourbon tipped over. The brown liquid flowed across the surface of the table and onto the shiny hardwood floor.

"I'm very sorry, Mr. Blair. Let me clean it up for you," Flannigan said.

Blair's face turned red, and he said, "That's quite all right. No harm was done, Mr. Flannigan. I have people that clean up my messes."

"Thank God it wasn't Irish whiskey. Now that would have been tragic," Flannigan said.

Blair looked at Flannigan for a few seconds and then said, "I'll have my driver take you back to the hotel."

The men shook hands and Flannigan and Charlie walked out the front door to the waiting carriage. Once they were in the carriage the driver turned the rig and took a right turn on the main road.

"Didn't we come from downtown? He should have turned left," Charlie said.

"Hey driver, our hotel is the other way," Flannigan said.

"Yes, sir. There's a problem on the road. I'm taking another way," the driver said.

Flannigan looked at Charlie, and they both turned to look

behind them. There were two men riding horses, and they were gaining on them. Charlie reached into the front of his pants and pulled out a small Derringer pistol. Flannigan did the same and pulled out a six-inch pocketknife and opened it.

Suddenly, the driver stopped the carriage and turned towards Charlie and Flannigan. He was holding a Colt 45. Before he could fire, Flannigan pushed his arm up with one hand and plunged the knife into his chest. The Colt fell at Charlie's feet. He picked it up and handed it to Flannigan as the driver fell out of the carriage.

The men riding the horses saw this and began to shoot at the carriage. The noise of the gunfire spooked the horses, and they began to run. With no driver to guide them the horses sped up trying to get away from the noise.

Flannigan shot at one of the men but missed because of gyrations of the carriage. He aimed again and waited for a moment when the movement wasn't so bad and fired. One of the men riding the horses fell to the road. The horses pulling the carriage were now out of control, and Charlie motioned to Flannigan indicating they should jump before the carriage turned over.

Both Flannigan and Charlie jumped at the same time, one from the right side and one from the left. They both rolled several times, and Flannigan quickly got into a crouching stance. Charlie wasn't as lucky. He landed in a ditch full of water.

As Charlie began to sit up, the second rider pointed his Colt at him. Flannigan fired the Colt Charlie took from the dead driver and hit the rider in the hip. The rider grabbed his injured hip and the horse he was riding reared up. As the horse came back down, Charlie was standing just a few feet from the rider. He had jumped up when the horse reared realizing it was probably his last chance to stay alive. Charlie fired the Derringer and hit the man in the head. The man fell off of the horse, shook for a second then lay still.

"Can you ride, Charlie," Flannigan asked.

"I have," Charlie said.

"We'll ride their horses back to the train station and take whatever train we can to get out of this town," Flannigan said.

"Good idea," Charlie said as he put his foot in the stirrup and pulled himself onto the horse.

Three hours later they were on a train headed to Savannah, Georgia. From there they bought tickets on a train going north to Philadelphia. It was a long way around, but at least they were out of Atlanta, where the police assuredly would be looking for them. Flannigan fell asleep five minutes after the train left the station.

"You fellas from up north," a man in a seat next to Charlie asked.

"Philadelphia," Charlie said.

"New York City here. Just down here seeing some clients. How about you?" the man said.

"Same thing," Charlie said.

"What's your game? I sell steam engines," the man said.

"Guns," Charlie answered.

"Colts and such?" the man asked.

"Yep, all types," Charlie said.

"How do you find selling to these rebels? I think they're all grin fuckers," the man said.

This interested Charlie and he asked the man, "What's a grin fucker?"

"Well, up north a client will tell you if they like your product or not. It's straight talk. If they don't like it, they tell you to fuck off. Here in the south, they tell you how wonderful your product is and how much they like it. They keep you in their office for hours just grinning and buttering you up. Once you leave they stab you in the back and buy from some other southerner.

"That is exactly my experience down here," Charlie said.

"How about your company? Do they use steam engines?"

Charlie looked at the man, and said, "Fuck off." Then he smiled, pulled his hat over his eyes and went to sleep.

CHAPTER 25

Cuban Coast - 1890

Captain Murphy slowed his ship as he negotiated the Islands off Cuba and waited for the small boats to secure themselves with lines his men had thrown them. Murphy had ten cases of Winchester Model 1886 rifles lined up on the deck for transfer to the Cuban rebel boats.

"Alfredo, my friend," Captain Murphy said as one of the Cuban's climbed over the rail. "It's good to see you again."

"Ah Capitán, you too are a pleasure for these old eyes," Alfredo said then handed Murphy a satchel. Alfredo said something in Spanish and several of his men started to lower the crates to the waiting boats.

"I also have something for you," Captain Murphy said and handed Alfredo a bottle of Jameson whiskey.

"You are too kind. Thank you," Alfredo said as he took the bottle.

"Alfredo, have a drink with me while your men load the rifles," Captain Murphy said and handed Alfredo a silver flask.

"I will and good health to you," Alfredo said and took a swig and handed it back.

Captain Murphy did the same, placed the cap back on the flask and put it in his pocket. A lookout suddenly yelled a warning, "Spanish patrol boat coming from the starboard side."

"Hurry, get back to your boat and hide behind the island. I'll keep her steady to block their view," Murphy said to Alfredo.

Alfredo quickly lowered himself to his boat. Murphy's crew cut the lines and the two boats headed for the outer island and cover. There were still two crates of rifles on the deck, and Captain Murphy orded them thrown overboard hoping they would sink before the Spaniards arrived.

A few minutes later, the Spanish patrol boat rounded the ship's aft and pulled up beside Murphy's ship. They politely asked permission to board, and Murphy bid them come aboard.

The Spanish officer saluted Murphy and said, "We must search your ship."

Murphy replied, "Have at it."

The Spanish crew searched the boat but found no contraband. This bewildered the Spanish officer because they had received intelligence that Murphy's ship was carrying weapons. He reluctantly apologized and started to get back in the patrol boat. Before he got to the railing, one of his men rushed up to him and said something in Spanish. He put his head over the rail and looked down. Then he pulled his pistol and walked back to Murphy and said, "You are under arrest for smuggling contraband into Cuba." He grabbed Murphy's arm, pulled him to the rail and said, "Look."

Murphy looked down into the water, and his heart leaped. There were two boxes with their ends sticking slightly up from the water line. They were branded Winchester. Murphy shook his head and said, "Fuck."

The Spaniards made Captain Murphy, at gunpoint, sail to Havana Harbor and once docked the entire crew was put under arrest. The ship was confiscated along with its cargo, and the crew incarcerated in a Havana prison. The U.S. consulate in Cuba protested the imprisonment of U.S. citizens and the seizing of a U.S registered ship. Their protests were ignored, and two weeks after the seizure the Spanish governor conducted a mock trial of the entire crew. It lasted one day, and they were all found guilty. The governor sentenced the entire crew to death by firing squad.

Yielding to protests by the U.S. government all of the crew, except Captain Murphy were pardoned and turned over to U.S. authorities. A week later Murphy was walked to a wall in the courtyard of the prison. Guards covered his head with a black hood. A line of seven Spanish soldiers stood at attention just ten yards from Murphy. The officer in charge yelled, "Ready, aim," and after a minute's pause, "Fire." Murphy fell to the ground, and the officer walked up and shot him in the head.

The execution caused an uproar in the United States and especially in Boston, Captain Murphy's hometown. The Boston Globe ran a story about Captain Murphy's contribution to commerce and included a photo of his wife and his three children. For the first two weeks, there were protests, threats against the Spanish Embassy and harassment of Spanish citizens. After the initial reactions things calmed down, but Spanish and American relations were damaged more than they already were.

Shortly after the execution of Murphy, John O'Shaughnessy received a letter from Tom Blair telling him that he was changing the terms he had made with Charlie Byrne. He now, in light of the loss of John's shipping connection, wanted 100% of the Cuban gunrunning business. While Blair didn't say it, John now knew that Blair was responsible for informing the Spanish government about Murphy. That same day he asked Charlie, Graham, Flannigan and Danny to meet with him at a bar they owned on Fifth Street.

John read the letter out loud, crumbled the paper, threw it on the table and said, "What do you think?"

"He dies. His whole crew dies. That bastard killed Murphy just the same as pulling the trigger himself. And he fucked up our business," Flannigan said.

"Flannigan's right," George said.

"We have other ships. The business won't be hurt that much. But, we can't let Blair get away with killing our friend," Danny said.

"John, I want to be the one that puts a bullet in his head," Flannigan said.

"Glad to hear you're all in agreement. George, can you pull together five good men we can send to Atlanta tomorrow?" John asked.

"Sure, what do you want them to do?"

"For now I want them to learn what they can about Blair. Where he eats, what he does. We'll meet them in Atlanta one week from today, and then we take Blair out. Be sure none of the men have Irish accents. That would tip him off. Tell them to dress up, and say they are businessmen from Chicago looking for investments. They can stay at the best hotel, eat at the best restaurants. Atlanta is a small city. There are only 60,000 people there, and you can be sure they'll be as noisy as an Irish grandmother in Kensington. Be sure they take their weapons," John said.

Graham nodded and said, "What's the plan?"

"Don't know yet, George. We'll put it together in Atlanta." John said

CHAPTER 26

Atlanta, Georgia 1890

Charlie and Flannigan traveled by train to Louisville, Kentucky and then boarded a different train to the southern city of Atlanta. Blair knew what they looked like and John believed Blair's men would be watching the trains coming in from New York and Philadelphia. The two men dressed so they would appear as ranchers from the deep west. A day later Graham, John and Danny boarded the train to Atlanta but disembarked in Greensville, South Carolina. They bought a carriage and two horses and traveled to Atlanta where they checked into the second-rate hotel where Charlie and Flannigan were staying.

The hotel was nice enough, and it was centrally located in Atlanta and away from Blair's home in the eastern suburb. John telegraphed Jimmy McLeod, the leader of the five men they sent to Atlanta to gather intelligence and suggested they meet at Jacob's Pharmacy across from the hotel on Marietta Street. The pharmacy had a large soda fountain area that also sold food. They would be able to sit next to each other and talk without attracting attention.

At the appointed time John walked across Marietta Street and entered the pharmacy. It was well appointed, clean and they sold all types of medicines and other sundries. He told himself to remember to look for a souvenir to bring his wife and new son.

John sat at the counter, and a young man cheerfully asked him what he would like to drink. John hesitated not knowing what to order. The young man sensed this and said, "Y'all not from here, are you?"

"No, just visiting from Chicago," John said.

"Well, if you don't mind, sir I suggest you have a nice slice of our homemade pecan pie and a cola," the young man said.

"What's a cola?" John asked.

The young man puffed up his chest and said, "Well sir, cola is a drink invented right here in Atlanta by a local pharmacist. It's both delicious and refreshing." The young man lowered his voice then said, "It even cures headaches and gives you energy."

"In that case, I'll have the pie and the cola," John said.

The young man smiled and said, "You won't be sorry, sir," And then he strode off to fetch the pie and cola.

Ten minutes later, Jimmy McLeod sat down next to John and said, "I see you found cola,"

"Yeah, this is pretty good," John said, holding up his glass of cola.

"It's kind of addictive. I've been drinking them since we got here," McLeod said.

The young counterman asked what he could get for McLeod. He ordered the same as John. Once the young man placed the pie and cola in front of McLeod and left, John said, "Okay, what'd you learn?"

"This guy Blair is a homebody. We've been here for a week, and he has only gone out twice. Once he went to an office he keeps on West Peachtree Street and another time to some kind of meeting at an office on Peachtree Street. You'll find these rebels have a lot of streets named Peachtree," Jimmy said.

"We'll have to hit him in his home. What's the layout like?" John asked.

"He lives in the middle of fourteen three-story row homes. It's called Baltimore Block, and it's on Baltimore Street. Nice homes and pretty big. There's an entrance in the front and one in the back. They're kind of like the houses in Kensington, but bigger and nicer," Jimmy answered.

"What about guards?" John asked.

"Two in the front, two in the back. Men are in and out of the house so maybe more inside," Jimmy said.

"Can we get in the windows?" John asked

"Not without being seen."

John thought for a few minutes and asked, "How about the roof or from another house on the row?"

"I looked at a home that was for sale on that block, and the agent told me that there was a double brick wall between each unit. There would be a lot of noise to break through. Same with the roof," Jimmy said.

"Damn it, looks like we're going to have to do this the hard way. Hit them from the front and back and barge our way in," John said.

"Yeah, but if we surprise them, it might work. I have an idea," Jimmy said.

"Spit it out," John said.

"There's an old mansion at the end of Baltimore Street. The man who showed me the home told me an old Atlanta family owned it. Twice a year they throw a rebel party to celebrate Jefferson Davis' birthday or some rebel general. He said many of Atlanta's elite come to celebrate. Maybe we should throw a party," Jimmy said.

"Go on," John said.

"They love that old Confederate battle flag. Maybe we do something with that. First, we'll have to take over that mansion," Jimmy said.

"I'll have to think about it, Jimmy. It could be risky," John said.

"No more than a direct assault," Jimmy said.

"We're at the hotel across the street. After dinner, bring your men and we'll mull it over and see if we can make a plan," John said.

That evening John and the nine other Johnny O. gang members met in John's hotel room. They all agreed that Jimmy's idea was good and that week they quietly prepared for the assault on Blair's home. They decided it should take place on a Saturday at five in the evening.

On Thursday after dinner, Jimmy and two of his men walked to the door of the mansion and knocked. An older servant woman answered the door, and Jimmy placed a pistol to her head and they forced their way into the home.

"I'm sorry, Misses. I mean you no harm as long as you do what I say. How many servants are working today?" Jimmy said.

The woman who was now sweating profusely, wiped her brow with her apron and answered, "Four, sir."

"How many of the owner's family?" Jimmy asked.

"Just the two, sir. The Misses and Mister Oglethorpe," the woman answered.

"No children?" Jimmy asked.

"They's grown up, sir. They don't visit much."

"What's your name?" Jimmy asked.

"Mabel, sir," she said.

"Mabel, I want you to go with these two gentlemen and collect the other servants. Find a nice room where you'll be comfortable. You're going to have a vacation for a couple of days. We won't hurt anyone. Can you do that for me?" Jimmy said.

"Yes, sir."

Before Mabel left with men, Jimmy said, "Mabel, where are the misses and mister?"

"They'll be on the back porch. Every day this time they like to have tea and watch the sunset," Mabel said.

Jimmy walked to the back porch and saw the Oglethorpes sitting close to each other in rocking chairs. They were holding hands and looking out at the expanse behind their home. Seeing an elderly couple being so intimate touched Jimmy's heart. He had never seen his mother and father hold hands and they were married for forty years.

He hated to interrupt and when he made himself known it startled the Oglethorpes. Jimmy explained that he and his men would be taking over their home for a couple of days and that no one would get hurt if they cooperated. Mr. Oglethorpe stood up and resisted at first, and John had to sit him back down. He did it gently as the man was in his late seventies.

Oglethorpe, it turns out had been a major in the Army of the South and fought at the Battle of Chickamauga and the Battle of Kennesaw Mountain where he took a bullet to his leg. That evening and the next Jimmy enjoyed hearing the old major's stories about the War Between the States. It bothered Jimmy that on Saturday morning he had to lock them in their bedroom.

At about ten Saturday morning a wagon pulled up, and two men hung a large Confederate battle Flag on one side of the front porch and a sign that said Happy Birthday on the other side. The caterers arrived at noon and Jimmy had them set up tables on the porch. He showed the cook to the kitchen and explained that in celebration of the birthday the servants were given the day off.

The band showed up at three in the afternoon and spent an hour and a half setting up. At five Jimmy escorted the Oglethorpes to the front porch, explaining that they should not talk and be calm. He had the four elderly servants placed behind the Oglethorpes. Jimmy nodded to the band leader.

The band started playing the Confederate version of the song Dixie. Men riding horses and dressed as Confederate cavalry turned onto Baltimore Street as the music began to play. They slowly rode towards the mansion. The riders' heads were lowered, and their hats pulled down to hide their faces. They were flying the Confederate battle flag and the Georgia state flag. The symbolism was impressive, and Jimmy noticed a tear rolling down old man Oglethorpe's cheek.

Tom Blair, on hearing the commotion came to his front door. Many other neighbors were already on their steps and shouting praises, and some were singing the lyrics to Dixie. Once he saw the Confederate cavalrymen, he began singing as well, and when the cavalrymen approached his home, Blair cheered them. He abruptly stopped cheering and looked carefully at one of the six men. He looked familiar, but he couldn't place from where he knew him.

George Graham pulled his revolver from the holster, pointed at one of Blair's guards and pulled the trigger. The guard fell backward into Blair knocking him down. The second guard fell to a bullet from Charlie Byrne's rifle. The third guard rushed inside, helped Blair up and pulled him along the hallway to the back door. Five of the six cavalrymen jumped from their horses and rushed the door to Blair's house. The band continued playing, and all but the closest neighbors continued to sing and cheered even louder, thinking the attack was all part of the pageantry.

When Blair and his guard reached the back door, the guard cautiously opened it to see if it was safe to leave. Flannigan, who was standing by to the side of the door stepped out and fired his pistol point-blank into the man's forehead. The guard, who was already dead, dropped forward as Blair pushed him into Flannigan. Flannigan fell down the stairway with the guard's body on top of him. Blair shut the door and bolted it. He ran to the basement door, entered the doorway and locked it before running down the steps.

Blair ran to the back of the basement, past the cooking kitchen and opened a cabinet door. He pulled out two Colt 45 revolvers, checked to see if they were loaded, then stood in the dark waiting.

Five minutes before Graham killed the first guard, the two men with Jimmy at the mansion left and circled behind the Baltimore Row homes where they met Flannigan. Together they overpowered Blair's two guards, and gagged and tied them to the wrought iron handrail and waited. John had ordered that Flannigan and the two men should remain outside to protect the rear entrance and to bring up the four horses they had waiting at the far end of the row homes.

When the shooting started Jimmy ushered the Oglethorpes and the servants inside the mansion to protect them from any stray bullets. Jimmy closed the door, turned and saw the last of the Johnny O. Gang enter Blair's home. They had left one man to guard the six horses. The plan was that he was to stay at the mansion until John and the crew exited Blair's home and then he was to run to the rear and join Flannigan.

Danny O'Boyle was the first to enter Blair's house. George came behind him, Charlie next, then John and the others. John sent Charlie and two men to search the second and third floors while he, George and Danny spread out on the first floor. John unlocked the door and pulled it open slowly to check on Flannigan. When he did the three men quickly pointed their revolvers at him.

"Whoa, it's me John," John yelled.

"Jesus Christ, John. We could have killed you," Flannigan said.

"Everything okay?" John asked.

"Aside from almost shooting you, yes everything's dandy. Blair's inside somewhere," Flannigan explained.

"He's not on the first floor," John said.

"There's a basement where they cook. The door should be on your left if I remember correctly," Flannigan said.

John pointed to the door to the basement, and George tried the door. It was locked. He pointed his revolver at the handle and fired and pulled the door open. George descended the long stairway quickly. There was no need for stealth now that he blasted the door open. Blair moved as far back as he could into a darkened place and crouched down to make a small target.

John followed George, and Danny was last to descend the steps. There was a small window in the front and rear of the basement that bathed the room in a dim early evening light making it difficult to see in the shadows. George slowly stepped into the room and his silhouette shown against the front window. Blair saw this and immediately took aim at George's head and fired two rounds.

George felt the first bullet as it skimmed past his ear and

because of his military training, he immediately fell to the ground as the second bullet whizzed by him.

"Blair, give it up," John said from the steps.

"I'm dead anyway, so fuck you," Blair said.

"Not so. If you agree to leave Atlanta and go west I'll let you live," John said.

"I'm to believe a lying Mick like you?"

"You have no choice, Blair. One way you're for sure dead and the other you have a chance at a new life. Throw your gun out and chose life," John reasoned.

Blair didn't answer for two full minutes, and then John said, "Come on, Blair. What's it to be?"

"Okay. Here's my gun," Blair said and then threw a revolver towards John.

"Hands on your head and walk out slowly," John said.

Blair did as ordered and walked out into the dimly lit room. John stepped out of the stairway and faced Blair who was twenty feet away. George held his pistol at the ready as Blair slowly walked towards them. Suddenly Blair dropped his right hand and pulled his second revolver out of the back of his waistband and fired at John. George responded and put four bullets in Blair's chest. Blair dropped to the floor, and his gun made a clang as it hit a cooking pot.

George checked Blair to be sure he was dead, and when he turned back, he saw John holding his side. Blood was oozing from between his fingers. John grunted and said, "Let's go."

George took John by the shoulder and helped him up the steps. Danny ran up the steps before them and yelled to Flannigan, "It's done. Time to leave." He waited for George to get John to the first floor then grabbed John's legs. He and George carried John out the front door and to the horses. They sat him on the closest one.

"Can you ride?" George asked John.

"I think so," John grunted.

"Hang on. I'll lead your horse," George said as he took John's horse's lead and mounted his horse.

Charlie and the two men that went to search the upper floors had heard the gunfire and had come down the stairs just as George and Danny carried John to the door. The six men started to ride north. As they rode they shed the Confederate uniforms revealing the civilian clothing that was underneath.

Jimmy saw them leave and started to step off the porch of the mansion to go meet Flannigan, when he heard Major Oglethorpe say, "Yankee scum." He turned to see Oglethorpe standing five feet away and holding his old service revolver. Before Jimmy could react, Oglethorpe fired. The bullet hit Jimmy in the middle of his chest. He fell off of the porch and landed in a small flower bed. Major Oglethorpe slowly walked over to him and pointed the weapon at Jimmy's head.

Flannigan heard the shot coming from the mansion and rushed to see if he could help. As he rounded the corner of the Baltimore Row homes, he saw an old man point his gun at someone lying in a flower bed and fire one round. When he realized it was Jimmy, rage coursed through his body and he started towards Oglethorpe who was about two hundred feet away. He intended to kill the old man. One of his men who had followed grabbed him by the shoulder and said, "No time, Flannigan. We have to leave now."

Flannigan took two shots at Oglethorpe and ran back to the horses. Neither hit the old man. Flannigan and the other two men mounted their horses and rode off leaving Jimmy's horse tied to a tree at the end of the row homes.

As planned Flannigan and his men rode to Chattanooga,

Tennessee. They left the horses and booked passage on a train going to Chicago. In Chicago, they caught a train to Philadelphia.

George, Danny, John, Charlie and two other men rode to Spartanburg, South Carolina. They found a doctor, who removed the bullet from John's side and stitched him up.

"Will he be okay?" George asked the doctor.

"He's lost a lot of blood. We have a good hospital in town. Take him there, and with enough rest, he should be okay. That's if the wound doesn't get infected. I believe the bullet didn't hit any critical organs, but I can't be sure. They have surgeons at the hospital that can open him up and check," the doctor said.

George saw a wheelchair in the corner of the room and asked, "How much for the wheelchair?" Then he pulled out a one hundred dollar note and held it out.

"That'll do," the doctor said, his eyes wide in astonishment of the amount of money.

George picked up John and placed him in the chair, thanked the doctor and rolled John outside.

"No fucking hospital. Just get me back to Philadelphia," John said.

"John, don't be a fool. You have to go to the hospital," Danny said.

"I mean it. I'm not going to some rebel hospital. Just get me back to Philadelphia," John said. "I'll be fine."

They were able to secure three cabins that slept two men each. Charlie stayed with John and helped him into the lower bunk. Then he went to the club car and ordered food for himself and John. He left the other four in the club car and returned to the cabin. John ate a little and drank some water and coffee. He told Charlie he was tired and needed to sleep. Charlie fixed John's blankets, doused the light and climbed to the second bunk.

By morning they were halfway home to Philadelphia. George banged on Charlie's cabin door at ten o'clock to see if he and John wanted breakfast. A bleary-eyed Charlie opened the door.

"You hungry, Charlie? We're in the club car. Come get something for John and yourself," George said.

"I'm okay, I don't want to wake John up. Doc said he needed rest," Charlie said.

"He needs to eat to get better. Come with me and bring something back. When he wakes up, make him eat," George said and opened the door.

Charlie left with George and ordered two breakfast trays delivered to the cabin. Then he returned to the room. The porter brought the trays and set them on a table that he pulled down from the wall. Charlie thanked him, gave him a dollar bill and lightly shook John to wake him.

John slowly opened his eyes, and Charlie asked, "You hungry? I got you some eggs, bacon and toast."

John uttered, "No. I'm tired. Just want to sleep."

"Okay, sleep some more. You can eat later," Charlie said. Then he picked up a magazine that someone had left. He thumbed through it and saw that it was just about politics and threw it in a small waste bucket. Charlie then climbed on his bunk and dozed off.

An hour later, Charlie heard a strange noise. He jumped down from the bunk and checked John. John was making gurgling sounds.

Charlie slapped him several times on the face to wake him, but it was to no avail. After a minute or so John stopped breathing. He checked John's pulse. There was none. He put his ear to John's chest and could hear no heartbeats. Charlie collapsed backward to the floor, his back on the wall. He put his hands over his eyes and moaned. His friend, his mentor was gone, and he wasn't coming back.

Chapter 27

John's wake and funeral were traditionally Irish. The hundred people who attended ate and drank their full in celebration of John's life, not the tragic events that took it. All the mirrors in John's home were covered and the windows open so his spirit could ascend to heaven. His tearful mother put a silver cross and a rosary by John's head. His wife lit three candles and placed them on a table. At the gravesite, bagpipers played Amazing Grace as John's coffin lowered into the grave.

The evening of the day they buried John, Charlie, George, Flannigan and Danny met at George's home. As they sat at the round dining room table, they shared stories about John that made them both laugh and want to cry. An empty chair was at the table, and George put a glass of Irish whiskey in front of the chair.

George stood up and said, "A better friend, no man could ever have. To you, John. May you rest in peace."

Charlie picked up John's glass and poured a portion of the whiskey on the floor. Then they all poured a small amount from their glasses on the floor and together yelled, "To you, John."

Flannigan filled the glasses and said, "And may Tom Blair rot in hell."

"I'll drink to that," Danny said, then held his glass up. The others followed, and the four men drank and sat down.

"I hate to bring this up now, but we need a new leader. I think it should be George," Charlie said.

"To George," Danny said and lifted his glass.

George looked down to hide the small tear that had formed in his eye and said, "I'm grateful. I am, but I can't do it."

"Why?" Charlie asked. "You're the best man for the job."

"I've been thinking of leaving," George said.

"Leaving Philadelphia?" Danny asked in astonishment.

"Yes Philadelphia, the gang. All of it," George said.

"Why?" Charlie asked.

"To be honest, Charlie, I don't know why. I just feel like I need to do something else. I've been running from Ireland for almost ten years now. I want to create some roots, have a family someday, do something my Ma can be proud of," George said.

"What would you do, George?" Danny asked.

"I was thinking about joining the army. They have a program where if you sign up for six years you can become a citizen. I want to be a citizen. They said they would make me a sergeant because of my legion experience," George said.

Charlie sat back in his chair, sighed and said, "So you already spoke to the army officials?"

"Yesterday," George answered.

Charlie shook his head trying to make George's decision go away. Then he sighed again, looked at Flannigan, already knowing the answer to the question he was about to ask. "How about you, Flannigan?

"I go where George goes," Flannigan said.

Charlie looked at Danny O'Boyle. Danny said, "Not me, Charlie. I'm running for city council. I got to keep my nose clean."

"Charlie, it's yours. You're the boss now," George said.

"It will never be only mine, George. It's ours, and when you're ready to come back, you and Flannigan will be welcomed," Charlie said. "Meanwhile, your families will be taken care of and if you ever need me, just ask. I hope I can do the same," Charlie said.

A week later, after a two day going away party, George and Flannigan boarded a train to Camden and then another that would get them as close as possible to Fort Hancock in Sandy Hook, New Jersey. They spent two weeks at the fort learning general U.S. military etiquette and nomenclature. After that training, they were sent via ship to Jacksonville, Florida and took up residence at Fort Jackson, a coastal fortification.

It took Charlie Byrne a few weeks to recover from the loss of John and departure of George and Flannigan. Danny was busy campaigning for a seat on the city council, and Charlie felt utterly alone. He had alternating bouts of despair, excitement and fear that he would fail. He knew people were counting on him, so he forced himself to make preparations to ensure his success. As he grappled with the issues and made his plans, he found that his fear and despair turned into confidence and enthusiasm.

He faced two major issues. The first was he needed to replace Danny, Flannigan and George. He found several good men amongst the Irish immigrants in Kensington that would become the "muscle" he required to keep the gunrunning in operation. Replacing Danny was harder. He needed a competent bookkeeper who was willing to bend the laws. His second issue was he needed Murphy's ship that was still being held by the Spanish authorities in Cuba. Danny had contacted several senators to see if they could help put pressure on Spain to release the ship. To date, nothing had come of his efforts.

One day, three weeks after John's funeral, Captain Murphy's widow knocked on his door. She had traveled from Boston with her two children and a newborn baby. Mrs. Murphy inquired about her husband's holdings and informed Charlie that the Spanish authorities in Cuba had released her husband's ship and she needed funds to hire a crew to sail the ship home.

"Mrs. Murphy, first let me put your heart at ease. Yes, I have money enough from the captain's holdings to both get a crew and to provide for you," Charlie said.

"Oh my, that is a relief. I have been working on my late husband's business books and wasn't sure where the money was. I hope you don't mind my intrusion on your time," Murphy's widow said.

"Of course not. Captain Murphy was a dear friend, and anything I can do for you and the children is my pleasure," Charlie said. He thought for a minute and then continued, "What are your plans for the Lincoln once we get it home?"

"I don't really know. I've been so focused on getting it back that I haven't thought that far ahead," Mrs. Murphy answered.

"Would you consider selling 50% of your two ships to me, and you and I can become partners?" Charlie asked.

"I... I don't know. I'm not a business person, Mr. Byrne. I just helped my husband with his bookkeeping, not business decisions," Mrs. Murphy said.

"But I am, and I can see you have what it takes to learn, Mrs. Murphy. Please, call me Charlie."

"And you may call me Ethel," Mrs. Murphy said.

Charlie's brain was racing with ideas. The first thing he would do is switch the ship that ran weapons to Ireland with the

SS Lincoln. The Spanish authorities in Cuba knew the Lincoln and would be on the lookout for her. The British authorities had never seen the Lincoln.

With Tom Blair dead and his gang gone, Charlie had free reign to sell weapons in Cuba. Mrs. Murphy had bookkeeping skills and must have been aware of her husband's less legal activities. She would be the perfect person to run his office.

"Mrs… I mean Ethel, would you consider moving to Philadelphia and becoming my bookkeeper as well as a partner in the shipping company?" Charlie asked.

Ethel looked at Charlie in surprise and replied, "Oh my, I don't know. This is all going so fast."

"The pay would be very good, plus you would have your partner's money from the ship revenues. You'll be quite well off," Charlie urged. "Philadelphia has good private schools. Your children will have every advantage. What do you say?"

Ethel sat silent for a few minutes mulling over Charlie's offer. "Yes. Yes, I'll do it," Ethel said and put her hand out to shake Charlie's hand and seal the deal.

Charlie took her hand and placed his left hand on hers and said, "You won't regret it. I promise you. Stop by tomorrow, and I'll have some cash for you so you can go back to Boston and settle your affairs. By the time you return, I'll have the paperwork ready, and you and your children can live in my home until you find a suitable residence."

"I don't know how to thank you, Charles. I came here dreading my circumstances, and now I'm embarking on a grand adventure. God does work in mysterious ways," Ethel said.

"He does that, Ethel. He does that."

Ethel got up to leave, and Charlie rose and walked her to the door. Before she left Charlie asked, "Ethel, do you know how to contact Ginger Muller, your husband's first mate? I've lost contact with him since he was released by the Spaniards."

"Why, yes I do. His correct name is Francis. He called on me a week ago to give his condolences. He said he was to be captain of a small freighter moving goods between Camden and Boston. That's why he was in Boston and could call on me. Do you have paper and a pen? I'll write down his address for you," Ethel said.

Ethel and Charlie walked back to Charlie's desk, and he placed a sheet of paper in front of her and handed her a pen. As she wrote the address, Charlie said, "Ethel, do you think Gin... sorry, Francis would make a good captain for the Lincoln,"

Ethel looked at Charlie and said, "I do."

CHAPTER 28

Fort Jackson - Jacksonville, Florida 1895

"Okay, you scruffy sons of bitches, mount up," Sergeant First Class William Flannigan yelled.

The twenty U.S. Army soldiers standing beside their horses did as ordered. Flannigan nodded to Master Sergeant George Graham then mounted his horse. Graham, who was already on his horse, gave the order to move out. Two by two the men followed Graham and Flannigan out of the gates of Fort Jackson.

It was mid-August and the Florida heat and humidity reminded George of his time in Cochinchina. As they rode, his mind replayed both the happy days in the French Foreign Legion and the dreadful scene that took the life of the only woman he had ever loved. He loved his family who was now safe from British rule and living in Philadelphia. But love for a woman was different and often confusing, and he wondered if he would ever feel about another woman as he had about Dat.

George's daydreaming was interrupted when Flannigan asked, "Where we going, George?"

George turned in his saddle to see how far the men were behind Flannigan and him. They established early on that each would address the other by their titles when their troops were in earshot. Otherwise, they would use first names. When he turned back, he said, "Ned Nokosi's gang was seen fifty miles inland."

Ned Nokosi led a band of men who were decedents of the Native American Seminole Tribe. Before the civil war, the U.S. fought three wars with the Seminoles and finally was able to move them to Oklahoma. A small group of one hundred or so Seminoles resisted moving and took refuge in the Everglades near Biscayne Bay. For almost forty-five years they kept to themselves and avoided the numerous settlers from the North, but by 1885 building developments close to and on the Seminole land were such that they melded into the white population. Ned Nokosi rebelled against this idea and formed a group of like-thinking men. Together began to harass various Southern Florida towns. Nokosi's gang favored robbing banks and they had recently traveled north.

The gang had even crossed the border into southern Georgia where they robbed three banks before returning to Florida. This caught the attention of a powerful Georgia senator who pressured the U.S. Army to do something about the Nokosi gang. What normally was a local law enforcement problem had now become a U.S. Army problem. George Graham's troop of twenty-two soldiers was the solution.

"Nokosi, I thought they were in the South?" Flannigan said.

"They're here now," George replied.

"How many men does he have?" Flannigan asked.

"Not sure. Maybe 30 or so," George answered.

"Oh, well. Glad we're not outnumbered," Flannigan said and shook his head.

George smiled, glanced back at his men and said, "These boys will do the job. When we get closer send Dittmar and Robinson to see if they can locate Nokosi."

"Yes, sir. I'll go tell them to get ready," Flannigan said, gave a wide smile and saluted.

"Asshole," George said, so only Flannigan could hear.

Flannigan smiled and said, "Yes, sir. That would be me."

At the appointed time, troopers Dittmar and Robinson broke off from the column and rode ahead. An hour later George called a halt and gave the command that they bivouac till first light. There was a small stream nearby, and the men filled their canteens and watered and fed the horses. They settled down around fires and ate the evening meal. Corporal Jeremiah Winters, who had been in his church's choir, began to sing *When Johnny Comes Marching Home.* It was a song most of the men knew well and that their fathers and grandfathers sang during the Civil War.

"WHEN JOHNNY COMES MARCHING HOME AGAIN
HURRAH! HURRAH!
WE'LL GIVE HIM A HEARTY WELCOME THEN
HURRAH! HURRAH!
THE MEN WILL CHEER, AND THE BOYS WILL SHOUT
THE LADIES THEY WILL ALL TURN OUT
AND WE'LL ALL FEEL GAY."

The rest of the men joined in after the first verse. George and Flannigan were sitting nearby close to a large sweetgum tree. Flannigan heard the men singing and asked George, "Do you ever feel homesick?"

"For Ireland? Yes a bit, but I do miss my family in Philly, Charlie and Danny as well. We have been through a lot together, and they're my brothers just as you are, Flannigan," George replied.

"You're right, we are all brothers, but I'm the most handsome brother," Flannigan said and smiled.

"Now you have to go to confession and tell the priest you lied. A big whopper of a lie, at that," George said.

"Yeah, well maybe. I guess John was a hair prettier than me. God rest his soul," Flannigan said.

George took a small flask from his saddlebag, looked around to be sure none of the men were looking, then poured a small amount of the contents on the ground. He held up the flask and said, "Till we meet again, John," then he took a swig of the Irish whiskey and handed it to Flannigan.

Flannigan said, "To John. May we meet again, but not for a long time." Then he finished the contents of the flask and handed it back to George. The men had changed songs and were singing another popular civil war tune. As George and Flannigan rolled out their blankets, the men began the chorus of the song.

TRAMP! TRAMP! TRAMP! THE BOYS ARE MARCHING,
CHEER UP, COMRADES, THEY WILL COME,
AND BENEATH THE STARRY FLAG
WE SHALL BREATHE THE AIR AGAIN
OF THE FREE LAND IN OUR OWN BELOVED HOME.

At daybreak, they ate breakfast and mounted up to continue their mission. Dittmar and Robinson returned before nightfall and reported that they had found Nokosi and his gang.

"They're about ten miles straight on and not hiding, Master Sergeant," Dittmar reported.

"How many?" George asked.

"Twenty-five or thirty I would guess, and there are women and children," Dittmar said.

"What were they doing?"

"Nothing much. Some men were cleaning their weapons, others just lying around. Thing is, they had made some pretty good shelters. I'm thinking this is their base," Dittmar said.

"Makes sense, Sergeant Major. They have their families with them," Flannigan said.

George shook his head and said, "Damn it! I didn't count on them having women and children with them."

"Doesn't seem like a problem to me, Master Sergeant. Nobody will care if we rid the world of some future injun warriors," Dittmar said.

George looked at Dittmar and asked, "Where are you from?"

"Ohio, why? "Dittmar asked.

"Where were your parents born?" George asked.

Dittmar straightened up and said proudly, "A small town in Germany."

"Why do you think they chose to come to America?" George asked.

"I don't have to suppose. They've told me many times. They came so their children would have a better life. In Germany, small farmers had no chance to advance, but in America, anyone who's willing to work hard can succeed. Here my father has his own farm," Dittmar said.

George shook his head back and forth and said, "And what do you think your mother and father would think about you being willing to kill children? These people from whom we forcibly stole their land have nowhere to go, no jobs and no security. They didn't have the same opportunity as your mother and father, so they rob banks to feed their children."

"I didn't think of it that way, Master Sergeant," Dittmar said.

"Okay, now you know. It helps when you think a bit before you talk." George paused for a few seconds and then asked Robinson, "Did you see anyone who looked like they were in charge? I have no idea what this Nokosi looks like," George asked Robinson.

"There was one man making his way around the camp talking to the others. He was wearing a black top hat with a feather. I thought that was a bit strange," Robinson replied.

"Okay, fall back in line. We'll be stopping for the night soon. Robinson, not you," George said. After Dittmar left George said to Robison, "I want you to go back to the Nokosi camp and hide nearby. As soon as you see Nokosi and his men leave, get your ass back here and tell me. Got it?"

"Yes Master Sergeant, but how long do you want me to stay there?" Robinson asked.

"Until Nokosi leaves," George said. He noticed Robinson's concern and continued, "We'll send Dittmar with food and water every twelve hours, and if it takes longer than three days he'll take your place."

Robinson held his thumb up and started to walk back to his horse." George called after him, "We'll be camped about two or three miles up this road by the river."

When Robison was out of earshot, Flannigan asked George, "What's the plan?"

"When Nokosi's men leave, I think we can take the camp with no shooting. Then when they return, we'll have their families as leverage. That should be enough to get them to talk to us," George said.

"Talk about what? Our orders are to kill him or bring Nokosi in for trial," Flannigan said.

"I'll deal with that when the time comes. For now, I just want to avoid a battle. I don't want to experience another Tonkin," George said.

Four days later Private Dittmar rode into the camp. His horse was streaked white with sweat, and both he and the horse had seen better days. He reported to George that Nokosi and his men had left their hideout and rode north. George assembled the men and gave them instructions to be as quiet as possible when they got close to the Nokosi camp. He told Flannigan to have the men circle the camp, stay hidden and when he gave the word to move in together. He reiterated that under only life-threatening conditions should anyone fire their weapons.

Flannigan gave the order to fix bayonets, and the men took their places. George took off his gun belt and hat. He had already rid himself of his coat when they left Fort Jackson.

"What are you doing, George?" Flannigan asked.

"I'm going to talk to the women and explain that we mean them no harm and that we just want to talk to Nokosi," George said.

"Are you out of your fucking mind? You think because they're women they won't kill you and cut you into little pieces," Flannigan said.

George shrugged his shoulders and said, "When I give the word have the men come into the camp, slowly, rifles in the air. If I get into trouble, then you can come save me. You'll be a hero." George smiled, and Flannigan shook his head. Then George started to walk down the road to Nokosi's camp.

CHAPTER 29

George entered the Nokosi camp with his hands in the air. He hoped the gesture would be enough to avoid being shot. Two teenage boys came at him with their pistols out and threw him to the ground. One of the boys searched George for weapons and not finding any allowed him to stand up. They kept their pistols pointed at George's back.

A group of women formed a circle around George. Some held knives and others had clubs. George put his hands up again. A woman that George guessed was in her early thirties approached him, looked him up and down and said, "You're army? What are you doing in our camp?"

He was surprised that her English was so good and that many people in the camp dressed like any other white resident of Florida. The woman who addressed him was wearing a unique looking feather and cloth headdress, a dress like one would buy from the Montgomery Ward catalog and a gun belt with a Colt 45 revolver hanging by her side. Her tanned skin and slightly slanted eyes reminded him of his lost love Dat.

“I’m here to make peace,” George said.

The woman laughed and replied, “We’re not at war. Those days are long over.”

“I understand, but your chief is robbing banks, and certain government officials don’t like that. It’s bad for business. So they sent me to bring him in for justice or kill him,” Graham said.

The woman put her hand on her gun, laughed and said, “And you think you can do that by yourself and the men you have hidden in the trees?”

This surprised Graham. He clearly underestimated these people. He shook his head back and forth and said, “I’m tired of war and killing. I’m here to see if we can work something out so that no one gets hurt.”

“Then why are your men pointing rifles at us?” the woman asked.

George yelled, “Flannigan, put your weapons down and come here.”

A few minutes later Flannigan walked out of the trees with his hands up. When he reached George, he stopped, looked at the women and waited for George to speak.

“Have the men pull back a mile or so and make camp. When they’ve settled comeback here. Just you and no weapons,” George ordered.

Flannigan looked at George and said, “Are you sure?”

“Yes, I’m sure. Go,” George said.

Flannigan stood tall and said, “Yes, Master Sergeant.” He wanted to make sure the women understood that George had the respect of his men. Flannigan turned and walked back into the trees.

The woman waved her hand and the women who had formed a circle around George left. The two teenagers remained. The women said, “Come with me.”

George followed her to a large hut with a thatched roof and open sides. There was a raised platform that George guessed was where these people slept. It made sense to him. The Seminoles lived in wetlands, not unlike some he had encountered in Cochinchina. Living off the ground not only kept them dry but also protected them from night creatures like snakes and alligators.

There were two rocking chairs on either side of a small table. The woman pointed to a chair, and when she sat down, he did the same. Another woman placed a bowl of mixed fruits on the table, then she poured an orange-colored liquid into two cups and placed one in front of the woman and another for George.

"Are you hungry…" The woman paused realizing she didn't know this soldier's name. She continued, "Solider?"

"Thank you, no. I ate breakfast. My name is George Graham," George answered.

"Then drink, Mr. Graham. It is hot today," the woman said.

George picked up the glass but hesitated. The woman noticed this then picked hers up and drank from the cup. George did the same.

"Mr. Graham, if we wanted to kill you it would have been done already," the woman said.

"And I appreciate that you didn't, Miss… Mrs…" George paused.

"Nokosi, Emily Nokosi. You may call me Emily."

"And please, call me George," George said.

Emily bent her head, and George continued, "I assume you are Ned Nokosi's wife?" George asked.

"Yes," Emily said.

"May I ask how it is that you have English names?" George asked.

"Both of our parents lived through the last Seminole war, and they felt that we would have better lives if we had English names. They were wrong, of course. We could change our names but not our skin, so nothing changed," Emily said.

"I'm sorry for that. My life in Ireland was similar. That's why I left," George said.

"I would like to hear your story about Ireland, but right now my children need me. Would you be able to wait for my husband's return? It should only be two or three days," Emily said.

"Yes, of course. I'll stay with my men, and when he returns, please send a messenger," George said.

"We would like it if you stayed in our camp. We have an empty chickee you can use," Emily said.

"A chickee?" George asked.

Emily looked surprised that George didn't know what a chickee was. She pointed to one of the thatched roof buildings and said, "chickee." She paused and said, "It's good that you stay with us and learn about the Seminoles you want to kill."

George knew arguing with Emily would do no good, so he just nodded his acceptance of her invitation. The last thing he wanted to do was kill any of these people, and he hoped it would not come to that.

Flannigan returned before nightfall, and both men were treated to a wonderful Seminole meal. There was a kind of corn soup the Seminoles called sofkey, fried bread and tasty roasted meat that Flannigan thought was chicken. They later discovered it was raccoon.

Flannigan and George spent the next three days learning about the Seminoles and telling their own stories of hardship in Ireland. Emily was a good hostess and was sure they met everyone living in the camp. She was also a smart hostess because she knew the better you got to know people, the harder it was to hurt them.

Ned Nokosi returned the evening of the third day and before he met with George and Flannigan, Emily told him what she had learned. The next morning Ned met with George and Flannigan.

"My wife speaks highly of you, George. I know this to be true because if she didn't like you, I would be meeting your corpse," Ned said.

"Ned, you have a fine woman. She explained how hard it was to find work and to provide for your clan," George said.

"What is a clan?" Ned asked.

"It's an Irish word that means a tribe or family," George answered.

"I'm not here to judge what you have done, Ned. I've done worse. I'm here to save your life and those of your people," George said.

Ned sat back in his chair and said, "How so?"

"Look, this bank robbing thing is not safe. Everything is becoming civilized, and it's too easy to get caught. Jessie James, the Younger Brothers and the Dalton gang, all bank robbers out west are dead or in jail. The U.S. government has the money and power to erase you from the earth. I was sent here to kill you and everyone in your gang if I had to. You need to do something else," George said.

"There is nothing else! White society has no room for us," Ned said.

"That's because you're not rich. Money talks in America. Money is freedom in America. Would you be interested in a new job that will make you rich, Ned? You'll be able to send your children to the best schools, buy homes where white people live, travel if you like. And it's much safer than bank robbery," George said.

"I'm thinking," Ned said and tapped his forehead and continued, "that this job may not be legal."

"You're right, it isn't, but it's safe because no one will know what you're doing. And even if our government learns about it they won't do anything. They even want you to do this," George said.

"Now you are lying to me," Ned said as he shook his head.

"No, I'm not. Let me explain. The U.S. government is feuding with the Spanish in Cuba. They don't like the fact that a foreign and potentially hostile government is so close to the U.S. The Cubans don't like the Spanish, and they've tried to rebel several times. They're building up to do it again. I was running guns to Cuba before I joined the army and my best friend still does. I can connect you with him so you can help him. I'm not sure how, but he's a smart man and will find ways for you to do well," George said.

Ned leaned forward and said, "How can I trust you? White men have made many promises, and not one was kept," Ned said.

"First off, if it doesn't work out you can go back to robbing banks any time you want. And I'm not just any white man. I have felt the boot of the English on my neck. I have lost family members to their oppression just as you have," George said.

"Someday, when this war between the Spanish and Americans is over, there will be no need for gunrunning. What do I do then?" Ned asked.

"By then, Ned, you will be rich. You'll have bought farmland and put your people to work. You'll buy land near the sea, and in the future, white Americans who love to vacation by the sea will buy it from you. There's a small town near the ocean where I come from called Cape May. It is booming, and every summer people rush to rent apartments and hotel rooms so that they can enjoy the water. Water surrounds Florida, and it is always summer in the south. Before you know it the white man will be kissing your ass just to talk to you," George said.

"I will speak to my tribe. I think it's best you go to your camp. Tomorrow I will send for you. If I don't then you know we have left and I do not want your job," Ned said.

George and Flannigan walked to the army camp and told the men that they had negotiated with the Seminoles and that in the morning, they would get Nokosi and bring him back to Fort Jackson for trial. The men were happy they were not going to fight with the possibility of being killed.

The next morning Emily Nokosi came to the soldiers' camp. George took a pair of shackles from his saddlebag and handed them to Flannigan, being sure the soldiers saw him. He ordered the soldiers to stay at camp until he returned.

When they arrived at the Nokosi camp, Ned explained that he would talk with George's friend, but made it clear that if it didn't work out, he would hold George responsible. The two men shook hands and Ned gave George an address of a man in Biscayne Bay who he trusted. The man would know where Ned and his people were staying. Both men shook hands to seal the deal.

"One more thing, Ned. I need your hat," George said.

"My hat. Why?" Ned asked.

"So I can prove I killed you," George said and smiled.

Ned took off his hat and handed it to George and said, "I want that back." Then he mounted his horse, and he and the tribe started on their southward journey.

"George, tell me how you're going to get Charlie to work with Ned and his people," Flannigan said.

George shrugged his shoulders.

Ten minutes after the last tribe member left the camp' George took out his revolver and fired two shots into the ground just in case anyone was in hearing distance. When they returned to the soldiers' camp, they said that everyone had left before they arrived except Nokosi. Then Nokosi had second thoughts and tried to attack Flannigan. Flannigan told the story of how George shot Nokosi twice, and they threw the body in the river. George held Nokosi's hat up to prove it. The men cheered, mostly because they would be happy to get back to the fort where there was good food, strong whiskey and women.

CHAPTER 30

Philadelphia 1895

Ethel Murphy and her children lived in Charlie Byrne's home for the first half of a year after she moved from Boston to Philadelphia to become Byrne's accountant and partner in the shipping firm. She was able to buy a home at 1008 Clinton Street in downtown Philadelphia. The home was built in 1850, and by city standards, it's over 4000 square feet of space was considered prestigious.

Charlie's plans had worked better than even he thought they would. The gunrunning business was brisk. Cuban rebels started a new campaign against the Spanish, and Irish resistance to English rule increased when it became evident that parliament would never pass home rule laws. This belief in Ireland created a big demand for weapons. Ethel Murphy's work was exemplary and allowed Charlie time to explore new sources for both weapons and his building business.

The construction company had built several factories, a church, a number of row homes and thanks to city council member Danny O'Boyle, he even had a contract to build a portion of the new Philadelphia city hall building. Danny's influence in Philadelphia politics had grown in the five years since he entered the political arena in 1890. Many local politicians claimed that he was on track to become mayor one day.

One situation Charlie did not foresee concerned his hiring of Francis Muller as Captain of the SS Lincoln. Muller was a fine Captain, and his affable nature allowed him to become friends with clients and customs officials both in Ireland and the U.S. Under his command weapons shipments to Ireland had doubled. During Muller's first year he worked closely with Ethel, and the two developed a mutual attraction. In 1893 Muller asked Charlie if he would be best man at his wedding to Ethel. Charlie was delighted because he was very fond of the couple.

The only issue Charlie faced was one of supply. If he could obtain more weapons, he was sure he could increase his business by fifty percent. So far the answer to that problem had eluded him. So when he received a telegram from George Graham inviting him to come to Jacksonville to discuss a potential business deal he was interested. He knew that George's "business deal" would involve gunrunning. George and Flannigan had helped him with several problems during the past year, including eliminating a potential competitor in Savannah. It had been six months since Charlie had seen his friends and he was excited at the prospect of drinking some Irish whiskey and reminiscing.

The trip to Jacksonville was as pleasant as first-class money could buy. The food was excellent, but even money couldn't abate the incessant noise and the black coal smoke that permeated everything including Charlie's lungs. He wasn't a fan of long train trips for these reasons. He thought about taking a steamer to Jacksonville, but it took longer, and he needed to finish his business with George and get back to Philly, so the train was his best choice.

George and Flannigan arranged to take a leave while Charlie was in Florida and they met him when his train arrived. They took a coach to the Jacksonville Grand Hotel where George had rented a suite for Charlie with adjacent rooms for Flannigan and himself. When they arrived at the suite three women from Madam Bouffant's house greeted them. Madam Bouffant advertised that they had the most beautiful and cleanest women in all of Florida. George and Flannigan were able to attest personally to this claim.

That evening George put off talking business, and the three men and their women just enjoyed each other's company, talked about the old days and drank a lot. Madam Bouffant's women left at the appointed time, and Charlie, Flannigan and George continued drinking and talking until the early hours of the morning.

Charlie woke at his normal time of seven o'clock and was bright and cheery as if he hadn't had a drop of whiskey the night before. He pushed a call buzzer, and a bellboy promptly knocked on the door. Charlie asked if he could get the room cleaned and ordered a full breakfast for three, with lots of coffee. At 8:30 he banged on George's door to wake him and yelled, "Get the hell up, you lazy bastard!"

Charlie put his ear to the door and listened. He heard a loud moan and yelled again, "Up! Get up, you Irish prick. We have business to do."

"For Christ's sake Charlie, shut up. I'm up," George yelled and then moaned again.

"Nine o'clock, breakfast," Charlie yelled and walked to Flannigan's door. He was about to bang on the door when it opened.

Flannigan stood in the doorway fully dressed and ready to go. He stepped to one side and said, "Thank you, Simone. I'll call on you in a week or two," Flannigan said.

Simone kissed him on the cheek and sashayed past Charlie and then walked out of the room. Charlie said, "I thought the girls left last night?"

"They did. I had Simone come in later. She's my regular," Flannigan said then looked around the room and continued, "Where's breakfast? I had a busy night, and I'm starving."

After breakfast, George told Charlie his story about the Nokosi gang and suggested that they would be perfect partners. "The more strained relationships are with Spain, the more weapons the U.S. Army is bringing into Florida. They are ripe for the picking. Nokosi and his gang can pick them for us," George said.

"Can you trust this guy?" Charlie asked.

"I trust that he wants to make money. I trust he wants to better his and his family's circumstances and I trust he won't have any qualms taking from the U.S. Army. After all, the government took all of Florida from his tribe," George said.

"From what you've told me about his escapades down here, there's no doubt he is capable but is he willing?" Charlie said.

"I've explained what we need from him, and he's willing to listen. I've arranged for a small steamer to take us to the Lake Worth area. There's a town there called West Palm Beach. Nokosi's camped near there," George said.

"When do we leave?" Charlie asked.

"Just as soon as I have another cup of coffee," George said.

"Okay, I'll go. But you have to promise me something," Charlie said.

"What?" George asked.

"If we do this deal I want you and Flannigan to manage these guys. Before you tell me any bullshit about you being in the army and having duties, just remember there are two of you. I'm sure you can handle it," Charlie said.

George looked at Flannigan who shrugged his shoulders indicating whatever George decided was fine with him. "You prick. You've been trying to get us back in the gang ever since we left. And now you finally did it," George said and put his hand out.

Charlie stood up and grabbed George's hand and shook it. Then he did the same with Flannigan. "God, it's good to have you both back," Charlie said.

Two hours later they were on a coastal steamer George had chartered for the trip to the Lake Worth area. The steamer hugged the coastline during the trip giving the men an opportunity to enjoy the majestic beauty of the beaches and surrounding land. This impressed Charlie, who was always on the lookout for places to build.

"One day, all of this land along the coast will be built out like Cape May," Charlie said.

"You think so? It's so wild, who would want to build here?" Flannigan said.

"Did you know that Cape May was a whaling station for fishermen from New England just a hundred fifty years ago? Now it's the most popular vacation spot, not just in New Jersey, but also the whole country," Charlie said.

"But isn't that because people from Philadelphia and New York want to get away from the heat of the cities? Florida's pretty much hot all year. I don't see people wanting to go to a place that's hotter," Flannigan said.

"What about in the winter, when the snow's blowing and you're freezing your ass off? Wouldn't you like to enjoy a little warm weather?" Charlie said.

Charlie's words about cold winters called up memories for George of his childhood home in Letterkenny, Ireland. It always seemed cold in Letterkenny. Suddenly, he was transformed to sitting behind large crates outside of old man O'Connor's warehouse waiting for O'Connor to leave so he could steal potatoes to feed his starving family. It was this single event that branded him as a potato thief and started him on a fantastic journey he, at the time, could not have imagined.

"George," Charlie said then touched George on the arm, "you okay?"

George snapped out of his daydream and said, "Yeah, I'm fine."

"I asked if you and Flannigan would enjoy a warm vacation in the middle of a Philadelphia winter," Charlie said.

"It's a good point, Charlie. I hate the winter," George said, not mentioning he already made this point to Nokosi.

"Of course, I'm right. All that's needed are good roads, and train service and Florida will explode with tourists. The next 50 to 100 years will be very exciting here. I wish I could be part of it, but I have my hands full with my work in Philly," Charlie said.

When they arrived at Lake Worth, the captain guided the steamer through the Lake Worth Inlet and then south on the inland waterway. Two miles from the village of West Palm Beach the captain dropped the anchors and had a small boat placed in the water. George, Charlie and Flannigan dropped over the side onto the boat, and two of the crew rowed them to a spot on the western side of the waterway. George told the crew members to wait for him and he, Flannigan and Charlie walked inland.

Suddenly, ten men rushed out of the trees each pointing either a pistol or rifle at the three men. Charlie and Flannigan pulled their side arms and pointed back.

CHAPTER 31

Near West Palm Beach, Florida 1895

"It's okay, these are Nokosi's men," George said. Then he pulled something out of a bag he was carrying and held it up for the men to see. It was Nokosi's hat.

Nokosi came from behind his men and walked to George. He shook his hand, smiled and said, "I see you have something for me."

George handed him the hat. Nokosi placed it on his head and said, "This is the first time a white man has done what he promised me. You have honor, George Graham."

"You remember Flannigan," George said. Flannigan shook Nokosi's hand. "And this is Charlie Byrne, the man I told you about."

Charlie shook Nokosi's hand and said, "Good to meet you, Ned. George says you are an honorable man as well."

"Come, let's talk," Nokosi said and led them back to the camp.

Emily was waiting for Nokosi to retune and had a plate of

fruit and drinks waiting. The men sat down at a round table that was placed just outside of the Nokosi chickee. After Nokosi introduced his wife to Charlie, Emily joined the men.

Charlie placed a black bag on the table and said, "Ned, if we come to an agreement today this bag is for you. It's enough money to allow you to buy a small farm and get established until the real money starts to flow."

Ned opened the bag and looked inside. He did not react and slid the bag to Emily who also looked inside. Her eyes widened a bit, but she was also silent.

"And what must we do for such a generous gift?" Nokosi asked.

"No more than what you have already been doing but with a lot less risk and a whole lot more money," Charlie said.

Nokosi leaned forward and said, "I'm listening."

Charlie reiterated that the military was increasing their forces in Florida because of the Spanish threat and that meant shipments of weapons to the area would also increase. Because of his connections with various arms manufacturers he was privy to details of when and where these shipments were going. It would be easy pickings for a team of seasoned bank robbers.

After two hours of discussions, questions, explanations and negotiations, Charlie asked, "Well Ned, what about it?"

"I have much to think about and to discuss with my people," Nokosi said and paused. Then he continued, "Be our guest tonight and in the morning you will have my answer."

That evening they ate a typical Seminole meal and drank heavily from several bottles of Jameson whiskey Charlie had imported from Ireland and had brought with him. Charlie understood it was a good time to bond with Nokosi and his people. He told humorous stories from his childhood in Philadelphia and talked about his rise from a poor Irish American family to the leader of a powerful organization. But most of all, he listened to the stories Nokosi, Emily, and others in the tribe told him about the trials and tribulations of these original people.

He, of course, knew what was happening in the American West with the various Indian tribes, but the newspapers always discussed how when we took land from these people we were doing them a favor. There was a common thought amongst Eastern men that the native people would benefit from the life imposed on them by American's politicians.

He never even thought about the east coast tribes, especially those in Georgia and Florida. No one in the north did. He and others just assumed they had assimilated into the communities. Charlie had no idea that most of the Seminole and other Florida and Georgia tribes had been forced to relocate to the west. Nokosi told him about the long walk on what he called the trail of tears, where thousands of men, women and children died. Charlie wondered how he would react in the same situation.

That night, the three men stayed in a chickee near Nokosi. George and Flannigan were used to sleeping in tents and outdoors, but Charlie wasn't. He was restless for an hour or so but finally fell asleep.

Once again, after a night of drinking, Charlie was up early, while George was still sleeping off the Jameson. Emily was also awake and offered him a cup of coffee from a pot she had cooking on the campfire. They both sat at the same round table they had the night before.

"Emily, is Ned awake?" Charlie asked.

"Yes, he's meeting with the tribal elders down by the river. When they're done he will have your answer," Emily said.

"I thought Ned was the leader. Isn't this his decision?" Charlie asked

"Yes, he is, but we revere our elder's opinions. They have lived long and experienced much. It would be foolish not to consult them," Emily said.

"And what about you? What would you answer?" George asked.

"Ned knows my thoughts on this matter. More coffee, Charlie?" Emily said.

Charlie, realizing he would get no useful information from Emily continued his conversation with small talk. He learned that Emily was the daughter of a Seminole woman and a British trader from Bermuda. Her father was killed during the third and last Seminole War. She was 37 years old and had never known her father. Emily and Ned Nokosi had three children, eighteen-year-old Nathanial, fourteen-year-old Jacob and eight-year-old Mary.

"Emily, I hope you don't mind me asking, but why don't you and your children have Seminole names?" Charlie asked.

"Well, my father's mother's name was Emily, so I was named after her. When I was five years old, Catholic missionaries came to our village and offered to teach the children reading, writing and arithmetic. We also had to learn about Christ. The elders agreed, understanding that if we were to prosper in the white man's world, we needed to learn these things. So I became a Catholic and spent ten years in the missionary school. Nathanial is named after the priest that taught us. Mary and Jacob get their names from the bible," Emily explained.

"I did nine years stretch in Catholic school in Philadelphia," Charlie said.

"You make it sound like jail," Emily said smiling.

"It kind of was. Nuns and priests can be harder than prison guards," Charlie said and grinned.

George and Flannigan walked up to the table, and Emily

asked them to sit down. She poured each a cup of coffee and offered them breakfast. Both men were feeling the effects of a hangover and declined.

"Any word?" George asked Charlie.

"Not yet. Ned's having a meeting with the elders. Emily was just telling me that she was brought up Catholic," Charlie answered.

George looked at Emily and said, "Well, maybe you can say a prayer for me to have this headache go away," George said and smiled.

"I can do better than that. Just wait here, I'll be back in a minute," Emily said.

A few minutes later she placed a small handfull of leaves on the table and said, "Eat four or five of these. In twenty minutes I promise your headache will be gone."

"What is it?" George asked.

"I don't really know our name for it, but in English, it's called Snakeroot. Eat it, you'll see," Emily said.

Flannigan made a face when he swallowed the chewed up leaves and said. "It's just what I thought something named snake-root would taste like."

When Ned Nokosi finished his meeting with the elders, he returned to his chickee. Charlie, George and Flannigan stood up as he approached. Emily hugged Ned, and he whispered something in her ear. She instinctively placed her hand on the Colt 45 she had holstered by her side.

Ned poured himself a coffee and refilled the others cups. He sat down and sipped his coffee, looked at Charlie, then Flannigan and finally George and said, "We have a deal."

"You won't regret this, Ned. Your and Emily's lives are about to change for the better," Charlie said and held his cup up for a toast. "Here's to a profitable partnership." They all clicked each other's cups.

"Ned, can you and your men meet us outside of Jacksonville in three days?" George asked.

"If we leave today, yes," Ned said.

"Before Charlie left Philadelphia he learned that a shipment of arms was coming from Philadelphia to Jacksonville. It arrives in four days, and we want you to meet it when it comes across the Georgia border and relieve it of those weapons. Can you do that?" George asked.

"Yes, it's just robbing a rolling bank to us," Ned said.

"Great," Charlie said, "George and Flannigan will meet you near Jacksonville and go along this first time. They'll have information for the location on the coast where a ship will meet you and take the weapons off your hands."

"Ned, just one other thing," George said. "The government thinks your dead, so you'll have to change your name. Charlie will have papers for you and your family made when he returns to Philadelphia. We thought it might be good if people thought you're Italian. You look Italian, and so do Emily and the children. How do you like the name Edoardo Natoli?"

CHAPTER 32

20 Miles from Jacksonville, Florida

Emily Nokosi pulled her Colt 45 from the holster and checked to be sure it was loaded. She placed it back in the holster and slid it in and out several times to be certain the humidity wasn't making the leather stick. It was a precaution Emily took when she rode with her husband and his men.

George watched Emily with interest. She obviously knew how to handle a gun, and she looked striking in her deerskin trousers, white shirt and Stetson hat. He hadn't seen a woman wearing trousers since leaving Cochinchina, and he suddenly felt the ache of sadness. George shook his head trying to rid of the horrific memory.

"Now that's my kind of woman," Flannigan said. "She's beautiful, smart and knows how to use a gun."

George grunted and moved his horse to where Ned Nokosi was overlooking the railroad tracks and said, "Remember Ned, no killing unless necessary. The officer in charge of detachment is on our payroll. He'll stand his men down when we attack."

"I heard you the first three times you told me, George. Stop worrying. My guys are ready and know what to do," Nokosi said.

"I know they are, Ned. Sorry." George said.

That morning Ned had his men cut down several large trees and place them alongside the train tracks. There was one train that was scheduled to arrive in Jacksonville before the one carrying the weapons. When it passed, the trees were placed on the tracks to block the weapons train that was two hours behind.

George pulled out a gold Waltham pocket watch, looked at it and said, "If the train's on schedule we have another 30 minutes to wait."

Ned's twenty men were hiding behind a ridge. The plan was to have ten men attack from the rear and the other ten to attack from the front once the train stopped. There were four large wagons that would be brought to the train when they were ready to load the weapons. If everything went as planned, they would be on the road in an hour to a location just south of Saint Augustine. Once there, they were to meet the ship that would take the weapons to the rebels in Cuba.

George took a flask from his saddlebag and handed it to Ned and said, "A little Irish courage, Ned."

"Seminoles don't need liquid courage. It's built into us," Ned said, then smiled and continued, "But I wouldn't want to insult you." Ned took a large quaff of the flask's contents and handed it back to George who did likewise and replaced the flask in the saddlebag.

It was forty-five minutes before Ned pointed to the smoke he saw several miles up the tracks. He took a red kerchief from his pocket and waved it in the air. Flannigan rode off to join the men who would attack the front of the train. George, Emily and Ned joined the men attacking from the rear. Everyone placed on the cloth hoods the women at the camp made before they rode off to attack the train.

When the train stopped to avoid hitting the felled trees on the track, Ned's men started shooting their weapons in the air. There were two train cars with the weapons and two additional cars with passengers. The five soldiers guarding the weapons immediately dropped their rifles as was planned. George and Flannigan each boarded one of the passenger cars and told the travelers that it was in their best interest to stay calm. A male passenger sitting near where George was standing pulled out his wallet, took the money he had in it and offered it to him.

"Put your money away. We're not here to rob you. We just want the weapons for the Cuban resistance against the Spanish overlords and their bitch Queen Maria and her whelp Alphonso. Fuck Spain. God bless America!" George yelled. He knew it was popular to support the Cuban rebels and bash the Spanish. Besides American's loved rebels and hated the European Monarchies. He hoped it would help to keep them calm. The train erupted in cheers and shouts of God Bless America.

George had thought that one day the United States would have to fight the Spanish. Now he believed it would be sooner rather than later.

Ned Nokosi supervised the loading of the wagons with the weapons, while Emily stood guard over the soldiers just in case one decided to be a hero. None did. When the wagons were loaded George and Flannigan left the train and Nokosi guided the wagons and his men to the road. As the Nokosi gang rode away, the passengers in the train where George had been, rushed out and stood by the side of the train cheering. As word spread to the other passenger car that the guns were for Cuban rebels they joined in the cheers. One man yelled, "God Bless America," and the crowd joined in.

Flannigan, riding beside George asked, “What the hell did you tell those people?”

Sitting on his horse several hundred yards away from the train, Captain Alejandro Delgado of the Spanish 55th Infantry Regiment looked on in disgust. He coughed up a glob of phlegm and spit it towards the train and said out loud, “Fucking Americans.” Then he rode off.

CHAPTER 33

Captain Alejandro Delgado was the eldest son of a wealthy landowner and merchant from Toledo, Spain. From a young age he was groomed to take over his father's business, but Delgado wanted a life of excitement and adventure, so he decided to join the military. Delgado was a natural warrior, arrogant and very ambitious. In less than six years he obtained the rank of Captain, a feat rarely achieved in the Spanish Army.

His rapid accession in the ranks was mainly due to the fact that Delgado took on assignments others avoided. If a mission was dangerous and difficult, his superiors could count on him to be the first to volunteer. He had no qualms about ordering his men into impossible situations. It was no surprise to the commanding general when Delgado gladly accepted an assignment to take fifteen handpicked soldiers to Florida with the mission to stop the flow of weapons to the Cuban rebels.

Delgado hired locals to report anything they heard about gunrunning operations. He had local agents throughout central and south Florida along the coast where shipping guns to Cuba would be most likely. One of his agents learned about the train robbery from a Nokosi man who while drinking at a local bar bragged that they were going to get rich working for a white man from up north. Then Delgado had the man followed back to Nokosi's camp. When the gang left to go to the robbery location, he and his men followed them and watched them rob the train.

He decided to wait until Nokosi delivered the weapons for transport to Cuba before attacking him. He hoped that he could also learn how they were getting them into the Spanish colony. At that point, the plan was to attack, destroy the weapons, kill as many of the gunrunners as possible. His superiors would calculate his success by the number of dead bodies, and the number of weapons destroyed, and Delgado was hell-bent to make the General happy. He certainly didn't want to stay a Captain much longer.

Delgado and his men stayed well behind as Nokosi traveled the road to the rendezvous location. It was easy to track them with as many men as Nokosi had with him, as well as the heavily laden wagons. Delgado knew that surprise would be his main advantage and he also knew he would need every advantage he could get. He would be outnumbered, but he believed the Seminole Indians like the Cubans were poor warriors. He would get extra credit for killing the two white men that were riding with the gang. They were, no doubt the gunrunners from the north.

George Graham and Flannigan rode ahead of the wagons looking for the markings that would indicate where the boats from the transport ship would be located. The sailors were supposed to place five rocks on the side of the road just before where they were to turn left towards the ocean. The shrubs and any trees were to be removed by the sailors by the time they arrived for easy access for the wagons.

"There it is," George said and pointed towards the five stones stacked so the appeared to be a mini pyramid. He and Flannigan galloped forward to inspect the newly made pathway. When the determined it was safe, they waved on the wagons. The pathway was approximately two hundred feet and just wide enough for the wagons to pass. When they arrived at a clearing, they could see five boats pulled up on a small beach. George assumed they where the ship's lifeboats. Each boat had four sailors standing in front of it.

Nokosi and Emily rode up and stopped beside George and Flannigan. He looked left and right out into the inland waterway and then gave the signal for his men to start unloading wagons. One of the sailor's walked to where the four were stopped, gave a sloppy salute and said, "Good afternoon, I'm Alfred Masterson, First Mate on the SS Jefferson."

George looked down at Masterson and said "Good to meet you, Mr. Masterson," and stuck his hand out. Masterson shook his hand, and George continued, "This is Flannigan, and this couple is Ned and Emily Nokosi."

Masterson shook Flannigan's hand, then Ned's and then took his hat off and bowed slightly to Emily and said, "Good to meet you, Madam."

Emily nodded her head slightly and smiled.

"Now if you'll excuse me I'll get my men to help load the weapons," Masterson said, then turned to walk back to his sailors. He took four steps and fell forward. A split second later the report of a rifle was heard. Then another shot, then several more.

George, Flannigan, Ned and Emily jumped from their mounts. The sailors, who were unarmed, took shelter behind the boats. Ned's men began to shoot back at about fifteen men who had come out from the surrounding forest. By the time

Emily hit the ground she had her pistol out and was shooting. George, Flannigan and Ned crawled behind one of the wagons, pulled their side arms and began shooting.

Two of Ned's men were laying in the pathway bleeding. Several attackers had been able to break through and were running towards the boats. All three were holding torches. Flannigan ran after them, shooting at one as he ran but missed. He caught up with and tackled the man closest to him. He pushed the man's face into the dirt, but the man was strong and was able to push Flannigan off. He smashed Flannigan in the face, and as blood flowed from Flannigan's eye, the man hit him again. Flannigan fell backward and lay on the ground stunned. The attacker stood up and pulled his holstered gun.

While Flannigan was chasing down his attackers, Emily aimed at the first man holding a torch and fired. The bullet hit the man on the side of the head pushing him to the right as he fell to the ground. A split second later she fired at the other torchbearer hitting him in the back. He tumbled several times and then lay withering in pain on the beach. Emily turned just as the man Flannigan was fighting drew his revolver and was about to shoot. Emily held the gun with two hands to steady her aim and squeezed the trigger. The front of the man's forehead exploded with blood and fragments of his brain as Emily's bullet exited his head.

Flannigan now covered in the man's blood and brains stood up, waved to Emily, picked up his weapon and joined the men fighting off the rest of Delgado's soldiers. Five minutes later all of Delgado's men lay dead or dying, their blood soaking into the rich Florida soil. Two sailors and three of Ned's men had also perished in the fighting.

George saw the man Emily had shot in the back crawling towards the trees, and he slowly walked over to him and put his foot on his head. He flipped the man over and said, "Who sent you?"

Delgado recoiled in pain, then in a halting voice said in English, "Eat shit, American."

George kneeled then placed the barrel of his revolver on Delgado's temple and said, "What's your name?"

Delgado closed his eyes and opened them again and said, "Captain Alejandro Delgado of his Majesty's Cuban Colonial Army." Delgado knew he would die either from his wound or a bullet from this American so why not tell him. At least these Americans would know it was him that had been so brave.

"Well, Captain you just killed all of your men."

Delgado closed his eyes as a searing pain in his back engulfed him. When he opened his eyes, he said, "They are warriors. They knew the price."

"How did you learn about us?" George asked.

"We have spies all over Florida and even in Washington. Fooling Americans is easy. You are like children." He smiled and continued, "I hope you go to war with Spain. We will show you how to fight," Delgado said.

"Tell that to the families of the men you just got killed. I was going to give you mercy and put a bullet in your brain, but now you can just suffer. Go ahead, crawl to the trees. Maybe you'll die before the alligators get you. Maybe, but I doubt it," George said.

Delgado rolled over and started to crawl again. Emily Nokosi walked up behind Delgado and fired one round into the back of his head. Then she said, "George we can't chance to leave anyone alive who knows who we are."

George shrugged his shoulders and walked back to the wagons. As he walked he heard gunfire as Nokosi's men made sure that none of Delgado's men survived.

Chapter 34

Philadelphia, PA 1895

Naval Lieutenant Henry Bannister sat impatiently on a wooden chair with no cushion. The longer he waited, the more agitated he got. It had been an hour since he walked into Charles Byrne's office and asked to see him. Byrne's secretary told the Lieutenant that as soon as he finished with his current important meeting, Byrne would decide if he had time to meet with him.

He will decide, Bannister thought. *That son of a bitch is lucky I don't have him tossed in jail.* Henry Bannister was not used to being kept waiting. He came from a wealthy and powerful family. People jumped when he came into a room. Even some admirals treated him as an equal. *Obviously, this Byrne character didn't know who he was,* he thought.

Bannister tried to calm himself. The president and naval command wanted this alliance with Byrne, and if he screwed it up, he would have people even more powerful than his father to answer to. He took a long breath and shifted in the chair to get more comfortable, and he waited.

An hour and a half after he arrived, a bell rang on Byrne's secretary's desk. She got up and walked into Charles Byrne's office and closed the door behind her. Bannister sat up straighter thinking he was about to be shown into Byrne's office. Ten minutes later she opened the office door, and a man holding several bolts of cloth and a small satchel walked out. A young man in an impeccably made suit followed him.

Charlie Byrne said, "Remember Carlo, one each, black, blue and gray."

Carlo bowed slightly and walked past Bannister and out the door. Bannister stood up as Charlie walked to his chair.

"Charles Byrne," he said and held out his hand.

Bannister shook his hand, presented a business card to Charlie, and said, "Henry Rosemont Bannister III."

"What business could a Naval Lieutenant with such a pretentious name have with me? If you're selling tickets to the Naval Ball, I don't dance?" Charlie said.

Bannister's face turned red, and he said, "May I have a word with you in private? I assure you that it is worth your time, sir."

"Okay. Come in," Charlie said and walked into his office. Bannister followed, and Charlie shut the door behind him and said, "Have a seat," and pointed to several chairs surrounding a round table.

"Can I get you something? Coffee, whiskey?" Charlie asked.

"No sir. Thank you."

Charlie sat down, leaned forward and starred at Bannister, waiting for him to speak. Bannister became even more agitated. *No niceties, no small talk, just get straight to the point,* Bannister thought. *What a clod this Byrne character was.*

"I'm here at the behest of the President of the United States," Bannister said. Charlie leaned back and starred more intently at Bannister as he continued. "We are aware of your business, Mr. Byrne. Not the construction business, the weapons business."

Now it was Charlie's turn to feel ill at ease. He said, "And just how did you come up with that fairytale?"

"You may have heard about the United States Secret Service. They are quite efficient," Bannister said and smiled.

"Well, they're wrong. I am a simple builder. That's all," Charlie said.

"Let's suppose you were in the illegal weapons business," Bannister said. Charlie started to interrupt him, but Bannister continued. "Consider it a work of fiction. If you were an illegal weapons dealer, I would have enough evidence to put you away for a long time. Or, I could make you a proposition that could be worth a fortune to you. At the same time, you would be providing an important service to your country."

"Okay, so let's say I am a character in this fiction novel you're writing. What would I have to do?" Charlie asked.

"The plot of this book is quite simple, Mr. Byrne. Our country is at odds with Spain over Cuba. Certain powerful men believe it's in our country's best interest to have the Spanish gone from an Island so close to us. So they would like you to continue to steal weapons and deliver them to the Cuban rebels. In fact, they wish to help you by providing you with times and locations of shipments. All you have to do is steal them and get them to Cuba," Bannister said.

"So you're saying the government wants me to steal weapons from them and give them to the Cubans?" Charlie asked. Bannister nodded in the affirmative, and Charlie continued, "Why? Why don't they just give them the fucking guns?"

"Politics Mr. Byrne, politics. If the Spanish found out that the government of the United States was shipping weapons to the rebels, they would declare war on us. Certain other powerful politicians don't want that to happen because they have a business interest in Cuba and other Spanish-held colonies. The powerful politicians I represent would love to have a war with Spain. They figure we can win and take over those colonies. It, however, is not in our best interest to go to war only two years after the greatest recession our nation has ever experienced. It will take a few more years before we're strong enough. Meanwhile, the rebels can soften up the Spaniards for us," Bannister explained.

"So what's in it for me if I agree," Charlie said.

"You get to keep ninety percent of everything you make. Ten percent is to be paid, in cash, to me on the first of each month," Bannister said.

"And if I refuse?"

"Then you, and Sergeants Graham and Flannigan go to jail for a very long time," Bannister said and smiled.

For the next hour, Bannister and Charlie worked out the details of the union of the United States government and the Johnny O. Gang.

CHAPTER 35

July 1897 Palm Springs, Florida

During the two years after joining forces with the Johnny O. Gang Ned Nokosi, now going under the name Edoardo (Ned) Natoli, had been able to buy and operate a large farm near West Palm Beach. At the suggestion of Charlie Byrne, he also purchased over 2,000 acres of beachfront property along the Florida coastline. His small tribe had flourished, and not a single member had lost their life robbing trains for weapons.

The United States government kept their promise and supplied Charlie Byrne with the dates and location of various shipments of weapons to military bases in Florida. Military escorts were ordered not to fire on train robbers. Very often it was the same soldiers escorting the weapons, so Ned and his men got to know them and would frequently exchange gifts and sometimes money with the soldiers. All in all, it was a good union of government and gunrunners.

Charlie Byrne, in late 1895, suggested that Ned consider sending his two sons, Nathanial and Jacob to Philadelphia to attend school. Both were intelligent kids, and Charlie used his influence to get Nathanial into the University of Pennsylvania where he was studying business administration. Jacob enrolled in one of the best private schools in Philadelphia.

While attending school Nathanial and Jacob lived with Charlie in his home' and when the school year ended they returned to their parents in Florida. Charlie became very fond of the boys, especially Jacob who he found to be adventurous, intelligent and quick-tempered like himself. Since Charlie had been the youngest in his family, he enjoyed his new role as big brother. The boy's mother, Emily, made Charlie promise that neither of her boys would be involved in any illegal business. Charlie kept that promise and took every opportunity to teach them about the construction business. Nathanial loved helping with the administrative aspects of the business and Jacob gravitated towards the actual building of homes and factories. He laid bricks, poured cement and pounded nails every chance he got.

George Graham and Flannigan often visited Ned and Emily's farm to discuss business. When the boys were home for the summer, they would take Ned's new sailboat and go fishing in the Atlantic Ocean. While they silently floated over the gently rolling waves, Flannigan would entertain the boys with stories of his and George's adventures in exotic places. The boys loved it, and even when Flannigan repeated a story they had heard their attention never wavered.

"Uncle Flannigan, tell us the story of when Uncle George beat up a man with a fruit," Jacob said.

"It was a durian," George said.

"I've done that once too often. How about a new story?" Flannigan asked.

Both boys just stared at Flannigan waiting for him to start.

"Do you remember the story I told you about us fighting off the pirate attack when we were traveling across the Pacific Ocean?" Flannigan asked.

Both boys said, "Yes."

"Well something far more dangerous and mysterious happened on that trip," Flannigan said, making his voice as dramatic as possible.

"What happened?" Jacob asked.

"One day, your Uncle George and a fellow named John, may he rest in peace," Flannigan made the sign of the cross and continued, "and another fellow named Danny, you know Danny O'Boyle, and me were sunning ourselves on the aft deck. It was one of those perfect days. You know the bright blue sky, no clouds and a light breeze. Suddenly the wind picked up, and the sky darkened with ominous black clouds. Waves started to batter the ship," Flannigan said, raising his voice to build suspense.

We heard the muffled sound of a small bell ringing. You know like the ones they have on ships to tell the time. Then we heard the bell again, a little louder this time. The rain started. It was a cold rain that felt as if pins were being stuck in your arms and face. The ship was rocking side to side, and Uncle George fell on the deck and slid towards an opening in the railings. I was just able to catch him before he fell overboard. As I picked him up from the deck, we heard the bell again. It was louder.

Danny and John joined us on the port side, and as we peered into dimness, the bell sounded again, then again. Each time louder. Our ship became engulfed in fog, and we could only see about 2two-hundred feet in front of us. I thought I saw something and at that moment the bell rang again, and again, and again each time a little louder. As we gazed out into the fog, we saw a faint shape of something coming closer and closer. I don't mind telling you I was scared," Flannigan paused for effect then continued. "I heard Uncle George gasp, and when I turned to look at him he was kneeling with his hands together. Then he said, "For all that is holy. God please save us."

When I looked back out to sea, I saw it, and my heart skipped a beat. A battered three-mast ship was emerging from the fog. It was an unsightly thing with torn sails and rotting wood. It looked like the spawn of the devil. At the helm was the ugliest looking man I have ever seen. He wore black clothing, and his eyes were evil and glowing red. He had two horns sticking out of a three-cornered hat.

The bell rang louder and louder as the ship came closer and closer to a collision with our vessel. Uncle George was crying now and praying, as were John and Danny. They were asking God to take them to heaven and not let Satan take them to hell. My legs were shaking, and I yelled loudly, "God, save my friends and take me instead."

George rolled his eyes. Nathanial smiled. Jacob sat still, intently listening to Flannigan.

Flannigan continued, "Then I remembered I was wearing a cross around my neck." Flannigan put his hand down his shirt and pulled out the cross that was on a gold chain and said, "This one. I held the cross up to that devil as his ghost ship bore down on us. I thought that I had taken my last breath but just 20 feet in front of us, the ghost ship dove down into the water and under our ship. Just like that, it was gone, and we were safe." Flannigan put his hand in his pocket and pulled out a medal the French Foreign Legion gave him and said, "See, I got this medal of valor for beating the Devil."

Flannigan sat silent for a minute then said, "And that is a true story."

Then a bell rang, and Jacob said, "Did you hear that?"

"What, I didn't hear anything," Flannigan said.

Then the bell rang a little louder and Jacob dove into Flannigan's arms and started to sob.

Flannigan pulled him up and said, "It's just a joke, Jacob. See, I gave Uncle George a small bell to ring. It's okay." George held up the bell.

Jacob sat back down, looked at Flannigan and said, "Jesus, Uncle Flannigan, I'm 16 years old. Do you really think I believed you?" Jacob said and held up the medal Flannigan showed him.

Flannigan checked his pocket and sure enough, the medal was missing. Jacob then held up Flannigan's wallet and said," Missing anything else?"

"Son of a bitch, how'd you do that?" Flannigan asked.

"Devil's magic, I guess," Jacob said and handed Flannigan his medal and wallet.

Flannigan picked up a bottle of beer and handed it to Jacob and said, "Here, you're right. You're not a kid anymore. For Christ's sake, do not tell your mother I gave you a beer."

That evening the Natoli family and their guests, George and Flannigan, sat down to an Italian meal. Emily had, to support the family's new name, learned to cook Italian dishes. She always included some of her Seminole foods when she had guests, telling people she learned these recipes from her farm workers. At heart, Emily and Ned would always be Seminole, but Jacob and Nathanial were rapidly adapting to their new personas. Nathanial was even learning the Italian language.

As Emily talked about the farm and the legal investments she and her husband made, Flannigan couldn't help but stare at her with admiration. This woman who was raised in the swamps of south Florida was now able to discuss money matters as if she had been born to a wealthy New York family. Flannigan admired her intelligence, courage and her tenacity.

Emily noticed Flannigan staring at her and said, “Flannigan, have you made any investments?”

“Oh no. I don’t have the brain for that. I send all my money to my Ma and my family in Ireland. They’ve done well, and I trust them,” Flannigan said.

“And you, George? Do you invest?” Emily asked.

“Some, I guess. I bought some land north of Philadelphia. Like Flannigan, I give most of the money I make to my family. They had it hard in Ireland, and I want it to be easier for them here. Danny O’Boyle set up a family trust for me, and my brother-in-law Paddy is the administrator. I’m like Flannigan here. I have no mind for investing. We’re both just soldiers.

“Nathanial, Jacob, could you leave us? We have some business to discuss with your uncles.,”Emily asked.

Nathanial and Jacob understood that they were not to be part of the business their parents had with George and Flannigan. Of course, they knew what that business was, and they wanted to be part of it. They said their goodnights and left the room.

When the boys were out of earshot, George said, “Charlie has had word from his government contact that shipments of weapons are going to increase. That means we’ll need to intercept more shipments. Things are heating up between Spain and the US. The prolonged fight between rebels and the Spanish military is hurting imports of sugar and other goods from Cuba, and important men want the fighting over. The contact said they expect that within a year the U.S. and the Spanish will be at war.”

“How many more shipments do they want us to divert,” Ned asked.

"It will have to increase by at least twenty-five percent," George said.

"I can handle that, but we don't have enough ships to deliver them to Cuba," Ned said.

"Charlie discussed that with them. The government is willing to put at our disposal ten unmarked smaller boats. Some will be fishing boats. Others will be pleasure craft. They are to be operated by U.S. sailors in civilian clothing."

"They've thought of everything," Ned said.

"They're serious, Ned. Pulitzer and Hearst are writing about Spanish atrocities in their newspapers daily. It's gotten U.S. citizens riled up, and many are calling on the U.S. to kick the Spanish out of Cuba. American businessmen who were against the war last year are now supporting it. As their import/export profits get lower, they get louder. If we know one thing about our United States it is that money talks. The war is going to happen sooner rather than later," George said.

"And when it does, that will be the end of our gunrunning. We've been anticipating that day by investing in land, cigar manufacturing and spirits distilleries, mainly rum. We'll be fine. One thing that Americans will never give up is smoking and drinking," Emily said.

"I know I won't," Ned said and laughed.

"What about the two of you and Charlie? What will you do?" Emily asked.

"Flannigan and I have the army. Our families are well off, and that's all that's important to me. Charlie has his construction business, and there's still Ireland. We have a part of that operation so we'll all be fine," George said.

George took a folded piece of paper out of his pocket and slid it to Ned and said, "Here's the latest list of shipments the government has targeted. You'll notice by the manifest that some of these shipments include cannon and machine guns."

"Really? That's a bit of a change," Ned said.

"I told you, they're serious. The U.S. government wants the rebels to be well armed," George said.

CHAPTER 36

November 1, 1897 - Philadelphia

Of all the Catholic churches in Philadelphia, Charlie Byrne's favorite was the Cathedral Basilica of Saints Peter and Paul. It wasn't because Charlie was a devout Catholic, but rather because he loved the architecture of the building.

The building of the cathedral started in 1846, just two years after the anti-Irish Catholic Nativist Riots. The riots were sporadic over the summer of 1844 and resulted in over twenty deaths and numerous injuries. There were protests about the building of the church, but the building continued. Charlie's grandfather worked as a laborer on the church during the years from 1846 to 1850. He and other laborers had to endure threats, name calling and the occasional stone throwing as tension between Catholics and Nativists continued. He told Charlie many stories, but the one that impressed Charlie the most was the story of the placement of the church's stained glass windows.

One day on the job site, the chief architect selected one of the stronger-looking laborers and had him throw large stones as high as he could. When the man finished throwing twenty or so stones, the architect handed him a silver dollar, thanked him and went back to his office. He pulled the building plans and modified the height of the windows to be higher than the laborer was able to throw the stones. This made Charlie love the building even more. It was a symbol of Catholic perseverance, and it was like giving the Nativists, who hated all foreigners and especial Catholics, the middle finger.

Before she allowed Nathanial and Jacob Natoli to come to Philadelphia to go to school, Emily Natoli made Charlie promise that both boys would attend church regularly. So on November 1st, All Saints Day, Charlie hired a carriage to take the boys and himself to the church so they could attend mass. Charlie lived at 9th and Callowhill Streets, so the driver took 9th Street to Race Street then on to 19th and Race the location of the cathedral. Charlie told the driver they would be an hour or so and to be sure he was parked in front when they were ready to leave.

During the mass all Charlie could think about was how much this bejeweled holy structure would cost to build in 1897 dollars. He estimated square footage size, mulled over the cost of the various fixtures and came up with a figure that would be at least three times what it cost in 1850. He hoped someday he would have the opportunity to build something that would last for hundreds of years.

Charlie was sitting daydreaming when a man abruptly plopped down next to him. The man then pushed Charlie over to make room for himself. Charlie woke from his daydream with a start, made a fist and turned to reward this arrogant churchgo-er with a knuckle sandwich. He stopped short of hitting him and said, "You asshole. It's good to see you, Danny." Then he shook Danny O'Boyle's hand.

"Yes, it has been a month of Sundays. Good to see you, Charlie," Danny said.

Several parishioners in adjacent pews looked at Charlie and Danny with disdain and put their fingers to their lips, indicating the two should shut the hell up. "Let's go outside and talk," Charlie said.

They sat on the front steps of the church and Charlie clapped Danny on the shoulder and said, "Danny O'Boyle soon-to-be Mayor of Philadelphia. Who would have thought?"

"Well, thanks for the vote, Charlie, but I won't even get a chance to be mayor for another four years at least, probably eight," Danny said.

"But you will be mayor, and I'll be helping you get there," Charlie said.

"Thanks, Charlie. I know you will," Danny said and patted Charlie on the back. Then he continued," Tell me, how are George and Flannigan?"

The two friends sat on the cathedral steps discussing politics, friends and sharing old memories until the door opened and the mass goers started to leave.

"Mrs. McGorry passed away," Danny said.

"No! I'm sorry, Danny. I know you thought highly of her," Charlie said.

"She was very kind to me, and I am happy I could make her life better," Danny said. Danny had been sending money to Mr. and Mrs. McGorry ever since he arrived in Philadelphia. When Mr. McGorry died, he bought Mrs. McGorry a small cottage. She retired from her job and lived the rest of her life enjoying her grandchildren. "I lit a candle for her earlier," Danny said.

Charlie made the sign of the cross and said,"May she rest in peace."

The two men sat in silence for a minute then Charlie asked, "Can I give you a ride back to City Hall, Danny,"

"That would be great. It'll give me a chance to talk to Nathanial and Jacob," Danny answered. "By the way, how's Jacob doing with his art lessons?"

"He's very creative, and his art teacher said he'd be a fine artist one day," Charlie answered. "I wish I could draw. I envy him as much as I'm proud of him."

When the driver returned Charlie and Danny sat in the carriage and waited for the boys, who were for some reason the last to exit the cathedral. Charlie was pretty sure it had something to do with the pretty young girl who exited with them. He didn't mind and would have done the same thing himself.

The last carriage pulled away as Nathanial and Jacob took their seats. Jacob sat next to Charlie and Nathanial sat next to Danny and said, "Sorry we were talking to someone we know from school."

Before Charlie could say anything, a police officer ran up to the carriage door and said, "Which of you is Mr. Byrne?"

"I am. What is it you want?"

"I have a message for you," the police officer said.

"From who""

The police officer pulled a Mauser Zig-Zag pistol from his coat and pointed it at Charlie and at the same time said, "The King of Spain."

In the split second it took the police officer to pull and point his weapon, Jacob analyzed the situation and acted. He pushed the man's arm up with all his strength and fell forward on top of him. As he did, the gun fired, but the bullet went harmlessly above Charlie's head. Nathanial immediately jumped from the carriage and helped Jacob subdue the officer. The Mauser fell to the ground, and Nathanial retrieved it and pointed at the man's head. Jacob yelled, "Don't kill him." Then he stepped out of the carriage and kicked the man in the head knocking him out.

"Help me get him in the carriage," Jacob said.

After the man was lying on the carriage floor, Danny searched him and found a twelve-inch long Spanish dagger. Nathanial, Danny, and Jacob put their feet on the man to hold him down should he regain consciousness. Charlie took a seat with the driver and told him to go to the Delaware Avenue ferry to Camden.

"What's your name?" Charlie asked the driver.

„Harry Hird, sir,"

"Look, I need you to forget what you saw. That man is not a cop. He's an agent of the Spanish King, and he was sent here to kill me. I can't get into details, but I'm part of a group that's helping to kick the Spanish out of Cuba. It's in our own government's interest that I find out everything I can from him. Will you help keep America safe?" Charlie asked.

"Yes, sir. I didn't see anything," Hird said. He had been a driver for several years and saw plenty happen in his carriage. Men and women fucking, men and men sucking each other off, and priests with prostitutes, were common occurrences. You didn't get repeat business by being a gossip monger. Anyway, none of it was his concern.

"Good, because if you tell anyone, the secret service would not look kindly on you," Charlie said.

"You can depend on me, sir," Hird said.

Charlie slapped Hird on the back and said, "Thank You."

By the time they arrived at the ferry, the Spanish agent had started to wake up. Danny smashed him on the head using the butt of the Mauser he confiscated. The agent lay still until they arrived at an abandoned lamp wick company Charlie had purchased a few months before. He planned to use it for storage of construction materials when he expanded his business to New Jersey. For now, it would work just fine for the interrogation of the Spanish agent.

Charlie asked the Harry to wait outside with Jacob while Nathanial and Danny dragged the agent into the building. Jacob didn't like to be left out, but Charlie insisted. They sat the agent on a large wooden crate and woke him up.

When the agent was coherent, Charlie asked, "Who hired you? And if you say, King Alfonso, I'll cut your fucking ear off."

The man said nothing, so Charlie asked, "You're not Spanish. Why are you willing to be maimed, tortured and murdered for some nitwit King thousands of miles away?"

Still, the man said nothing. Charlie hit his head with the palm of his hand and said, "I get it. Really I do. You think I won't hurt you. You think I'm a milksop. Am I right? Is that what you think?"

The agent remained silent. Charlie held his hand out to Danny and Danny placed the Spanish dagger he took from the agent in Charlie's hand. Charlie said, "Hold him." Danny and Nathanial took the man by his arms and held tight. Charlie placed the point of the dagger in the man's palm and pushed. The agent screamed in pain. Charlie twisted the dagger, and the man screamed again, and then Charlie slowly slid the dagger out and placed it on the man's other hand.

"Okay, the Spanish Ambassador. He gave me five hundred dollars." The man stopped and grimaced in pain, then continued. "He gave me the pistol, a dagger and a picture of you and said kill this hijo de puta."

“What’s that mean?” Charlie asked.

“I don’t know. I don’t speak Spanish,” the agent said.

“It means son of a bitch,” Nathanial said.

“How does he know me?” Charlie asked.

“I don’t know. He didn’t say,” the agent answered.

“Charlie pushed the knife into the man’s palm. The man screamed and when he was able said, “I swear I don’t know nothing else. Just kill me if that’s what you’re going to do.”

Charlie looked at the man, pulled the blade out and quickly cut the man’s jugular vein and said, “Okay, if that’s what you want.”

Nathanial stepped back not to get blood on his clothing. He looked at Charlie and said, “Did you have to kill him?”

“Yes. Yes, I did. If I didn’t, he would keep trying. This guy made his living assassinating people. Now I can use him to send a message to the ambassador.”

Danny pointed to the dead agent and asked, “What do we do with him?”

“Leave him. I’ll send someone to take care of it. Not a word of this to anyone, especially Jacob. And for Christ’s sake never mention this to your mother.

Two days later the groundskeeper at the Spanish embassy in Washington, DC found a body hanging from a lamppost outside of the ambassador’s office. There was a note pinned to his shirt. It read *Next time this happens, it will be the ambassador hanging from this lamppost.* It was signed *Las Hijo de Puta.*

CHAPTER 37

February 18th, 1898 - Philadelphia, Pennsylvania

Two days after the sinking of the battleship Maine in Havana Harbor, George Graham and Flannigan were on a train to Philadelphia. George had received a cryptic telegram from Charlie telling him that they must be in Philadelphia no later than February 18th. They were equally surprised when their commanding officer handed them train tickets and orders stating that they were both reassigned to a special task force.

As military men, they didn't question orders given them by their superiors and immediately prepared to leave. They had an idea it concerned the sinking of the Maine, but why them and what this task force was about they had no idea.

The train pulled into the Broad Street station in Philadelphia at 10:45 am, and when they entered the main room of the station they saw a man holding a placard with their names on it.

George walked up to the man and said, "I'm Graham, and this is Flannigan."

"Welcome to Philadelphia. My name is Harry Hird. If you come with me, I'll take you to Mr. Byrne's home," Hird said.

Charlie hired Harry Hird several days after the assassination attempt. He had been impressed with Hird's unflappable attitude and the fact that Hird spent six-teen years in the army, ten of them fighting in the Indian Wars. Hird was to be both bodyguard and driver for Charlie.

"May I get your luggage?" Hird asked.

"No, we made arrangements to have them taken to Charlie's house," Flannigan said.

"Okay, then if you follow me I'll get you to the house," Hird said and started walking to the main entrance.

When they exited the station, George was surprised to see an automobile. He was even more surprised to see four mounted police officers, two in front and two behind the car.

"Is that Charlie's?" George asked, pointing at the vehicle.

"Yes, sir. It's a new Olds Automobile from the Olds Motor Works in Ohio. Mr. Byrne bought it last month," Harry said.

"What's with the police?" Flannigan asked.

I have no idea. They just showed up at the house before I left and stayed with me all the way here," Hird replied.

Neither George nor Flannigan had ever ridden in an automobile. The exhaust from the gasoline engine was smelly, and the ride on the cobblestone roads was very rough, but never-to-less it was exciting. It was a short ride to Charlie's house, and when they arrived, Charlie, Jacob and Nathanial were outside waiting for them.

Once they greeted each other Charlie told Jacob and Nathanial to meet them for lunch at 1 pm, and then he showed George and Flannigan to his office. He poured three glasses of Jameson, spilled a small amount in the fireplace and said, "To John, may he rest in peace."

After another drink, George asked," What's this all about Charlie? Police escort, reassignment to a special task force. It's all a bit much."

"You know as much as I do. In about fifteen minutes a naval captain named Henry Bannister will be here to explain. So for now, let's get caught up. What have you two been up to?" Charlie asked.

Fifteen minutes later the housekeeper knocked on the door and announced that Captain Bannister had arrived. She showed him into the room and closed the door as she left. Charlie pointed to the bottle of Jameson and said, "Drink, Captain?"

"Thank you, no. I have a lunch meeting with the secretary of defense later."

Charlie was used to Bannister's name-dropping and better-than-thou attitude. Bannister always made it clear that he was very busy and connected to the highest authorities in the U.S. government.

"Have a seat, Captain," Charlie said. "I believe you know George Graham and Bill Flannigan."

"I know of them, but we haven't met yet," Bannister said and shook each of their hands then sat down.

"Let me get to the point. As you know, the Spanish sunk our battleship Maine a few days ago. That was the straw that broke the camel's back. There will be war. No stopping it now.

"The papers are saying that there is an investigation as to what happened to the Maine. What if the Spanish didn't sink her?" Charlie said.

"It doesn't matter. Powerful men want this war, and the sinking of the Maine is their excuse to start it. The newspapers have already begun to rile up our citizens. By April they will insist we declare war on Spain," Bannister said.

"Why would anyone want war?" Flannigan asked.

"For the same reason they didn't want war ten years ago, sugar. Sugar is big money and Cuba has a lot of it. When the rebels were quiet it was in the sugar industry's best interest to ignore the Spanish. Now that the rebels are at war with Spain sugar exports have slowed. That means these men are losing money. So we kick Spain's ass out of Cuba, and these sugar barons take control. That's the simple reason," Bannister said.

"Captain, if you're here to tell us that our gunrunning days are over when the war starts, we already know that," Charlie said.

"Yes, that's part of it. From this moment on you're not to take any more shipments. We're going to need everything we can get for the war. Also, I have been authorized to offer you and everyone involved in your scheme a pardon," Bannister said.

"Will that be in writing?" Charlie asked.

"Yes," Bannister said.

"And what must we do to get such a favor?" Charlie asked.

"There are two conditions. The first is that you, Mr. Graham, Mr. Flannigan and one other man of your choice will travel to Cuba no later than April 1st. You will connect with your rebel clients and coordinate their efforts to defeat the Spanish with ours," Bannister said.

"Why us?" Charlie asked.

"Because you have a relationship with them already and they trust you. We need the rebels. There's no bargaining with this, Mr. Byrne. Either you go, or we put you in jail for the rest of your life. That includes Mr. and Mrs. Nokosi or should I say, Natoli," Bannister said.

"What precisely must we do if we decide to agree?" Flannigan asked.

"A week before March 1st a man will join you. He will be your interpreter, and he will have your orders. I am sure I don't have to remind you, Mr. Flannigan and Mr. Graham that you are in the U.S. military. Your noncompliance will result in a firing squad for both of you," Bannister said with a wry smile.

"And the second stipulation?" Charlie asked.

Bannister shifted in his chair and looked at Charlie and said, "You will deliver to me fifty thousand dollars along with the payment from the last high jacking by mid-March. Remember, if you do these two things you will never be prosecuted for your past crimes. You will be free to be law-abiding citizens. And you will be doing your duty to the United States of America."

Charlie stood up and put his hand out and said, "Well, I guess we have no choice then. I'm in."

Bannister stood up and shook Charlie's hand and then looked at George and Flannigan. George slowly rose from his chair and shook Bannister's hand, and then Flannigan did the same and said, "Fuck."

"The government of the United States of America thanks you, gentlemen," Bannister said.

Bannister turned and made his way to the office door. Before he left, he turned back and said, "By the way, Mr. Graham, Mr. Flannigan, when this mission is over, you'll be honorably discharged from the army with full benefits."

CHAPTER 38

Coast of Cuba - March 10, 1898

When the battleship Maine deployed to Havana, the U.S. government also moved a large portion of the American fleet to locations near Cuba, the Philippines and Puerto Rico. The public was told there was a diplomatic solution that would avoid a war with Spain. The various large news media organizations, however, continued to antagonize the general public by reporting real or imagined atrocities committed by the Spanish. In fact, government officials were sure there would be war and even wanted it as much as the sugar businesses. Secretly they prepared for it.

It was under this veil of war preparation that a small vessel made its way to an isolated beach near the village of Santa Cruz on the southern side of Cuba. The vessel beached, and Cuban rebels unloaded crates of rifles and two Gatlin guns along with five Americans.

A Cuban rebel officer greeted Charlie Byrne. "Mr. Byrne,

my name is Alfredo Cardosa. It is so good to meet you. Captain Murphy, God rest his soul, spoke highly of you." He shook Charlie's hand.

"And he of you, General Cardosa," Charlie said, paused then continued."This is George Graham and Billy Flannigan."

"Ahh yes, I have heard many stories of the two U.S. soldiers who have supplied us with weapons for all these years." General Cardosa stood at attention and saluted the two men and said, "The revolution salutes and thanks to you for your service."

Graham and Flannigan, by force of habit, returned the salute and George said, "Thank you General. Let me introduce you to Harry Hird, U.S. cavalry retired and Jefferson Waddell, currently on special assignment from 10th cavalry. You might also know them as the Buffalo Soldiers. Waddell holds the rank of sergeant major and is a Gatling gun expert as well as a Spanish speaker."

Hird and Waddell stood at attention and saluted the General. The General returned the salute and in Spanish addressed Waddell, "Welcome to Cuba sergeant major Waddell. We are in sore need your expertise." In English, he addressed Hird, "Welcome, Mr. Hird. cavalry is not our strong suit. We do have some horses, and perhaps you can provide us with some education of their use in war."

"Of course, General," Hird replied.

"We have a three-hour trip to get to our camp, so I suggest we start now to avoid traveling in the dark."

The Cuban rebel camp was situated on high ground overlooking a large forest. To the far north there were the pristine fields of a tobacco farm, and to the south there was a sugarcane farm. The access to the camp was blocked by a thicket of trees that would make it difficult for an enemy to attack. It was an ideal location.

For the next 40 days, Harry Hird taught the small rebel cavalry contingent how to shoot while riding and how to control and care for their horses. Jefferson Waddell focused on creating well-trained Gatling gun teams. Cardosa had four old style Gatling guns and a large store of ammunition, but his men could not accurately shoot and repair them when necessary. After Waddell's training he bragged that his Cuban teams were as good as any he had trained in the United States Army.

Charlie, Flannigan and Graham spent their time exploring the lands around the camp and traveling to the beach near Santa Cruz. They had dug a large hole and hid it by covering it with dirt and vegetation. Sailors in small boats would leave supplies and communications from U.S. military once a week. The communications were usually general information, but on April 24th when Charlie, George and Flannigan arrived at the beach they were greeted by Captain Henry Bannister. They had not seen Bannister since they left the U.S.

"Gentlemen," Bannister said and did not offer his hand in greeting.

Charlie noticed Flannigan's face flush red and he quickly stood in front of him to avoid an altercation with Bannister.

"Bannister, you truly do have deplorable manners," Charlie said.

"That's Captain Bannister," Bannister said.

"Did your dear old Da buy you that title," George asked.

"Must I remind you, sergeant Graham, that you're still in the army and that I outrank you," Bannister said.

"As you so politely informed us, after this war I won't be in the army any longer. Perhaps we can meet at that time," George said.

"Bannister, why are you here?" Charlie asked.

"I have orders for you to convey to General Cardosa," Bannister said and handed Charlie a letter.

Charlie read the letter and handed it to Graham. He looked at Bannister and asked, "Do you know what this says?"

"Of course."

"So the war has started?" Charlie asked.

"It will tomorrow. On April 25th the United States will officially be at war with the country of Spain," Bannister said.

"The orders say we're to convince General Cordosa to move his forces to the Guantanamo Bay area to harass Spanish fortifications and create as much mayhem as possible. That can only mean one thing. We'll attack Guantanamo. When does that happen?" Graham asked.

"I have no idea, but I can tell you that on April 20th, President McKinley signed a resolution demanding that Spanish forces leave Cuba. On April 21st our Navy began a blockade of the Island. No reinforcements or supplies for the Spanish will be coming to Cuba. We have a saying in the Navy - ours is not to reason why, ours is but to do or die. I suggest you do one or the other. You're dismissed," Bannister said.

Bannister stood stone-faced waiting for Flannigan and Graham to salute him. Graham quickly performed a sloppy salute, and Flannigan stood at attention, lifted his hand to the brim of his hat. Then he curled all but his middle finger inward.

"That's just what I'd expect from Irish hooligans," Bannister said, then turned and walked back to the boat.

"What a twit. Every schoolboy knows that's from Tennyson's Charge of the Light Brigade. He didn't even say it right, Flannigan said, then recited the correct quote.

> "THEIRS NOT TO MAKE REPLY,
>
> THEIRS NOT TO REASON WHY,
>
> THEIRS BUT TO DO AND DIE."

"Okay professor, let's get out of here," Charlie said.

> "HALF A LEAGUE, HALF A LEAGUE,
> HALF A LEAGUE ONWARD,
> ALL IN THE VALLEY OF DEATH,

Rode the six hundred," Flannigan said, then followed Charlie.

"How'd you know that poem, anyway?" Graham asked.

"Danny read it to me. I liked it. Six hundred Englishmen died," Flannigan said.

The next morning General Cardosa ordered half of his detachment, about two hundred men, to travel with the Americans to Guantanamo. They arrived in the province of Santiago De Cuba on May 1st and immediately began harassing Spanish encampments in and around the villages of Bayamo, Manzanillo and San Luis. It was hit and run guerrilla tactics.

On May 11th, Charlie was directed by the U.S. command to cut telegraph cables to Manzanillo and Guantanamo. This was to be done in conjunction with a naval attack to cut the various underwater telegraph cables at a site near the city of Cienfuegos.

By the end of may Charlie received word that the war was going well in Asia. The Spanish fleet in Manila Bay was destroyed, and because of this, the Philippines was likely to fall by July or August. Spanish defenses were destroyed in Puerto Rico as well.

On June 4th, a messenger arrived with new orders for Charlie. His men were to take out several Spanish cannon emplacements overlooking Guantanamo Bay. It was imperative that the cannons be destroyed before six in the morning on June 6th. Charlie chose forty of the best Cuban rebel soldiers and assigned twenty to George and Flannigan to take out the cannons on the north ridge. The other twenty, including Jefferson Waddell, followed him to the south ridge. Hird's fifteen-man cavalry unit traveled with them but were kept in reserve should they need help during the attack.

Under cover of darkness, both groups made their way to their targets and silently waited until five when they believed the gunners would be asleep or at least groggy. Crawling on the dew-wet ground each team made their way to the first two targets. The strategy was to try to silently take out the Spanish gunners in the first two emplacements and then hit the third target.

Flannigan was the first to draw blood. A Spanish soldier was on guard duty just outside the first emplacement. Flannigan came up behind the man, put his hand over the man's mouth and drew his razor-sharp knife across his neck. Flannigan held tight as the blood flowed down the man's chest and out of his nose. The man ceased to struggle, and Flannigan dropped him. After wiping his hands on the man's tunic, he waved to the other team members. George Graham and the others rushed into the bunker and quietly dispatched the sleeping soldiers inside. They placed explosives at the base of each cannon as well as inside and waited.

As the first team was setting their charges, Charlie Byrne rushed the man guarding the second target. He grabbed the man, putting his hand over his mouth and attempted to cut the soldier's throat. The soldier immediately dropped to the ground making Charlie lose his grip. The soldier turned and pulled Charlie's legs out from under him. As Charlie hit the ground, the soldier pounced on him. He rapidly punched Charlie twice in the face, but to Charlie's surprise the soldier's hands dropped to his sides. It took Charlie a few seconds to realize that Waddell was standing behind the soldier and had driven his bayonet into the base of the man's neck.

Waddell pushed the now dead man off of Charlie and extended his hand and pulled Charlie up. As soon as Charlie was upright, a gunshot rang out and he and Waddell dove to the ground. One of the Spanish soldiers had heard the commotion and came out of the bunker to investigate. Charlie had no choice but to shoot back or be killed. Waddell and Charlie both shot the Spanish soldier. Realizing any hope of a surprise attack was gone, Charlie ordered his men to charge the bunker. This happened so quickly that the sleeping soldiers had little time to react and all killed.

George Graham heard the gunfire and yelled, "Light the fuses and get the fuck out of here." His men obeyed, and George waited until they all left the bunker and then he followed. When he was fifty yards away the bunker exploded in a ball of fire. There was no doubt now that the Spanish soldiers camped along the shore of Guantanamo Bay knew there was an attack.

George's team made their way to assist Charlie. When they were halfway there, they heard another explosion. Charlie had destroyed the cannon at target two. Both teams met up and made their way to the third and final target. This time the ten-man Spanish gun crew knew they were under attack and were ready.

Charlie saw that the soldiers on the beach were getting into formation. He knew that if they didn't take the bunker quickly, they would be outgunned. He ordered his men to fire everything they had, including tossing any excess explosives at the bunker.

The noise was deafening as the bunker lit up with explosions and hot lead chipped away at the façade. It was like an inferno from hell, and after five uninterrupted minutes of pandemonium, a white flag on a pole appeared at one of the windows. Charlie had Waddell tell the Spanish soldiers to push their guns out of the window and come outside. Guns immediately started falling out of the window.

When all ten Spanish soldiers were standing in front of Charlie, he told Waddell to tell them to take off their boots and start running down towards the beach. Charlie had never seen men run so fast.

The charges were set, and they waited a safe distance away until the explosions took out the guns. Then Charlie ordered his men to make their way back to their camp. The group started towards a clump of trees, but before they took three steps a rebel in front of George fell from gunfire coming from trees. Immediately more gunshots rang out, and several more of Charlie's men fell.

"Take cover," Charlie yelled. The problem was there wasn't much cover as the group was in an open area.

Charlie and Waddell fell to the ground in front of a small boulder that scarcely hid them, and Charlie said, "Fuck, they got around us somehow. We're surrounded."

"I'd say twenty men or so, but there's a whole lot more coming up that ridge. We need to get out of here pronto," Waddell yelled over the gunfire.

Feeling confident, the commander of the Spanish troops attacking from the trees then made a mistake. He ordered his men to advance. As they came from behind the tree cover, Charlie ordered his men to fire. The Spaniards knelt and fired back at about the same time the men attacking from the beach reached the ridge's summit and also began firing on Charlie's force.

Charles's heart skipped a beat as he realized he was outnumbered and outgunned. He quickly recited an act of contrition and opened fire hitting the commander of the forward-attacking men in the head. As the commander fell Charlie put a shot into the trooper next in line.

George Graham, Flannigan and their men had turned and were firing at the Spaniards attacking from the rear. Two of George's men fell. He then emptied his Colt at the attacking Spaniards. As he quickly reloaded he had a fleeting regret that he had never married or had a child, and now he was going to die and never would.

Charlie ran out of ammunition and grabbed a rifle lying beside a fallen rebel and started firing again. He thought, *Fuck it! If I'm going to die, I'm taking as many Spaniards with me as I can.* Charlie sensed movement rather than heard it coming from the left of the battlefield, and he quickly turned his rifle in that direction. About two hundred feet away, shrouded in fog and gunpowder smoke, he saw the image of a man on a horse. He pointed his rifle at the man's torso and waited until the rider was fully visible. He began to squeeze the trigger and abruptly stopped, and his jaw dropped.

Harry Hird came out of the fog, his pistol in his right hand and a sword in the left. Behind him were the fifteen men of the rebel cavalry. Charlie couldn't believe it. It was like the passages of books he read as a child. The gallant and dashing cavalry officer saves the day. But in this story, it's retired Sergeant Harry Hird from the Kensington section of Philadelphia. Charlie grinned as Harry's cavalry galloped by and opened fire on the Spanish soldiers.

Charlie yelled, "Attack!" and started to run towards the now decimated Spanish troops in front of him. His men followed and finished what Harry had started. Harry's cavalry turned and put themselves between George and Flannigan's men and the Spanish troops that had come from the beach. George immediately ordered his men to turn and run for the trees where they met up with Charlie. Harry and his men passed by the surprised

Spaniards, opened fire and then turned to join the others in the forest.

Harry guided his men through the trees and took up a post behind Charlie, George, Flannigan and their men. The Spanish had enough and did not pursue. The Americans and Cuban rebels returned to their camp.

CHAPTER 39

Near Santiago, Cuba - July 1, 1998

Guantanamo Bay fell to U.S. troops on June 10th and shortly after Charlie's men rejoined General Cordosa's army, was directed to go to the town of Aguacate and wait for orders. Henry Bannister met Charlie, George, Flannigan, Harry and Waddell and gave them orders to join Colonel E.P. Pearson, Commander of the 2nd Brigade who was located near San Juan Heights. Waddell requested that he be allowed to rejoin the Buffalo Soldiers who were part of the 10th cavalry regiment stationed nearby.

Colonel Pearson had no idea of what to do with two civilians and two soon-to-be retired sergeants and told them to find their own way. "Do whatever you fucking like. Just don't bother me," was the Colonel's exact words. So the four men found Waddell with the Buffalo Soldiers and offered their services. Waddell took them to the Regimental Quartermaster Lieutenant John Pershing, who was able to get the bedding and Waddell had them stay in his tent.

They did very little for the next few weeks, except to watch the troops train. They particularly enjoyed watching a cavalry detachment the men called the Rough Riders. Their commander Colonel Theodor Roosevelt was a flamboyant man, and his antics were entertaining. On June 30th the 10th Calvary Regiment, known by all as the Buffalo Soldiers, was told they would be part of the effort to take San Juan Heights. The attack was to take place on July 1st.

On the morning of July 1st, the 10th cavalry Regiment was ordered to advance towards the Spanish lines. The battle for San Juan Heights began. Horses could not be used because of the steepness of the hill so these cavalrymen would now be infantry.

As the American forces half crawled, half walked up the hill, the Spanish opened fire with their Mauser rifles. The .44 caliber bullets whizzed past their heads and at one point, Graham's campaign hat flew from his head. A soldier behind Graham picked it up and tossed it to him and said, "Gonna need some patching up Sarge."

"Thanks pal," George said, putting his finger in the hole the bullet had made.

Before the man could say anything else, he was hit in the head with a Mauser round and fell backward down the hill. George quickly turned and began returning fire. He hit a Spanish soldier who poked his head out of his trench, and George prayed that it was the one that had fired the shot that killed his fellow soldier. Waddell gave him the thumbs up.

Flannigan crawled up beside George and said, "Like the old days in Indochina, huh George?"

"Yeah, except we didn't have these goddamn cactus," George replied as he pulled a cactus barb from his leg.

Harry Hird and Charlie had gotten separated from Waddell,

Flannigan and George who were about 100 feet to the left. The battlefield experience was new for Charlie, but Harry was a seasoned veteran. He warned Charlie to keep as low a profile as possible and to keep firing as they ascended the hill.

The Spanish were rumored to have just under a thousand men on the hill and were outnumbered by the 19,000 American and rebel soldiers. But the Spaniards had the advantage of the high ground and were making it very difficult.

When Flannigan, Waddell and George were about halfway, the Spanish unleashed their Maxim machine gun. The Maxim could fire at the rate of six hundred rounds per minute. It was belt feed and deadly. American soldiers were dropping like flies until Flannigan stood up during a lull and was able to put a bullet in the shooter's eye. Before he could get down again, a Spanish soldier shot Flannigan. He fell backward, rolled down the hill several yards and was stopped by a small boulder.

George saw this and crawled back down to help Flannigan. He rolled Flannigan over and saw he was still alive. He needed immediate medical assistance, so George started to drag Flannigan down the hill. He didn't get more than ten feet before the Maxim opened up again and George was hit in the left arm and the right leg. He fell on top of Flannigan and passed out.

Charlie had seen Flannigan and George get hit, and a stab of fear for his friends ran through his body. "Harry, stay here," Charlie yelled, then stood up and ran across the battlefield, bullets hitting the dirt where he had just stood. When he was fifteen feet away, he flopped headfirst and slid on the dirt stopping next to George. He pulled George from Flannigan and smacked him on the face to wake him up.

Flannigan was conscious and gave a big grin and said, "What the fuck was that? You gotta be out of your mind."

"Shit, Flannigan I thought you were dead," Charlie said.

"Not yet. How's George?" Flannigan asked.

"Breathing."

Waddell crawled over and asked, "How are they?"

"Alive," Charlie answered. "I'm going to get them down to medical. You keep going, and I'll catch up later."

Waddell nodded in the affirmative, patted Flannigan on the head and started crawling up the hill.

Charlie couldn't wake George up so he told Flannigan to stay put and he started dragging George down the hill. It was dicey going, but finally he was at the bottom, and two medics rolled George on a stretcher and took him off to the doctor. Charlie started up the hill again. As he did, he heard a familiar rat-ta-tat-tat-tat sound. He instinctively knew that was the sound of Gatling guns. He turned and saw that the army had set up four guns and were shooting up the hill at the Spanish troops.

The constant barrage from the Gatling guns caused a lull in the shooting from the Spanish. Taking advantage of that Charlie sprinted up the hill, picked up Flannigan, threw him over his shoulder and ran back down. This time he ran all the way to the medical tents. He turned Flannigan over to a medic and said he was going back up the hill.

"I think we need to take care of that before you do any more fighting," the medic said and pointed to Charlie's crotch.

Charlie got a puzzled look on his face and looked down. Sticking into Charlie's privates were several cactus scrubs. The medics put him on a stretcher and took him with Flannigan.

"Oh fuck!" Charlie said.

By three o'clock the doctors had removed twenty cactus spines from Charlie's penis and testicles. They also cleaned and treated Flannigan's wounds. The bullet had broken his bone, and the medics put his leg in a cast. George was still unconscious, but the doctors were hopeful he would recover. The battle of San Juan Heights ended with an American victory an hour later.

On July 3rd, the U.S. Navy destroyed several Spanish warships in Santiago Bay and lay siege to the city. On July 5th Graham, who had come out of his coma and was doing well, Flannigan, Charlie and Harry Hird boarded a ship to the U.S. Waddell stayed with the 10th cavalry in Cuba. When they arrived in Jacksonville, Flannigan and George received an honorable discharge from the U.S. Army. Three days later they were cleared by the doctor to travel.

Charlie arranged to rent a full Pullman car, and on July 12th they boarded the train to Philadelphia. The Pullman was plush with sleeping cabins, a full bar and two porters to serve them.

"Charlie, I've meant to ask you something," Flannigan said.

"What's that?" Charlie asked.

"How did it feel to have twenty cactus spines stuck in your cock? Did it make you hard?" Flannigan said and laughed.

"That's funny. Ha, ha," Charlie said.

"You should have seen him. Dives like he was Phillies' Billy Hallman sliding into home base. Except Charlie here, lands on a bunch of Cuban scrub cactus. Didn't even know it until some doc told him," Flannigan said. They all laughed.

"I have a new name for Charlie. Want to hear it?" Flannigan asked.

"Do we have a choice?" George said.

"Charlie numbnuts," Flannigan said and laughed so hard he fell off the chair.

"Fuck you, Flannigan. I thought I did a good slide. Well, except for the cactus. I don't think I'll be getting any hard-ons for a while," Charlie said.

"Charlie, seriously, it was really something, dodging bullets as you ran across the hill. When you pulled George off of me..." Flannigan paused for a second. "Well, I almost cried. I didn't know if George was alive or if I would survive. You saved our lives," Flannigan said.

"If you were in the army you would have gotten a medal. You're a hero Charlie, and I will never forget it. We owe you our lives," George said as he held up his glass of Irish whiskey.

"Here, Here," Harry said and then all four men clinked glasses and drank.

"To tell the truth, I would have pissed myself if I hadn't had cactus spines in my dick," Charlie said.

They all laughed and finally George asked," What now, Charlie?"

"Well," Charlie said and paused. "Well, we go home, and we go straight. No more gunrunning. That's over now. Now we build Philadelphia. Things are happening again, and there's going to be a real need for housing, especially in North Philly. So we go home and make Byrne's Construction the best Philly has ever seen. All of us," Charlie said.

CHAPTER 40

Philadelphia 1899

George and Flannigan spent a couple of months healing from their wounds before joining Charlie at Byrne Construction. The company was doing well, thanks to Danny O'Boyle's influence. O'Boyle was now head of the zoning commission and introduced Charlie to several investors who had an interest in building out sections of North Philadelphia.

Charlie put together a plan to construct two-thousand row homes near Girard Avenue. The investors were impressed and put up the funds, with the promise that there would be more if Charlie's plans were successful. Just three months after the Spanish American War ended on August 13, 1898, Charlie broke ground on the first row of homes. Charlie was now the President of Philadelphia's fastest growing construction company.

As is often the case, success brings animosity. The USA's success over Spain added Cuba, Puerto Rico, Guam and the Philippines to its geography. By February 1899, fierce fighting broke out between the rebels of the First Philippine Republic and the United States. Jefferson Waddell and the Buffalo Soldiers were deployed to the Philippine Islands to fight that war.

For Charlie and Byrne Construction the animosity came from two established Philadelphia construction companies, Taylor and Sons, and Raymond Evans Construction. At first, they sought legal means to stop Charlie and when that failed they used slander. Articles were written in the local newspaper accusing Charlie of running a criminal enterprise, of using faulty materials to build homes and for employing Italian immigrant labor. The writers of the articles, who were being paid by Charlie's competition, called him a Mick, Harpy, Hibe and many other names derogatory to the Irish Catholics.

When this failed to discredit Byrne Construction, they hired remnants of a group of thugs from the Bloody Tubs gang which disbanded in the 1880s. The members were notorious practitioners of Nativism and hated all immigrants, especially Irish Catholics. At the beginning of the summer of 1899, several of Byrne's construction sites were vandalized and materials were stolen. Throughout the summer the attacks increased.

The police could do nothing to stop the vandalism. Charlie hired men from Kensington to guard the sites, but the Bloody Tubs beat one of Charlie's guards to death. That was the straw that broke the camel's back for Charlie. On September 4th he asked Danny O'Boyle, George, Flannigan and Harry Hird to dinner to discuss the problem and how to solve it.

Charlie poured each man a Jameson and then poured a small amount in the fireplace and said, "To John, wherever he may be." The others said, "To John."

"Charlie, where are Nathanial and Jacob? I have a small graduation gift for both of them," Danny asked.

"They took off last month for Florida to be with Ned and Emily. Jacob will be back later this month to start his first year at Penn. Nathanial's staying in Florida to help out with his parents' business. I'll miss him. Those boys are more like my brothers than my own brother," Charlie said.

"They're good kids," George said. Maybe it's good they're not here to see what we have to do."

"What's that? What are we going to do with these fucking Bloody Tubs and their bosses?" Flannigan asked.

"Since we got back from Cuba we've been trying to go straight and narrow. We stopped running guns to Ireland as the government asked. I don't want to give them any reason to dump on us, but we can't let those bastards get away with killing one of our men. We'll lose the respect of our construction crews," Charlie said.

"So what do we do? Come on, Charlie. Say it," Flannigan asked.

"We hit them where it hurts most. In the pocketbook. We do ten times the damage they do to us. No killing. Break an arm or leg if you have to, but no killing," Charlie said.

"And how do we pay for that? We don't have the money to fund an army of men," Danny said.

"We start running guns to Ireland again. I talked to Ginger Muller and his wife Ethel, and they are willing to run whatever we want to Ireland. They have the two ships. I still have contacts at several arms manufacturers, so supply won't be a problem. George, can you take care of that?" Charlie asked.

George nodded in the affirmative. There was no need to say anything as Charlie and he had already discussed this option.

"Flannigan, are you up to taking charge of the retribution?" Charlie asked.

"You really have to ask? Those sons of bitches won't know what hit them," Flannigan said then smiled.

"No killing, Flannigan. You okay with that?" Charlie said.

"Not really, but if you say so that's the way it will be. One exception though," Flannigan said. "If I find out who murdered Kevin O'Farrell, I'll kill him whether you like it or not. Kevin's mother and my sister are friends." Flannigan's family had moved to Philadelphia when his mother passed away in 1897. "And I made a promise. The guy had two young children for Christ's sake,"

Charlie looked at Flannigan for a full thirty seconds before he said, "Okay, but keep it low key,"

"Don't worry, Charlie. You won't even know when it happens," Flannigan said.

Charlie poured each man another Jameson, held up his glass and said, "Here's hoping this will be our last war."

Three days later Flannigan and ten of his men set fire to a large factory that was under construction by Taylor and Sons located at 3rd Street and Girard Avenue. The next evening they destroyed the interior of an almost finished office building built by Evans Construction located at 21st Street and Oregon Avenue. During the month Flannigan hit ten different construction sites.

At first, Taylor and Evans retaliated, but their efforts were weak and eventually stopped. By late November Charlie was convinced that his war with his competition was over. Graham continued to assemble weapons to send to Ireland to help build their war chest. Captain Muller scheduled the Lincoln to set sail to the port of Calais, France on December 1st, 1899. Once in Calais the weapons would be transferred to smaller fishing boats, sailed around England and on to Ireland and the resistance.

During one of his raids, Flannigan convinced a captured member of the Bloody Tubs gang to give him the name of the man who murdered Kevin O'Farrell. It took five broken fingers, but eventually, the gang member blurted out, “Tom Abbott.” The gang member was given $100 and put on a train to Chicago, with a warning that if he came back, he would be killed.

After days of following Tom Abbott, Flannigan and three of his men caught up with him the evening of November 30th as he left a bar alone. Flannigan told Abbott that he was going to beat him to death for killing Kevin O’Farrell, but that if Abbott were able to kill him first, he would be let go. Abbott was three inches taller than Flannigan and at least fifty pounds heavier, so he was not worried.

“You fucking Mick bastard. I’ll crush your skull like I did O’Farrell’s,” Abbott growled. Then suddenly he rushed towards Flannigan, knocking him down. He hit Flannigan in the face twice, before Flannigan was able to roll Abbott off. Both men quickly got to their feet, Flannigan threw a left punch at Abbott’s face and connected. Abbott backed up a few feet and shook his head to clear it then lunged out with a right hand. Flannigan stepped to the side, making Abbott miss.

As Abbott’s body came forward with his fist extended, Flannigan smashed his left fist into Abbott’s face and then his right hit with a crunch. As Abbott staggered backward Flannigan kicked Abbott in the groin. Abbott grabbed his privates, bent over and fell to the ground. Flannigan jumped on top of him and began to pummel Abbott’s head. As Flannigan administered his punishment he yelled, “Kevin had two sons, Sean and Jimmy. Now they have no father. His wife is a widow. His mother and father will never see him again. Remember this when you spend an eternity in hell.”

When it was evident that Abbott was dead, Flannigan’s men pulled him off of the body. They wrapped Abbott in a bed sheet and threw him in the back of their carriage.

"We'll take care of this, but first you need a doctor. Looks to me like you might have broken your hand," one of Flannigan's men said.

Flannigan looked at his hands, tried to move his right hand and couldn't and said, "Looks like it."

They dropped Flannigan off at a doctor that Charlie paid on retainer and then drove Abbott's body to the SS Lincoln. Muller had the body placed in a safe area. When the ship was in the middle of the Atlantic Ocean, Abbott's body was pitched over the side.

CHAPTER 41

Things between Charlie and his rivals remained quiet as Christmas approached. Philadelphia was, however, a hubbub of holiday activity. Store owners decorated their shops with lavish colors, John Wanamaker's department store held nightly concerts, and for the first time, the Salvation Army had placed red kettles outside major stores to collect money to feed the hungry. Next to the kettles, both to protect the donations and to foster collections, men dressed as Santa Claus rang bells to get attention. As was the custom, there were plenty of Christmas parties with good food and excellent spirits to drink.

Byrne's Construction held a large party for vendors, employees and their families on December 9th. It was a fun event and ended with employees receiving Christmas bonuses. Charlie always had his Christmas party and gave out bonuses early in the month because he remembered how hard it was for his parents to afford the trappings of the holiday. He wanted his employees to have both the money and time to buy their children gifts.

This year Mrs. Muller, Captain Muller's wife, and the widow of Captain Sean Murphy had hired a man to play Santa Claus and give children small gifts of candy. It was a big hit. Ethel Muller had started to organize the Byrne Construction event after the first year. That year Charlie, George Graham and Flannigan had ordered copious amounts of liquor but forgot to have food available. The next year she forbade, using her formidable Yankee attitude, to have any one of them involved. She said, "You three are the worst party givers I have ever met. I'll handle it from now on. You just pay for it and enjoy yourselves." No one argued and since then, the party had been a big hit.

Charlie and George Graham were watching Flannigan who was standing in line to see Santa Claus. "What the hell is Flannigan doing?" George asked.

"He said he never got a present from Father Christmas before and that he would be damned if he didn't get one now," Charlie said.

As they watched, Flannigan sat on Santa's lap making Santa a bit apprehensive. Charlie and Graham laughed as Santa placed two bags of candy in Flannigan's hands and pushed him off. Flannigan proudly walked off the platform and towards George and Charlie. He handed George a bag of candy and said, "Here, Santa said this is for you."

"Where's mine?" Charlie asked, making believe he was disappointed.

"Sorry Charlie, he said you've been a bad boy, and all you get is ashes in your stocking," Flannigan said.

"Is that so," Charlie said then grabbed the bag of candy from Flannigan.

"Hey, give me that back," Flannigan said, then grabbed Charlie and put him in a headlock.

All three men were laughing when Harry Hird walked up to them and said, "Is this a good time to introduce my Niece?"

George and Flannigan looked at Harry then at his niece. George sucked in a breath of air. She was the most beautiful woman he had ever seen. He couldn't talk so Flannigan said, still holding Charlie in a headlock, "Yes, of course."

Harry nodded his head and looked down at Charlie and opened his eyes wide. Flannigan looked down and realized he still had Charlie in a headlock and let him go. Charlie stood up, shook his head, brushed back his hair and smiled.

"That's better. Gentlemen, please meet my niece, Mercy Hird. Mercy, this wrestler is Flannigan," Harry said.

"Merry Christmas, Mr. Flannigan," Mercy said.

"And Merry Christmas to You, Miss Hird," Flannigan said.

"This rather tall gentleman is George Graham," Harry said.

"Merry Christmas, Mr. Graham," Mercy said.

George's mouth became so dry he couldn't properly talk. He croaked, "Merry Christmas, Miss Hird.

"Mr. Graham, are you ill? I suggest a cup of tea with honey and a bit of Jameson," Mercy said.

"No, no. I'm fine. Just a bit parched," George said.

"I'm glad to hear it, Mr. Graham."

"And last but not least, this is Charlie Byrne," Harry said.

"Merry Christmas, Mr. Byrne," Mercy said.

Charlie took Mercy's right hand and slowly bent over and kissed it and said, "Merry Christmas, Mercy."

"Mr. Byrne, it seems you've dropped your bag of candy," Mercy said, then she bent over and picked up the bag. She handed it to Charlie.

Charlie took the bag from Mercy, and in doing so, his fingers brushed against her hand. A warm feeling came over Charlie, and he said, "Thank you."

"If you fellows are available, I'm having a pre-Christmas dinner next Saturday. Bring Jacob with you, Charlie?" Harry asked.

All three men answered at the same time that they would be honored to attend. Charlie added, "Jacob will be traveling to Florida to be with his family for Christmas this Friday, so he won't be able to make it."

"Sorry Jacob won't be there, but Mrs. Hird and I are happy you can make it," Harry said.

"As am I," Mercy added.

"Where is Mrs. Hird?" Charlie asked.

"She's off with the grandkids sampling your fine food," Harry said. "I think we should go find her before the kids get sick on sweets. I'll see you Monday at work.

"And I'll see all of you next Saturday. Good day, gentlemen," Mercy said.

The three men watched as Mercy and Harry walked off. Mercy was stunning in her blue dress, white short-wasted jacket and her white hat with blue feathers.

Charlie drove Jacob to the train that Friday. The weather had changed, and there was a light covering of snow on the ground. The Olds was dong more sliding than rolling, but they arrived at the train station safe and sound.

"Pretty impressive, Uncle Charlie," Jacob remarked.

"What was impressive?" Charlie asked.

"Your driving in this snow," Jacob said.

"Oh, well that might have been more luck than skill," Charlie said. "How're your driving lessons going?"

"Great. Uncle Harry's a good teacher. He says that when I come back from break, he'll let me take out the Olds by myself," Jacob said and smiled broadly.

Charlie reached into the back seat and pulled a large bag decorated with a Santa Claus photo and said, "When you get home, give this to your Mom to put under the tree. It's just a few gifts from Flannigan, Uncle George and me."

"Thanks, Uncle Charlie, Jacob said and took the bag. "That reminds me. I have a gift for you," Jacob said and handed Charlie a small box. "You can open it now."

Charlie took the box, pulled the decorated paper off and opened the lid. Inside the box was a key. He smiled and asked, "What's this?"

"On Christmas Day before dinner, go to my room and open the door. Your gift will be there," Jacob said.

Charlie smiled again and said, "Okay, thank you." and then put the key in his suit pocket.

"You won't find a present in that bag from me. I've decided since you're a big college man now that when you get back from break, I am going to buy you an automobile. Any make you want, within reason," Charlie said.

"Are you kidding me?" Jacob said.

"No, I'm very serious. Look Jacob, you've done so well here. Finished high school at the top of your class and now your going to the University of Pennsylvania. You deserve it," Charlie said.

"I can't believe it. You're such a good friend, Uncle Charlie," Jacob said and hugged Charlie.

Charlie was a bit uneasy with the hugging. It wasn't something Irish men often did, but this was Jacob. As he hugged Jacob back, he said, "Jacob, you're family, not just a friend."

When Jacob let go of Charlie, he wiped tears from his eyes and said, "Okay, I have to go now. I'll see you next year." He jumped out of the Olds and started towards the terminal, the porter behind him with his luggage.

"Jacob. You forget something?" Charlie yelled and held up the bag of gifts.

The next day Charlie, George and Flannigan dressed in their finest suits and met at Charlie's house. They walked five city blocks to Harry Hird's home where they were attending an early Christmas dinner. As they walked three abreast down the Philadelphia streets, women couldn't help but look at them wishing their husbands were so well dressed. Charlie was sporting a three-button dark gray suit and a white shirt with a royal blue ascot. His dark gray Homburg hat tilted at just the right angle, and his overcoat was unbuttoned to show off his gold watch chain.

Flannigan was wearing a five-button unconventional brown suit, no overcoat and a Stetson hat tilted down to just cover the tips of his eyebrows. George, who towered over both Flannigan and Charlie, was wearing a navy blue suit, a long black overcoat and a black Homburg hat placed squarely on his head.

Halfway there, George noticed a man walking towards them. He was weaving back and forth and was obviously drunk. Still, George stuck his hand in his overcoat pocket and grabbed the handle of his Colt revolver. The man had his head down and just as he passed the trio, he weaved in front of Flannigan, and the two men collided.

"Hey pal, watch where you're going," Flannigan yelled.

The man just grunted and continued to walk. George watched him until he was a safe distance away.

By the time they had walked another block, Flannigan was complaining about being cold.

"Damn it, it's cold," Flannigan said.

"I told you to wear a coat," George said.

Well, I fucked up. What can I say," Flannigan said.

"You could have said, you're right, George. I'll go get my coat," George said.

"Jesus Flannigan, if you're that cold, do you want my coat?" Charlie asked.

"Yes, that would be very kind of you, Charlie," Flannigan said.

"Well, keep wanting and remember every decision you make has a consequence," Charlie said.

"Fucking asshole," Flannigan said. All three men laughed.

Harry Hird's home was a three story row home that Harry purchased six months after returning from Cuba. That particular row of homes was larger than most of the others in the area. Charlie used the brass door knocker, and Harry's wife Ellen answered the door.

"Oh don't you boys look handsome. Come in. It's cold out," Ellen said. When she saw Flannigan had no coat, she said, "Mr. Flannigan, where's your coat? You're going to catch your death. Come with me. I'll get you some spirits to warm you up."

Flannigan went off with Ellen Hird to get a drink, and Charlie and George walked over to a table where Danny O'Boyle was discussing politics with Harry Hird.

"All I know, Harry is they're saying city hall will be completed and opened by mid-year 1901," Danny said.

George put his arm around Danny's head and rubbed the back of his neck with his knuckles and said, "You got a haircut, Danny."

"Cut it out, George before I get angry and lay you out."

"Oh, in that case, I'll let you go. Wouldn't want to get Danny angry," George said and let Danny go.

Danny got up and shook George's hand and said, "It's good to see you guys. It's been too long." Then he shook Charlie's hand and said, "Where's that savage Flannigan?"

"Off with Harry's wife to get a drink," Charlie answered.

"I'd better go save him. She'll be mothering him all night.

Danny, come with me, and you can say hello to Flannigan. Charlie, George, Mercy's in the kitchen if you'd like to greet her," Harry said.

"Yes sir, Sergeant," Charlie said and saluted.

"Sorry. Old habits are hard to change," Harry said.

Charlie and George stood in the doorway to the kitchen gaping at Mercy. She was wearing a dark green gown and had a red choker around her neck. Mercy also was wearing a white apron and was stacking cookies and small cakes on platters. When she saw Charlie and George, she said, "Don't move. I'll come to you." She grabbed two cookies and walked to the doorway.

"Here, try these and tell me if you like them," Mercy said and placed one cookie each in Charlie and George's mouth. "Go ahead, chew."

Charlie was the first to finish the cookie and said, "Wonderful." George still eating nodded his affirmation.

"Gentlemen," Mercy said, "you're standing in a very dangerous spot,"

Charlie and George quickly looked around, and when they saw nothing, they looked back at Mercy. Mercy stuck her index finger out and pointed up. George and Charlie followed her finger and saw a large sprig of mistletoe attached to the top of the doorway.

"The legend says if I don't kiss you I'll have bad luck all year," Mercy said, then leaned over and kissed George on his lips. He immediately turned red. Charlie stood waiting with anticipation for Mercy's red lips to connect with his. She sensed this and purposely waited a minute and then kissed Charlie on his right cheek.

Charlie smiled and thought, *this is my kind of woman. She knows how to handle me.* Then Mercy kissed him on the lips and said, "Come on, you two can help me take these platters to the dessert table."

Harry Hird's wife, daughters, Mercy and several other women began preparing the dinner at five that morning to get it ready by three in the afternoon. It was a feast to behold. They served roast turkey with cranberry sauce, rice croquettes, asparagus tips, braised duck, baked macaroni, lettuce salad, wafers and Brie cheese, English plum pudding with brandy sauce, coffee, nuts, fruits and sugar plums. Of course, the wine, brandy, and whiskey flowed freely.

By the time Ellen served the coffee, Charlie, Danny and George had to loosen their belts. Flannigan, who ate sparingly and drank copiously, was falling asleep at the table. After coffee, the men moved to the living room, and Harry poured them a Jameson.

Harry held his glass up and said Merry Christmas. The men replied in same, and they downed their shots. Harry filled their glasses again. Flannigan had several more drinks and finally fell asleep on the sofa.

"Should I wake him?" George asked.

"No, let him sleep. He can stay here tonight. I have a spare room on the third floor," Harry said.

George nodded and picked up Flannigan in his arms and started towards the stairs. "George, what are you doing?" Harry asked.

"I'm putting him to bed. He'll not wake until tomorrow. It happens more often than not," George said, then turned and walked up to the third floor, plopped Flannigan in the bed and put a blanket on him.

Within an hour the women joined the men, bringing with them dishes of nuts, dried fruit and a pitcher of eggnog. The men refused their offer of eggnog, so the women filled their own glasses. Harry stood up again and said, "To a wonderful meal prepared by the fairest beauties of the realm." Everyone said, "Here, here" and drank their drinks.

Danny O'Boyle asked to be pardoned. He had a city event he was obligated to attend. "Goodbye Mr. Mayor," Charlie said and smiled.

"Funny man. Maybe someday?" Danny said.

"We're all voting for you Danny," Harry said. Danny waved goodbye and left.

"Mrs. Hird, George, I and Flannigan, if he were awake, want to thank you for allowing us to be part of your wonderful family's celebration of Christ's birthday and a meal I consider to be the best I have ever consumed," Charlie said.

"You're most welcome anytime, Charlie," Mrs. Hird said.

"I was wondering if you could answer a question for me?" Charlie asked.

"Of course," Mrs. Hird answered.

"Why is it you have your Christmas dinner five days before Christmas? Is there a religious significance?"

"In a way there is. You see, on Christmas Eve we make food, and on Christmas day we take it to Old Saint Mary's Church and feed the poor and homeless. It was Mercy's idea, and we've been doing it, as a family, for three years now. It's so heartwarming to see the children open the small gifts we give them. For some it's the only Christmas gift they have ever received," Mrs. Hird said.

Charlie stared at Mercy for a long minute and said, "What a great idea, Mercy. George and I would love to make a donation to the cause. Would $2,000 be enough?" Charlie said. While he spoke, Charlie thought *What a beautiful woman she is inside and out.*

Harry Hird who was drinking coffee when Charlie made his offer, choked. Mrs. Hird hit Harry on the back to help him swallow whatever he was choking on.

Mercy said, "Oh my. That's a considerable sum. Are you sure?"

"Absolutely, it's the duty of every God blessed person with wealth to share it with the needy," Charlie said.

A tear rolled down Mercy's cheek, and she said, "I don't know what to say. That's so kind of you. Thank you."

"I'll add another $500," George said. "I remember all too well how it feels to go hungry. Flannigan will give $500 as well."

"Are you sure, George? Mr. Flannigan is in no shape to make that offer," Mercy said.

"I'm sure. Flannigan also knows what it's like to have his family go hungry. It's the least we can do," George said.

"Thank you, George, and please thank Mr. Flannigan," Mercy said.

Mercy stood up and kissed George on the cheek and then did likewise to Charlie, and said, "I have a wonderful idea. Why don't you and George come help us serve on Christmas day? Bring Mr. Flannigan if he wishes to come."

"Well," Charlie paused to think then said, "Yes of course. I would love to."

"Count Flannigan and me in, Mercy," George said.

"Wonderful," Mercy said. "Oh, we're all going to the Arch Street Opera House on the 23rd at seven to see a performance of A Christmas Carol. It stars Billy Hallman as Mr. Scrooge. Would you like to go?" Mercy asked.

Realizing it was another chance to be with Mercy, Charlie immediately said, "Yes, I love hearing those old carols."

"No Charlie, it's a play, but I do think they sing a carol or two," Mercy said.

"Oh! Better yet. Yes, I would love to go," Charlie said.

"I'm sorry, I promised my family I would spend a couple of days with them so I won't be able to go," George said.

"And Mr. Flannigan?" Mercy asked.

"He'll be with me," George answered.

"You said Billy Hallman was playing Mr. Scrooge. Is that the baseball player?" Charlie asked.

"Yes, he's also an actor during the off seasons." Mercy said.

"I didn't know that. He's one of my favorite Phillies," Charlie said.

"Yes, he's quite accomplished," Mercy said.

At around eight that evening Mrs. Hird served ham sandwiches, cookies Mercy had made and coffee. After coffee and the snack, George and Charlie said their goodbyes and began to walk back to Charlie's house. George was staying the evening at Charlie's since his family still lived in Kensington, and it would be a long trip at night.

After walking around a city block, George saw four men standing on the corner across the street from them and pointed them out to Charlie.

"Probably leaving a party just like us," Charlie said.

George wasn't so sure and grabbed the handle of his Colt. The men crossed the street when they got closer. Charlie tensed but kept walking. George suddenly recognized the drunk who had fallen against Flannigan. He pulled the Colt from his pocket and put his hand behind his back.

"One of those guys is that fucking drunk we ran into coming over here," George said.

"See the red bands around their arms? These boys are Bloody Tubs," Charlie said. George and Charlie stopped walking and waited for the four thugs to come to them.

CHAPTER 42

The four Bloody Tub gang members stopped about twenty feet from Charlie and George. A man as tall as George stepped forward a couple of feet and said, "Where you Micks going? No fish eating fucking Irish bastards are allowed on this street. This," he paused and spread his arms," is a Bloody Tub's street. Turn around and run off like good little boys."

"I don't think so. My feet hurt and we're pretty close to our house. So we'll just keep going," George said.

The man took two more steps closer and said, "You're not walking down this street without us breaking your fucking Mick heads."

"What's your name?" George asked.

"Tim," The man lied.

Tim, let's settle this like men. You and me, one on one, no holds barred. I win, you and your men let us continue. You win, and we'll turn around. What do you say?" George said.

"I say you're in for the beating of your life," the man said and rushed at George. George quickly stepped to his left, swung his arm with the gun in it around and hit the man in the temple. The man was stunned but didn't go down, so George hit him three more times in very fast succession. The man fell to the ground, and George jumped on top of him and smashed the gun in the man's face several times.

The other Bloody Tubs started towards George's, fists at the ready. George leveled the Colt at them and said, "I'd love to blow one or all of your brains out." They stopped in their tracks.

"Hands up. knees on the ground," George ordered.

Charlie walked behind the men and searched them. He found knives but no guns. Then he tapped on one of the men's head and said, "Crawl over there and check to see if your boss is still alive."

The man did as Charlie ordered and put his head on the boss's chest to listen for a heartbeat. "He's alive."

"Good, but he won't be for long unless you tell me who put you up to this. In fact, none of you will," George said.

One of the men kneeling said, "No one."

George took the gun and placed the barrel in the man's mouth closest to him and said, "Speak up, I didn't hear you."

"Okay, okay. Raymond Evans gave us a fiver each to rough you up."

"You don't say. Well, when you wake up, you tell Tim here that you fucking rubba dub tub boys are going to have to get a lot tougher if you want to fuck with the Irish," George said and then kicked the man in the face knocking him out. Charlie did the same to the two men kneeling. When all four of the Bloody Tub gangsters were unconscious on the street, Charlie and George walked home.

The next evening George assembled nine men. Five went with Charlie to kidnap Francis Taylor, and four went with

George and a still suffering from a hangover Flannigan to take Raymond Evans.

Taylor lived in South Philadelphia and Evans in West Philly. Both snatches were pretty easy. Charlie's and George's men put hoods over their heads, knocked on the door and when the housekeeper answered they went in the house, blinded folded the target and marched him out. They were at one of Charlie's warehouses before the police even knew about the kidnappings.

Charlie sat Evans and Taylor at a table that had a white linen cloth on it. There were whiskey, wine and several different snacks. He, George and Flannigan sat in the seats across from Taylor and Evans. Then Charlie had his men untie and take the hoods off of his guests,

Immediately, Taylor yelled, "What the fuck is going on? Do you know who I am?" When his eyes adjusted to the light, he saw Charlie and said, "You bastard. How do you get the balls to kidnap me?"

"You're not kidnapped, Francis. We just wanted to have a meeting with you and Raymond. So be quiet for a minute, and I'll tell you what we want," Charlie said.

"What you want? Fuck you. Let me tell you what I want. I want to put my foot up your ass," Taylor said.

Charlie nodded to one of his men, who immediately put a gag in Taylor's mouth. Charlie said, "Just listen, Francis. When you calm down, we'll take the gag out and you can have a drink. Raymond, can I pour you something?" Charlie said.

"Whiskey," Raymond Evans said. Charlie poured Evans a Jameson, then one for George and himself. Flannigan had sworn off drinking at least until the next party.

"To your health, gentlemen," Charlie said and drank his Jameson, as did the others, then he said, "Francis, can I take out that gag? Will you just take a few minutes to listen to me?" Francis Taylor nodded yes. Charlie motioned to one of his men and he took the gag from Taylor.

Charlie poured Taylor a drink, then Evans, George and himself and said, "Here's to a profitable relationship for all three of us."

"Profitable, eh. How so?" Taylor asked.

"This fight between us cost a lot of money for both of us. You burn our houses down, I burn your factories. You hire men to do it. I hire men to stop you. It's all unproductive and very expensive. Philadelphia is big enough for all three of us. Things are happening here, and we can capitalize on the growth. Look, a new century starts in ten days. 1900 will be the beginning of a new era, and we can help build that," Charlie said.

"What do you propose?" Evans asked.

"Frances, you have all of South Philly. Raymond, you have West Philly, and we have North Philly. Downtown and anything out of the city will be open for competitive fair bidding. We all get our piece of the pie," Charlie said.

"How would that work? Our clients are going to want bids from all parts of Philadelphia," Taylor said.

"We bid on all, only if it's a bid for North Philly, you overbid to ensure I'm the low bidder. I do the same for both of you in your territories. If we have any differences, we sit down like reasonable men and work them out and not burn down each other's buildings. What do you say?"

"What happens if we don't agree?" Evans asked.

Flannigan smiled and said, "I murder you in your sleep."

After four more drinks and more clarification, Taylor and Evans agreed. They had a few more drinks, shook hands and Taylor and Evans were taken home. The story for the police and families was that they had joined a new club and the fake kidnapping was part of the initiation.

With the Taylor and Evans troubles now behind them, 1900 was starting to look like it would truly be a prosperous year. Charlie made arrangements for Captain Muller and Ethel to take over the gunrunning to Ireland operation. For the first time in a very long time Charlie, George and Flannigan were one hundred percent legal.

On December 23rd, Charlie went to see A Christmas Carol with the Hird family. He and Mercy sat next to each other and during the scary parts of the play, Mercy would grab Charlie's hand. It wasn't that Mercy was really afraid or for that matter required protection. Even in the modern era of 1899 soon to be 1900, it was not seemly for a woman to profess her attraction to a man to whom she was not married. That declaration required the woman's subtle actions such as grabbing a man's hand in a scary situation. Other methods included brushing up against the man, or in cases where the woman wanted to meet someone they didn't know dropping a scarf, glove or kerchief. In Mercy's case, she already decided that Charles Byrne would be her husband. Now all she had to do was make him feel the same way.

When the show was over, the family went to Bookbinder's, new restaurant at Second and Walnut Streets to have supper then home to Harry's house.

"Charlie, I am so happy you could make it tonight. I hope you liked the show," Mercy said.

"Thank you for inviting me. I did like the play. But I liked the company better," Charlie said.

"So I'll see you Christmas morning then?" Mercy asked.

"Of course. What time do you want me here?" Charlie asked.

"We start serving at noon, so can you be here at six in the morning?"

"Okay. I'll tell George and Flannigan to meet us at the church," Charlie said. He pulled an envelope from his suit pocket, handed it to Mercy and said, "As promised $3000 for the poor."

"This is beyond generous, Charlie. Please thank George and Flannigan. This money will feed a lot of people all year," Mercy said.

Mercy leaned forward and kissed Charlie on the lips and said, "Thank you, Charlie. You're truly a good Christian. I'll light a candle for your continued good health and prosperity."

"I already feel blessed," Charlie said then kissed Mercy.

At noon on Christmas day Harry Hird opened the doors to the church's hall. Hundreds of people flooded in and took their places in line to receive Christmas dinner. Even though most of the country was segregated, the Hird's Community Christmas dinner was open to all races, religions, and people with different national origins. It truly reflected the melting pot of people that made up the United States.

The hall was set up with twenty long tables. Each table had large pitchers of apple cider and bowls of candied fruits placed at intervals. By one in the afternoon, the tables were full of families and single people who were enjoying their first hot meal in months.

Mercy and her volunteers had come to the hall on Christmas Eve day and decorated it to reflect the Christmas spirit. A large Christmas tree stood in the southwest corner of the hall. Under it was hundreds of small bags of candy for the children. Flannigan was designated by Mercy to stand by the tree and pass out the candy. To help make it more festive, she had Flannigan wear a red coat and a green top hat she had gotten for a past Saint Patrick's Day parade.

George Graham's job was to stand at the entrance and be sure that the crowds remained orderly. There were a couple of small incidents when street thugs tried to bully their way to the front of the line, but George handled them. In one case he took the man by the back of his britches and tossed him out the door as the crowd cheered.

Charlie was in charge of keeping the cider pitchers full. As he went from table to table, he talked to the guests and was truly interested to hear their stories. Some stories revealed that the people were in this situation because of their own actions. Others were destitute for no reason other than fate. It surprised Charlie to see so many military veterans. They served in America's many wars dating back to the Civil War and now couldn't get jobs. After a couple of hours of hearing stories, Charlie realized that it didn't matter why these people were here. It only mattered that they needed help.

There was a young boy about eight years old sitting by himself. His head was bent over, and he was crying. His plate was full, but he had not touched it.

"What's the matter, kiddo?" Charlie asked the child.

The child just kept his head down and said nothing. Charlie said, "It's okay. You can tell me. Did someone hurt you?"

"No," the boy replied weakly.

"Then what is it? Why are you crying?" Charlie persisted.

"It's my Ma. She's sick," the boy said and sobbed.

"Where is she?"

"Outside in the courtyard," the boy said.

"Why didn't she come in?"

"She made me come in and eat. She said she was too weak and wasn't hungry."

"Come on, let's go see her," Charlie said and took the boy's hand.

Charlie found the boy's mother slumped against the courtyard fence. She was semi-conscious and looked awful. Charlie picked the woman up in his arms and rushed back to the hall. He asked George Graham to send someone to fetch the doctor he kept on retainer. "Write a note and tell the doctor I don't care if it's Christmas, get his ass down here as fast as you can," Charlie said.

Charlie found a small room that had a sofa. He laid the woman on it and said to the boy, "Go to the hall and ask someone who Mercy is and bring her back here."

When Mercy arrived, he explained what was happening and that he needed some blankets for the woman. Mercy ran to the rectory and had the housekeeper give her two warm blankets. She rubbed the woman's hands to help warm them and said a prayer for her.

The doctor arrived thirty minutes later, examined the woman and suggested that they take her to the new Hahnemann Hospital on North 15th Street.

"Doc, tell the hospital that I'll pay the bills. I want her to get first class treatment. I'll bring her boy after he eats and we close," Charlie said. Then he asked the boy, "What's your Ma's name?"

"Morris," the boy said.

"What's her first name?"

"Ma."

Charlie smiled and guessed he didn't know his mother's name when he was eight either."

"What's your name?" Charlie asked.

"Paddy."

"Paddy, the doctor is going to take your mother to the hospital. I want you to stay here and get a good meal. I'll take you to see your Ma when we're done. Is that okay?" Charlie asked.

"Yes, sir."

Charlie sent someone to find a taxi. When it arrived, he carried Mrs. Morris outside and placed her on one of the seats. The doctor jumped in and said, "Hahnemann Hospital, North 15th Street."

Once the taxi was away, Charlie and Mercy took Paddy back in the hall and had Flannigan give him two bags of candy. Flannigan said, trying to act like Saint Nicolas, "Paddy, you be a good boy and eat your supper before you eat this candy."

"Yes sir, I will."

Once he got Paddy situated, Charlie started filling cider pitchers again. At four Harry Hird closed the doors. The Christmas dinner was over. At five the last person left the hall, save for Paddy Morris who was waiting for Charlie to take him to the hospital to see his Ma.

Mercy insisted that she go with Charlie and Paddy to see Mrs. Morris. When they arrived at Hahnemann hospital, Charlie's doctor was just leaving. Mercy took Paddy to sit in a small waiting room while Charlie asked about Mrs. Morris.

"Mrs. Morris, we believe, is suffering from malnutrition. She is as thin as a rail. I'm assuming she has been feeding her son at her own expense. She'll need to stay in the hospital a few days. I think some good meals will do her wonders. Now if you don't mind, Mr. Byrne I'm going home and finish my Christmas dinner," the doctor explained.

"Of course, Doc. I really appreciate your helping out. My appreciation will be in your next payment," Charlie said.

The doctor nodded his head and left the hospital. Thirty minutes later Paddy and his mother were reunited. Charlie made arrangements for Paddy to stay in his mother's room while she was in the hospital. Then he wrote a letter saying that when Mrs. Morris was able, she was to talk to Ethel Muller in his office. It stated that Ethel find suitable employment for Mrs. Morris if she desired it. If not she was to give her $200 cash.

By the time Charlie escorted Mercy home and then walked the five blocks to his house, he was bone tired. Good works were more strenuous than Charlie thought.

When he opened the door to his house, there was a telegram lying on the floor. It surprised Charlie until he realized that he had given his housekeeper off for Christmas. He picked up the telegram and laid it on a small table next to his favorite chair. He then poured himself a large glass of Jameson and sat down. He reflected on what wonderful things had happened that week. He was officially courting Mercy, the problems with competition were over, and he had truly helped people in need. He was proud of himself and vowed to do more. He was a happy man.

He took a sip of Jameson and opened the telegram.

CHAPTER 43

Charlie read the telegram three times before it registered in his mind. He stood up but his knees buckled, and he fell to the floor. Charlie's heart started to beat fast, and he became dizzy. He wanted to scream but he couldn't, so he just pounded his fists on the wooden floor. Finally, he yelled, "No, no. Not him."

He stood up and walked to the telephone, almost falling twice. He picked up the phone and hit the cradle a few times. His voice was so shaky the operator had to ask him to repeat the number three times. Finally, there was an answer.

"George, come to my house now. I need to talk to you. Bring Flannigan," Charlie said, his voice still quivering.

"Christ Charlie, I just got home. I'm tired," George said.

"Now George. Come to my fucking house now," Charlie yelled.

George realized something was seriously wrong and said, "We'll be there as soon as we can." Charlie hung up, poured another whiskey and sat in his chair. He placed the telegram on the table, put his hands over his eyes and started to cry.

Thirty minutes later George found Charlie in the same

position. Realizing George and Flannigan were in his house Charlie took his hands from his eyes, picked up the telegram and handed it to George. Both George and Flannigan were alarmed at how bad Charlie looked.

George read the telegram and said, "No, this can't be true. God no."

Flannigan grabbed the telegram from George and read it out loud. "December 25, 1899. Ned, Jacob lost at sea 12/23/99. Presumed dead. It's signed by Nathanial,"

Flannigan sat down heavily on the sofa, letting the telegram fall from his hand. The three men sat for over an hour saying nothing.

Charlie finally said, "We have to go to Florida."

They couldn't sleep that night and the next morning while George and Flannigan made arrangements to travel to Florida, Charlie went to see Mercy.

When Charlie told Mercy about the death of Jacob and Ned, she immediately put her arms around him and hugged him tightly. It felt good to Charlie. Her arms were like a temporary refuge against the horror of Jacob's and Ned's deaths.

"I have to go to Florida, Mercy. I want to be with you for New Year's Eve, but I won't be back until at least a week later," Charlie said, wiping the tears from his eyes, so Mercy didn't see his weakness.

"Of course you do," Mercy said. Warm tears rolled down Mercy's alabaster cheeks. She didn't know Jacob and Ned, but she felt Charlie's pain, and that hurt her. She had, in just a few short weeks, fallen madly in love. She continued, "Charlie, don't worry about me. We'll have a lifetime together."

Charlie looked into Mercy's eyes and saw true compassion. He kissed her and said, "Yes, we will."

Later that day, while packing for his trip to Florida, Charlie decided that he would take a few of Jacob's personal items to give to his mother. The rest he would have shipped to her. He dreaded going into Jacob's bedroom and avoided it most of the day until he remembered the key Jacob had given him. He told Charlie that when he opened the door, his Christmas present would be in his room. Charlie found the key in the watch pocket of the suit he wore when he took Jacob to the train station.

With great trepidation, Charlie placed the key in the lock and opened the door to Jacob's bedroom. The first thing he saw was a painter's easel, with a painting on it that was covered by a large cloth. There was a note on the cloth that said, For Uncle Charlie, Love Jacob. Jacob's smell permeated the room. It was a combination of teenage sweat, shaving soap and a lotion Charlie had bought for Jacob to control his facial blemishes.

Charlie slowly approached the painting and lifted the cloth. Under the cloth was a portrait of Jacob and Charlie standing in front of the Cathedral Basilica of Saints Peter and Paul. It was signed by Jacob. He used his real last name Nokosi.

When Charlie, George and Flannigan disembarked from the train in West Palm Beach, the temperature was a warm and breezy seventy-five degrees. It was like spring in Philadelphia. Nathanial was waiting with a carriage and took them to the Natoli home. When they turned into the entrance to the farm, they noticed that field hands were harvesting crops of tomatoes. Philadelphia wouldn't see tomatoes until July.

On the way to see Emily Nathanial explained what they knew about the accident that took his Father and brother's lives. "My Dad wanted to go fishing and asked Jacob and me if we wanted to go with him. I had work to do so I declined. Jacob was excited to go. I took them to the boat on the morning of the 23rd and waited until they set sail then came home.

We expected them to be out all day, but when they hadn't returned by eight that evening we began to worry. I thought maybe they lost a sail or something and were stranded in the water somewhere off the coast. The next morning I contacted the U.S. Life Saving Service, and they conducted a search. Later that day a fisherman from Palm Beach found the boat capsized about a mile out in the Atlantic." When Nathanial finished his story, his eyes were glistening.

Emily Natoli (formally Nokosi) was a strong woman, and she maintained her composure until the day of the memorial for Ned and Jacob. They took a large powered boat to the spot the fisherman had found the capsized boat and laid a wreath in the ocean. In reverence to the ancient Seminole tradition, Emily threw several personal items for both Ned and Jacob in the ocean.

They returned to land and had a memorial ceremony at the Natoli farm where Emily had a large stone engraved with an inscription that read *Love begins in a moment, grows over time, and lasts an eternity.* After the priest performed the Rite of Committal and said the Lord's Prayer, the small group of attendees laid flowers on the gravestone. Emily kneeled in front of the stone, made a hole in the ground and placed Ned's wedding ring and a small gold necklace Jacob had worn as a child in it and covered it with dirt. This was too much, even for a woman as strong as Emily. She placed her forehead on the dirt and sobbed.

While the world celebrated the turning of the century on New Year's Eve the Natoli family, Charlie, George and Flannigan sat quietly in Emily's living room. Mary Natoli began to cry, and her mother Emily consoled her.

"My mother believed that when a person dies, they become part of nature. While we cannot see or hear them, they are all around us. What they gave of their self to us when they were alive lives on in us. As a Catholic, I believe in heaven and everlasting life and that someday we will see the departed again. I hope both are true," Emily said.

Charlie lifted his glass of Champaign and said, "To Ned and Jacob. May they always be with us."

Chapter 44

Philadelphia - New Year's Day 1901

When the clock struck midnight, Charlie kissed Mercy and wished her a Happy New Year. He then asked her to sit down. He kneeled in front of her, held out a small box and opened it. In the box was a diamond ring. A tear rolled down Mercy's cheek as Charlie asked, "Mercy, will you marry me?"

"Oh Charlie, I am going to have to think about that," Mercy said and paused. Charlie's smile faded. "Of course I'll marry you," Mercy continued.

"Jesus Christ, you almost gave me a heart attack," Charlie said and kissed Mercy.

"Charles Connor Byrne, no cursing please," Mercy chided then smiled and kissed him.

"I have another gift for you," Charlie said as he pulled from his pocket a diamond-encrusted locket on a gold chain. He opened the locket and showed Mercy, and said, "I want you to always remember me as I was the day I proposed."

Mercy took the locket and said, "And a very handsome man he is. My picture's not too bad either. Thank you, Charlie. When we celebrate our fiftieth anniversary, with our children, grandchildren and great grandchildren surrounding us, you can be sure I'll still be wearing this around my neck and close to my heart." Mercy kissed Charlie first on the forehead, then on each cheek and finally on his lips.

"You made me a very happy man. So happy I want to dance," Charlie said. Then he took Mercy's hand and led her back to the ballroom. The band was playing an Irish waltz. As Mercy and Charlie danced, George and Flannigan stood watching. When they caught Charlie's eye, Flannigan held his hands out and made a face, in effect asking Charlie if she said yes. As Charlie turned, he made the okay sign.

George and Flannigan clicked their glasses together and toasted. They had endured two months of Charlie's worrying, indecision about which ring to chose and hesitation due to fear of rejection and they were happy it all had a positive outcome.

As the couple danced, George thought, *if the circumstances had been different, I might be marrying Mercy.* Oddly, George wasn't jealous. He loved both Charlie and Mercy and hoped only the best for them. He had long ago determined that he was destined to be a bachelor and he reconciled himself to that fact of his life.

"When are you going to tell Charlie?" George asked Flannigan.

"Not tonight. He's happy, and I don't want to take away from that. I'll do it Tuesday when we meet at his office.

Charlie, George, Flannigan and sometimes Danny met every Tuesday at Charlie's office for a business lunch. In reality, it was just an opportunity to get together, have a few drinks and reminisce. Mercy told Charlie the only difference between a men's business lunch and a women's tee party was that the men drank

Jameson and the women preferred Gin. In both cases, it was a chance to gossip, reminisce and let off steam.

Flannigan raised his glass and said, "Congratulations to Charlie and Mercy on their impending wedding. My Pa, rest his soul, had a blessing he said at every wedding. If I may, I would like to say it for you, Charlie."

Charlie answered, "I'd be honored."

"Okay then, here it is. For you Charlie and your wonderful bride Mercy," Flannigan said, and then look down.

"MAY YOU ALWAYS WALK IN THE SUNSHINE.
MAY YOU NEVER WANT FOR MORE.
MAY IRISH ANGELS REST THEIR WINGS
RIGHT BESIDE YOUR DOOR.
MAY YOUR TROUBLES BE LESS,
AND YOUR BLESSINGS BE MORE.
AND NOTHING BUT HAPPINESS,
COME THROUGH YOUR DOOR."

"Thank you, Flannigan," Charlie said, paused and continued. "Now who wants a bit of Jameson?"

George, Flannigan and Danny pushed their glasses to the center of the table. Charlie filled them with Jameson. Then he held up his glass and said, "To John, may he rest in peace. I owe him much. If he hadn't brought the three of you to Philadelphia, we would never have met," Charlie said, then poured a small amount of the whiskey on the floor. The four men held their glasses up and drank the whiskey.

"You know Charlie, if George here hadn't stolen that sack of potatoes back in Letterkenny, I would have never met him in prison. George and I would not have found Danny on our way to

Dublin, and the three of us wouldn't have met Sergeant McGrath and joined the Foreign Legion. If we weren't in the legion, we would never have met John who brought us to Philadelphia where we met you. And if we didn't meet you, it's doubtful you would have met Mercy. So it was George that was responsible for you and Mercy getting married," Flannigan said.

"You're right, Flannigan. I propose a toast to the potato thief, George Graham. He's my friend, and he is my brother, as are all of you. May we always be together," Charlie said."

Flannigan squirmed in his chair then said, "Charlie, Danny I have something to tell you."

Charlie and Danny looked at Flannigan and waited. After a pause, Flannigan said, "I'm moving to Florida to be with Emily Natoli."

"What do you mean moving to Florida? Do you mean for good?" Danny asked.

Flannigan turned red. "Yes, I am hoping that I can get her to marry me one day."

"When did this all happen? Damn Flannigan, I don't want you to go," Charlie said.

"Charlie, I don't want to leave, but I love her. It's time I settled down," Flannigan said.

"What about your family? It took you years to convince them to leave Ireland, and now you're moving away from them," Charlie said.

"They're moving with me, Charlie," Flannigan said.

"So you're dead set on moving. Nothing I can say or do to keep you here?" Charlie asked.

"I've thought about this for a long time and I dreaded telling you, and telling George was like putting a knife in my liver. We've not been apart since we met in prison. Charlie, you have Mercy,

Danny's got his wife, and he'll be mayor hopefully next year, and George has you, and he'll find a wife soon. Is it so wrong that I want the same thing?" Flannigan asked.

Charlie looked at Flannigan for a long time then said, "You deserve the best life has to offer. If that's Emily, I hope to God it works out for you. We love you, Flannigan. Promise me you'll visit at least once a year."

"I promise."

"Okay then. Let me fill up your glasses," Charlie said and once he did he continued, "Flannigan, I'm going to miss you more than you can imagine. To Bill Flannigan, the finest hooligan I have ever met."

Flannigan laughed and said, "Hooligan is it?" and grabbed Charlie by the head. He rubbed Charlie's scalp with his knuckles and said, "Take it back, Charlie. Take it back."

"Okay, okay. Let me go, and I'll take it back."

"Hooligan, my ass," Flannigan said and let Charlie go.

Charlie filled the glasses one more time and said, "I'm sorry for calling you a hooligan. Let me try again. To Bill Flannigan, the finest thug I have ever met."

"That's better," Flannigan said.

Charlie and Mercy married at the Cathedral Basilica of Saints Peter and Paul on July 6th, 1901. Harry Hird gave away the bride, young Paddy Morris was the ring bearer, and George Graham was best man. Danny and Flannigan were groomsmen. It was a typical Kensington wedding with simple and delicious foods, lots to drink and Irish music. Charlie could have afforded an elaborate wedding as his business was booming, but Mercy insisted they keep it simple and donate the savings to charity instead.

William Flannigan and Emily Natoli were married in West Palm Beach, Florida on April 12, 1902. The newspapers reported that the marriage of two of the county's most influential citizens was an unusual event. West Palm Beach notables as well as an entire tribe of local Seminole Indians attended it. Father James O'Reilly from the archdiocese of Philadelphia conducted the Catholic wedding ceremony and the bride's adult son Nathanial Natoli, as is the custom, conducted the Seminole rites of marriage.

On October 16, 1903 Mercy Hird Byrne was rushed to the Women's Hospital of Philadelphia where she gave birth to an eight pound healthy baby boy. A week later Charlie Byrne and George Graham waited patiently as the nurses prepared Mercy and Charlie's newborn son to go home.

"What's it feel like to be a father, Charlie? George asked.

"I'm not sure. I'm a little numb, George. On one hand I'm excited and on the other hand I'm terrified. What if I screw this up?" Charlie said.

"You won't. Your kid is going to have advantages we didn't. He'll go to the best schools, and won't have to worry where his next meal is coming from. The kid's got it made. The country's at peace and imagine what wonders will be invented during his life. When you were a kid, could you have imagined that we would have telephones, electric lights and automobiles? The kid's got it made," George said.

"I hope you're right George. I know one thing. With you as his godfather I know he'll be safe," Charlie said.

George's eyes opened wide and he said, "Me. Godfather. Are you kidding me, Charlie?»

"No, I'm not kidding. Will you be my son's godfather?" Charlie asked.

George just looked at Charlie for a long time and Charlie eventually said, "Just say yes, George."

"Yes, of course. Yes," George replied. "What's my godson's name going to be? Have you decided yet?"

"Yes Mercy and I decided to name him after Jacob and the most important man in our lives, George Graham. His name is Jacob George Byrne.

George smiled, then wiped the tears from his eyes.

AUTHOR COMMENTS

Growing up in the inner city of Philadelphia in the 40s and 50's afforded me the opportunity to meet a large, diverse group of people. I learned at an early age to accept people who spoke with different accents, ate different foods, worshiped different religions and had different complexions. I hope where it is historically accurate this rings true in my writing.

The Kensington section of Philadelphia was traditionally made up of poor Irish immigrants who worked in the various factories. By the time I was born other immigrants such as the Polish, Italians, Hungarians, Germans, and other Europeans made Kensington their home. In those days, Kensington was considered what use to be called "a tough neighborhood" and that's an accurate description. There were bars on every corner, and they were full by 5:30 PM.

Yes, it was a tough place, but it was full of caring and wonderful people. People who were and still are fiercely proud of Kensington and Philadelphia. I suggest you visit www.facebook.com/groups/

KensingtonAlumnae/ and check out the comments and you will see what I mean. I would also suggest you visit www.facebook.com/oldimagesofphiladelphia/ to see historic photos of Philadelphia. It will give you a feeling of what the city was, and still is.

Most people in Kensington didn't care if you collected trash, worked in a factory, dug ditches, ran a multi-million dollar company, or were a cop or a gangster. If you treated them well and respected them, they returned that in kind.

I try to reflect that attitude in my writing. In my Mercy Row series, my characters and heroes have to do some very bad things, but I still show them as normal human beings with families, friends, loves, hates, and problems.

I hope as you read The Potato Thief that you experienced the thread of anti-colonialism. Colonialism never works out for the natives of the countries being colonized. The United States fought a war to be free of our overlords. In the book, I try to show how the Irish suffered under English rule, the Vietnamese under French rule, the Cubans under Spanish rule and the Native Americans under U.S. rule. While not in this novel, colonization and slavery has happened on every continent.

Where possible, you will find that the historical aspects of my books are accurate. When I mention a city, a street, a church or a place they were and still may be real. Historical fiction isn't foolproof, and if I got something wrong, I'm sorry. If you're interested in the history of any era or place I write about, I suggest you research it on the Internet or read non fiction history books of which there are many.

In closing, I want to thank you for reading my books. I never take for granted someone will read what I write, let alone like it. But I hope you did. I'm touched by the comments from readers on my Facebook.com/mercyrownovel page. Many people in or around my age read my books, and suddenly they are reliving their childhoods growing up in Philadelphia and other large northern cities. I am not ashamed to tell you I often end up dropping a few tears while writing. The act of writing brings back memories of my childhood with my grandparents Ethel and Harry, my parents Florence and Harry, my siblings Roberta and Bill and my myriad of friends. Many have departed this world now, and I hope they somehow ended up in a place as good as Kensington, Philadelphia, Pa. Someday I hope I join them, but not until I write a lot more novels.

Author's Biography

Harry Hallman

Harry Hallman is the author of the Mercy Row series of novels about the North Philadelphia Irish mob. He was born in the Kensington section of North Philadelphia in the summer of 1944. Hallman's father was Harry Hallman, Sr., a champion pool player who also owned a poolroom called Circle Billiards, located at Allegheny Avenue and Lee Street in Philadelphia. The younger Hallman spent many hours after school at his father's poolroom. The people he met, some belonging to the real K&A Gang, influenced his writing of the Mercy Row series.

He spent four years in the United States Air Force as a photographer, two of them in Vietnam. His first tour was at Ton Son Nhat Airbase where he processed film shot by U2 aircraft over North Vietnam and China. He returned to the same place for his second tour, and processed film shot by U.S. fighter recon aircraft. He is married to Duoc Hallman, whom he met in

Vietnam, and has two children, Bill and Nancy, and one grandchild, Ava.

Hallman is a serial entrepreneur who has created several marketing services and digital media companies and continues to work as a marketing consultant while writing novels and short stories. His works include Mercy Row, Mercy Row Clann, Mercy Row Retribution, the prequel The Potato Thief and Word, a short story. All his works are available on Amazon.com and other suppliers of printed books, eBooks, and Audio books.

Email Hallman at harry@mercyrow.com. Keep informed at www.mercyrow.com or on Facebook at www.facebook.com/mercyrownovel.